Dedication

To my favorite and best gift from God, my amazing
husband Billy.

THE CAT LADY'S SECRET

Linda W. Yezak

THE CAT LADY'S SECRET

Contact Information: titleadmin@pelicanbookgroup.com

Scripture quotations, unless otherwise indicated are taken from the King James translation, public domain.

Cover Art by *Nicola Martinez*

Harbourlight Books, a division of Pelican Ventures, LLC
www.pelicanbookgroup.com PO Box 1738 *Aztec, NM * 87410

Harbourlight Books sail and mast logo is a trademark of Pelican Ventures, LLC

Publishing History
First Harbourlight Edition, 2014
Paperback Edition ISBN 978-1-61116-353-7
Electronic Edition ISBN 978-1-61116-352-0
Published in the United States of America

"…as we forgive those who trespass against us."

1

With the ties of her green apron flopping with each step, Annie Crawley rushes out of the Down Home Diner and quicksteps across the red brick street, just beating the traffic light. She swipes her mud-brown hair from her forehead, mouths "Hi, Millie" at me, and plops on the other end of my bench on the courthouse lawn with a phone at her ear. Her place on the bench is perfect, because now I can eavesdrop. And judging by the angle of her brows over her nose, I certainly need to. If anyone can help her with whatever etched those stress lines around her lips, it's me. Well, me and Emily Taylor. But Annie doesn't need to know about Em. No one does.

"I don't understand. What's keeping you?" Annie says into her phone. Just last month, she showed up in town with one bag and a red pickup, both of which have seen better days. She got herself a job at the diner and an apartment at Lawn View—something else that has seen better days.

I don't want to be too obvious about how far my ear is stretched in her direction, so I keep my eye on a yellow tabby sitting in the shade under the boxwood hedge outlining the courthouse. If I wasn't busy stickin' my nose into Annie's business, I'd grab the long-handled fish net resting against my knee and go after it. That's something else I do—catch stray cats, though I've never used the net.

"You *lost* it? How?"

The tabby's ears prick forward at Annie's raised voice. So do mine.

"*Stolen?*"

That did it. Annie's shout sends the cat darting across the lawn and behind the courthouse's air conditioning unit. But it's not like he's safe. I know where he is.

"How long will it take?" Annie rubs her temple. "I love you, too. Bye."

"Trouble?" I ask as she snaps her phone closed.

"That was my husband, Kyle." The weak smile she gives me doesn't erase the worry lines plowing across her forehead. "He was supposed to finish his job in Waco and join me here in Dogwood."

"But...?"

"But he closed our bank account and got a cashier's check so we could open an account here, and he left it in the truck overnight and"— tears brim in her dark eyes, and her soft voice pitches to a high wail— "someone stole it!"

"The check?"

"No, the truck! Now he's not just broke, he can't even get here. Oh, Millie, what are we going to do?"

Fat teardrops dive down her cheeks and splash on her quivering lips.

I scoot over to her and wrap her shaking shoulders in a hug. Rubbing her arm, I let her cry until her nose is good and red and her eyes are puffier than plump pillows.

"I'm sorry." She dabs at the wet spot on my

shoulder. "I just miss him so much."

"I know you do. It'll be all right. You'll see."

She nods but doesn't look convinced. In fact, she looks like a cat stole her ice cream. Well, good thing I'm here. I reckon this is a problem Emily can fix.

"The diner's filling up again. I have to get back to work." Still sniffing, she rises and smoothes the wrinkles out of her waitress uniform. "Come by after the rush, and I'll fix you some soup."

"Too hot for soup."

She laughs. "A sandwich, then."

Such a sweet lady.

I watch her cross the street, grab my tote and net, and get up from the bench. I've got a cat to catch.

No more than halfway around the courthouse building, my feet start hurting, but I glimpse a yellow tail between the air conditioner unit and the brick wall. The cat's facing away from me, and in this stifling August heat, the AC fan is whirring loud enough to drown out my footfalls. I drop the tote and slip my net behind me. I don't want to scare it and certainly don't want to use the net if I don't have to. Cats go bonkers when caught in the nylon and wear themselves out trying to get free. I've never had to use it and don't want to start now.

I get fairly close, drop to my knees, and start cooing at the critter. Maybe I can coax it out without having to chase it. Sometimes I can do that, if the cat's not too wild. As I inch toward it, getting dirt and grass stains on my hands and knees, the back door to the courthouse pops open.

The noisiest gaggle of humans known to man swoops and clatters down the stairs, and the cat takes off.

I struggle to my feet to watch the commotion. Maybe some of these folks will head for the diner and leave Annie a big tip—

Heaven, help me—there are journalists in that group! Press passes big as day displayed on their chests. One of 'em turns his camera toward me, and I skedaddle before it clicks. If he gets a picture at all, it'll be a blur of floppy hat, orange t-shirt, and purple polyester pants.

Even that's too much.

2

"Annie Crawley's husband, Kyle, is stuck in Waco." In the bedroom of her downtown apartment, Emily Taylor propped a cordless phone on her shoulder and reworked her hair into its clip. The sun had given her dark hair chestnut highlights and the effect made her smile. Couldn't buy *that* in a bottle. "Someone stole his truck along with a cashier's check for their entire savings."

"Where do you find these people?" Connor Matthews's brusque voice fit a rotund lawyer in a vested suit, like the one he always wore to the office. But he didn't intimidate Emily. A friend of her parents, he'd been part of her life since childhood. Now she considered him the best financial adviser, confidante, and go-to guy whenever she needed something done.

"Millie tells me. You know how she is."

"I don't know a thing about her. I've seen her around town a time or two, but haven't met her yet. When are you going to arrange that?"

"Oh...someday. Anyway, can you get Kyle here? Maybe give him a few extra bucks?"

"How much?"

She nabbed a quickly calculated figure from her mind and gave it to him. "But please handle it yourself. No secretaries."

"I always protect your anonymity, Emily, although it would be easier if you trusted Kellie. She'd keep the time of day secret if I asked her to." He emitted a light snort. "But I know how you feel. I'll manage this myself."

"Thanks. I really appreciate your humoring me about this." Emily smiled at an image of Connor's chubby assistant scrambling up the courthouse steeple and draping a sheet over the clock.

She walked barefoot on the carpet through the living room to the kitchen and pulled a water bottle from the fridge. "How is my charities account doing? I haven't been using too much of it, have I?"

"Unlike your personal account—which desperately needs a cash infusion—it's still flush with your inheritance from your parents' estate. You didn't use it too much in Houston."

"I didn't need it then. As long as I could organize a fundraiser, I could raise enough money for just about any cause."

"It's a shame you can't do that now."

"I wouldn't dare. If anything about me leaks back—"

"I know, I know. This is all about Wade Coulter and what he did to you in Houston." His tone changed, became gentler. "You'll have to forgive him, you know."

"Forgive him? He ruined me. Ruined my business, my reputation." Her anger was tempered by fear of the man. The look he'd given her as she'd testified against him—a look of savage hatred—haunted her to this day. If he discovered where she was, would he come after her?

"I understand your feelings. After that fiasco, it's a wonder you're still charitable at all."

The thought of stopping what she so enjoyed

doing weighed heavily on her mind. She couldn't possibly. "In spite of what he did, I can't stop caring, can't stop wanting to give to people and help them." Emily's heart clutched as a wistful feeling washed over her. "And it's not like it's all out of good intentions. I get something out of it, too. This...connection, I guess, that I feel with my parents is important to me."

"They were the most generous people I knew."

"Yeah, they were." She sighed.

The car accident occurred over six years ago, but the pain of losing them hadn't diminished. Doing what she could to live by their example seemed even more vital now that she'd returned to her hometown. She couldn't abandon their legacy. "I want to follow in their footsteps, but I must remain anonymous. Nothing about me can get back to Houston. You wouldn't believe what a close call Millie had with a journalist at the courthouse today. Someday, she's going to wind up right on the front page of the *Dogwood Daily*."

"I don't understand what you need her for." Connor's chair squeaked. He mumbled something to someone in his office and then returned to Emily. "I'm sure you get solicitations in the mail, just like the rest of us. Pick a cause and go for it."

"Oh, but it's so impersonal. Besides, once you start that, you can never escape. It's like you're on a secret list of contributors that's passed around to everyone who needs money. And *everyone* needs money. My problem is I can't say no." Her blood pressure spiked at the thought of the stacks of letters and phone messages on her desk in Houston from organizations wanting her funds. Save the whales, support wind energy, rebuild the town hall, contribute to the firemen's retirement fund. The list grew exponentially, and actual contributions only led to more solicitations. "Millie discovers the people who need help but don't ask. They're the ones I want to find. And no one needs to know."

"Well, no one will find out through me or my office. I'll get the Crawleys set up, anonymously as usual."

She'd always known she could count on him, but his assurance brought her a surprising sense of relief. "You're the best, Connor. Thanks."

As she disconnected, the doorbell rang downstairs, and she headed to answer. Her apartment was on the second floor of the old Woolworth's building in downtown Dogwood. The first floor served as a cat refuge, The Litter Box. As she crossed to the front door, the resident felines eyed her lazily from gray, carpeted structures intended to keep them happy and playful. She scooped up a calico to keep it from dashing outside and toed away a neon-green tennis ball from the glass paneled door. Pulling aside the blue full-length drapes she'd had made for privacy, she peeked out.

Dr. Scott Barlow stood on the other side of the glass, juggling a thirty-pound bag of kitty litter and another of dry cat food. His smile had made her heart mushy since they were kids. Funny how the tables had turned. Back then, he'd been too timid to ask her out. Now, she was the one who shied from his invitations.

With a smile, she unlocked the door and pulled it open. "What's this?"

"A little present from Barlow Animal Clinic. Where do you want them?"

"You are too sweet for words, you know that? Bring them back here." She led the way to the storeroom, snaking around cat toys, oversized litter boxes, and half-empty food bowls.

Scott sidestepped a gray tom bolting across his path. "I noticed the building next door has a fresh coat of graffiti. It's a wonder they haven't hit your place." His voice developed a serious tone. "I worry about you here. When are you going to move?"

"Soon, I hope." She'd be able to shop for a new place when the second installment came from the sale of Deck the Walls, her interior decorating and design firm in Houston. Between the semiannual purchase installments and the royalties from her wallpaper designs, she had more than she needed in her personal account to pay the mortgage on this building without delving into her charities fund, but she'd have to delay buying a house.

One of the downsides of agreeing to heed the words of a financial advisor was the promise to wait for his approval to make large expenditures. And judging by the "cash infusion" comment Connor had made earlier, he wouldn't be granting his approval until the next installment.

"But it's safe here. I've never had reason to be afraid." She pulled open the storeroom door and pointed to the corner. "You can put the bags here."

But Scott didn't follow her. He dropped the bags in front of an old glass display counter several feet away and stooped his lean frame to peek into a tan pet carrier.

She backtracked to join him.

On the countertop, a yellow tabby cowered in the corner of the molded plastic carrier. Emily lowered her head next to Scott's and glanced in. "This is Daisy. Millie thought you'd like her."

"She does know how to pick her cats."

The musky fragrance of Scott's cologne zinged Emily's senses into full-alert mode, and she took a step back.

"So, when do I get to meet Millie?" He straightened and shifted his hazel eyes to her. "Is she here?"

"She is, but she's resting. The heat really takes it out of her." Emily rubbed her hands together. "Shall we get started? We only have four this time. Two were adopted last week."

"I need to put these up first." Scott hoisted the bags and carried them to the storeroom. "Just shots and exams today?"

"Yes, except for Daisy."

He emerged from the storeroom. "I'll take her back to the clinic with me. Let me get my bag."

Two hours later, after the resident cats had endured a needle and a quick exam, Emily rested a hand on Daisy's carrier. "You be a good girl. Don't go giving the doctor trouble."

"Oh, she won't. By the time I'm done with her, she'll sleep a good twenty-four hours." His strong, surgeon-soft hand covered hers, warming it like a kiss from the sun. "The church is hosting a concert tonight. Would you like to come with me?"

She slid her hand from his and looked away. Why hadn't he asked her out years ago? Her life might've taken a different turn if he'd been as persistent about dating her when they were younger. "Thanks, no. I have...things to do."

With the tip of his finger, he turned her chin to face him. "Em, what happened in Houston? When are you going to tell me about it?"

"You don't want to know." She closed her eyes to

shut out the compassion his expression offered. "Please don't ask me again."

After a long moment, he agreed, with sad resignation in his voice. He rubbed her shoulder. "I guess I'd better get back to the clinic."

She nodded. Her heart grew heavier with every step he took toward the door. But she was right to keep their relationship on the level of friends. After everything that happened in Houston, dating him now was out of the question.

****

With the cats on the first floor fed, watered, and pampered for the night, Emily settled in front of the TV in her apartment with a lonely supper of leftover tuna casserole and a diet soda. Lonely wasn't a good word choice. Being alone wasn't the same as being lonely, and being alone had its benefits. She could eat what she wanted, when she wanted, and didn't have as many dishes to wash. She could watch old movies, one of which flickered on the screen now. She could...

She could stop trying to convince herself that being alone was fine. It wasn't. It was just for the best. Still, in the year she'd been back in Dogwood, she'd learned to appreciate her freedom.

The silence had oozed into her awareness only because Scott had made his house call earlier. Having him at the refuge had been fun, and she'd enjoyed herself. Enjoyed laughing with him. But that didn't mean she was ready to give up her new lifestyle. She wasn't lonely.

To prove it to herself she cranked up the volume on the movie, and then flipped through the mail she'd left on the table earlier. Another money request from a green organization. Would those people *ever* give up? The bulk of her mail was the same. Send money for this, donate to that. She dropped the unopened solicitations on the floor to toss in the trash later.

The next envelope held a Houston return address. Another installment check for Deck the Walls... already?

Emily jumped from the sofa to double check her calendar. The payment wasn't due until the following month, but who cared? Now she could start house hunting!

She grabbed the phone. She couldn't wait to tell Connor about the check.

3

"Come here, baby. Come on." I don't know why it is my voice goes up an octave whenever I'm calling a critter. Rarely works. No amount of high-pitched *here, kitty, kitty* will get a feral cat to come.

But I keep trying. Have to. Just because a new house is in the plans, doesn't mean The Litter Box will be closed. As long as there's a stray cat to find, I'm gonna find it—along with anything else of interest.

This week's been slower than winter molasses, and I haven't found another cat downtown since Daisy. That can only mean the downtown area is stray-free, thank you very much, and it's time to move on. Besides, I haven't worked the bus station in a month. With all the fast-food dives around here, it's a prime location.

I caught sight of this stray a few moments ago, and now I'm on my knees with my backside in the air and my face poked under the driver's door of a rusty convertible, trying to coax the long-haired gray cat closer. Can't use my net. She'd dash off like a pit bull's on her tail, and I'd never catch up with her.

She stares at me, smoky blue eyes wide and wary, and stays scrunched up against the right back tire. Car engines rumble in the lot, their exhaust mixing with the fumes from the bus idling nearby. I choke on a cough.

"Come on, kitty. I won't hurt you."

Feminine laughter pierces the air, accompanied by a deeper chuckle, and I see two pairs of legs pass by the other side of the car. Squeezing tighter against the tire, Kitty twitches her ears to the voices behind her. But she keeps her focus on me.

"Hey, lady, need some help?" A kid with four studs in each ear, a torn t-shirt, and a sweet smile squats down near me.

I smile at him. "No, thanks. I can handle it."

"Suit yourself." He rises and moves on.

I look under the car. The cat's gone. Oh, well. There's bound to be another around somewhere.

Using the car door for support, I hoist myself up, grab my net, and hobble past a small group of people to a bench. My feet always hurt, so it's mighty nice to have so many benches around. This one is covered with advertisements: a real estate office, Down Home Diner, Carter's Floral Emporium. I sit down and lean back next to Parker Milligan's face grinning from his insurance company ad. Such a nice man. Kind eyes.

Another bus pulls up, and its brakes huff a dying breath as it stops. The doors whisk open, allowing four people to file out.

"Kyle!"

Racing past me, Annie launches herself into the arms of a young man with dark eyes and a black t-shirt stretched over bulging muscles. He picks her up and swirls her around. The long, loving kiss they share warms my heart. So nice to see folks in love.

Just behind them, a blonde woman crumbles, weeping into the arms of another who'd just stepped from the bus. "Oh, Mom, he's worse."

"What does the doctor say?"

"They can't do any more for him here." Her sobs

draw everyone's attention.

Mom wraps both arms around her daughter, shielding her from the curious, and starts the awkward walk to the parking lot.

Dear Father in Heaven, they look so shattered. As they pass me, I hear the mother shushing and cooing. "Let me drive. You're in no state. What room...?" Her voice fades as they drift away from me.

"Hey, Millie!" Annie drags my attention from the two. "This is Kyle. He's here. Isn't it wonderful?"

I push to my feet and give them my best smile, but they don't see it. They see only each other. "Well, I'm glad you could make it happen."

Annie looks at me brows raised. "I didn't do it. I don't know how it happened. Two days after I talked to you, he calls and says he got a bus ticket in the mail. A bus ticket and a *check*."

"Isn't that nice."

Kyle flashes his crooked-toothed grin. "The check is for more than what was stolen from me."

"Much more," Annie says. "Enough that we can open our restaurant."

"A&K's Barbecue." He puffs out his impressive chest like a cartoon rooster.

"And you come by whenever you want, Millie." Annie lays a hand on my arm.

I pat her fingers. "I'll be your first customer."

Smiling and beaming love at each other, the two walk to the parking lot, their arms wrapped around each other so tight dust mites wouldn't fit between them.

I sigh and watch them ride cloud nine to the parking lot. Kyle opens the door to their old red pickup, and Annie leaves his grasp long enough to jump in. When he plops down in the driver's seat, she leans over for another kiss.

I grab my net and hook the tote bag on my shoulder. Time to stop ogling the lovebirds and go for a walk.

****

From the bus station to the hospital is a long five blocks—a miserable walk anytime, but especially in the mid-morning heat. My net is too short to use as a staff, so the best I can do is just limp along.

The hospital entrance doors slide open. Frigid air from inside blasts out, evaporates the sweat on my face, and feels heaven-sent.

People stare as I cross the polished gray floor to the elevator bank, same as they stared while I walked over here. I greet them head-on. I know I'm a sight. Who wouldn't stare at an old woman in a bright green t-shirt and baggy plaid pants? Can't blame them for that.

The elevator dings and the glossy doors split. I walk in and lean against the wall across from a couple who look to be in their late thirties.

"Down?" The man asks.

I nod.

He looks gray and crumpled, crinkled all over like he'd slept in his clothes. The woman with him looks worse. The dark rings under her eyes would spook a goblin.

I take a closer look at her. She's the crying lady from the bus stop. Just who I was looking for. God saved me from a room-to-room search.

With another ding, the doors slide open again, and

I follow the two out, juggling my net while I fish change from my pocket. I may not have caught a cat at the bus station, but I did come up with a few quarters.

Although yummy scents tempt me to turn left to the cafeteria, I go right, following a few steps behind the couple. Just ahead is a wall of vending machines. Their backlit blues, reds, and greens shimmer like semi-precious stones. I'm parched, so the only one that interests me is the one with the water. Give me good ol' water anytime.

"Mama wants cheese crackers." The woman stops at the snack machine next to me. She frowns and whispers to her husband. "I don't care what we have to do. If they find out he can be helped in Dallas, we're going to Dallas."

"I'm not arguing with you." His voice is low, weary. He drops some change into the chip machine and makes a selection. "But I have to figure out..."

I look from the vending machine to the three quarters in my hand and back again. A bottle of water is a buck and a half? Highway robbery! Where'd it come from? The fountain of youth?

"There must be a way. He needs to go, and I need to be with him. I'll drive to Dallas and live in the car if I have to."

"No, I can't let you do that." His change clinks in the slot, and the machine spits out another selection. "Maybe I could take out a second mortgage on the house."

With another quarter, I could buy a soda. Why is *water* more expensive than sodas? Doesn't matter. I don't have another quarter.

"A little short?"

I drag my gaze from the unattainable blue bottles.

He has such sweet gray eyes. Pained. Hurts me to see that in anyone.

I nod.

"Water?" He digs in his pocket and pulls out more change.

"Yes, please."

He feeds the robber an entrée of coins, pokes the button, and smiles at me. "There you go."

"Thanks, Mister...?"

"Sawyer. Milt Sawyer. And you're welcome."

He turns to his wife, who gives me a strained smile, and the two of them walk back to the elevator. I want to holler out that I'll be praying for them, but that would be admitting I was eavesdropping. Not that I could help hearing, since we were standing right next to each other at the machines.

I cradle my net in my elbow, twist open the bottle, and chug until the cold water gives me an ice-cream headache. But it's not ice cream. It's water. Just plain old, can't-believe-it's-a-buck-and-a-half water.

Making my way back to the elevators, I keep my brain busy running the man's name through my head. Seems like a Sawyer landed in the paper not long ago.

The doors open at the same time my memory does. I snap my fingers and shout, "Mitchell Sawyer!"

People look askance and sidestep around me as they leave the elevator. I smile at them as I enter and poke the button for the first floor.

Mitchell Sawyer. He was in the paper just this past Wednesday. Bald head and all. His friends were crowded around him, each sporting chrome domes and grinning at the camera. Brain cancer, the article said. A promising football star and the only child of an electrician and a secretary. Just sixteen.

4

"That's a tall order, Em. Do you realize what you're getting yourself into? The expense involved will be massive." Connor regarded her from over the half-moons of his glasses. "Don't the Sawyers have insurance?"

"I'm sure they do, but deductibles and co-pays alone can send them into bankruptcy." Although she tried to maintain a calm demeanor, her hands were locked together in a death grasp in her lap. The burgundy-leather client chair in Connor's masculine, spacious office was comfortable enough, but she perched primly on its edge, convinced he would try to talk her out of her plans.

Connor was right about the cost, but she desperately wanted to help this family. True, they could take out a second mortgage, but if Mitchell survived, they would need to build up his college fund. And if he didn't...she couldn't bear to think of that. But he'd have no chance at all if they couldn't send him to Dallas, and she was determined to get him there. "Don't I have enough in the charities account to cover his bills?"

Connor's fat, ruddy cheeks puffed with a breath he quickly expelled. "I don't know. Too much factors into it. We may be able to get the ball rolling. Medical bills don't usually come in until the patient is released, so that buys time. If we have to, we can feed the account with your wallpaper royalties." He rubbed the deep creases in his forehead, studied her bank ledger, which sat open on his glossy mahogany desk, and grumbled to himself. "It may be doable depending on their insurance...I'll have to look into it. See what I can arrange. Maybe the hospital can offer a discount."

With every mumbled word, Emily's hope rose. If there was any way to get this done, Connor would find it, she felt certain. If not for his own soft heart, he'd try harder to dissuade her, but even though he was a grizzly of a man on the outside, inside, he was just a teddy bear.

He leveled his piercing blue eyes at her. "You'll have to stay out of this account until all his bills are paid. Do you think you can handle that?"

Emily's spirits lifted as if suddenly inflated with helium. "I can. I promise. Cross my heart!"

"That means you'll have to turn down anyone else in need for a while. I've never known you to be able to do that."

"I'll behave. If anything else comes up, I'll take it out of my personal account."

Connor scowled at her. "You have to go easy on that account, too. You're going to buy a house, remember?"

"Oh, I can put that off." She waved a hand in dismissal. "My apartment is comfortable."

"Yes, but I worry about your safety. I'd like to see you get out of the downtown area."

"You and Scott both. He's afraid the graffiti painters will hit my building next." Although she resisted the urge to roll her eyes, the attitude was evident in her voice.

"Well, he could be right—or it could be worse.

He's a good man. You should listen to him."

She jumped from her seat to circle the desk and give Connor a hug. "You're a good man, too. With you advising me, who else could I possibly need?"

He chuckled and then raised a hand to her cheek. "You are your mother's child. You have her heart. She would've been proud of you. Both your parents would."

Her breath hitched. No other words could touch her more. She kissed his balding head, whispered a thank you, and swept from his office before her tears could escape.

****

The next day on her way to the Barlow Animal Clinic, Emily slammed on the brakes hard enough to leave rubber on the road. She shifted her convertible into reverse and backed up to an ancient house with a *For Sale* sign posted in a yard riddled with weeds. A quaint Victorian in the Queen Anne style, painted in the pitiable shades of pea green and beige, sat on roughly two acres of a once-landscaped lawn. It was the kind of house that would be appealing only to someone with degrees in interior decorating and architectural history. Someone like her.

When she'd left Connor's office yesterday, she'd decided to put off looking for a house, in spite of his worries about her safety. He and Scott were being silly. She was perfectly safe in her apartment. Of course, she wanted a house of her own someday, but for now, she needed to see what she was in for with the Sawyers.

But today, she saw the Queen Anne.

She never would've believed she'd find the house

of her dreams so quickly—and totally by accident. Her brain kicked into gear, analyzing the condition of the Victorian before she even put the car in park.

This house design was most popular between 1880 and 1910, and since Dogwood was founded in 1893, Emily wouldn't be surprised if this was one of the original homes. So why hadn't she seen it before? Granted, today she'd followed a different route from what she usually took to Scott's clinic, but surely, *sometime* in her life, she'd driven past it.

Didn't matter. The best time for her to find it was right now, with its "for sale" sign planted in the lawn. She grabbed her keys, cast a glance at the caged calico in the passenger seat, and stepped from the car, continuing her analysis as her foot hit the cracked sidewalk.

The Victorian was at least twenty-five hundred square feet. One turret, two gables, and a balcony off the second floor. Gingerbread trim. Beautiful etched-glass bay windows. Twin chimneys pointing at the clouds. Shingles missing.

She waded through shin-deep grass and weeds to the back. The porch was a three-quarter wrap-around. One of the pillars in the back tilted to the right. The steps looked rotten, too. On the left side, a breezeway led to a three-bay garage/storehouse with a sagging roof. A stripped-paint carriage house deteriorated on the back of the lot.

Perfect.

Now she needed a peek inside. She completed the circuit around the house, looking for an uncovered window. No such luck.

Back at her car, she poked the realtor's number into her cell and drove to the animal clinic while she waited for a response, but she got a recording instead. After leaving a message, she disconnected and sighed her disappointment. Remodeling a Queen Anne would be a dream come true. Stately old houses like that one demanded color and grandeur. And she possessed the talent and ability to bring it back to its original glory.

Even with her promise to help the Sawyers, she may be able to afford a modest house—and judging by the deterioration, maybe this one was modest enough. She couldn't wait to find out.

A quick calculation based on what she believed the house to be worth in its current condition and what she could afford for a down payment—not to mention a few repairs and renovations to make the place liveable—and she determined an offer that would be fair to both seller and buyer, and still leave her with grocery and utility money until the next installment from Deck the Walls.

By the time she reached Scott's clinic, she was practically giddy with plans and had already run several color schemes through her mind. She parked the car in the lot, grabbed the pet carrier, and went inside.

In back, cats and dogs meowed and howled their protests, but silence reigned in the reception area. "Hey, Dani. Slow day?"

"Steady." Scott's receptionist peeked at the calico. "Millie at it again so soon?"

"She always is, just got lucky twice this month. She found this one near the hospital yesterday."

"I thought I heard your voice." From the hall behind Dani's desk, Scott followed on the heels of a bright-eyed boy holding a bandaged ferret. The boy continued out the front door, and Scott stopped beside

Emily. "What have you got for me?"

She lifted the cage so he could look inside. He released a low whistle. "This one'll be a real beauty with a little meat on her bones."

"And a bath," Emily added. "Got room for her?"

"Sure. Come on back."

He took the carrier from her and led the way to the cats' side of his practice. Felines either eyed them suspiciously or lounged on their sides and ignored them altogether. Some slept off their anesthesia, while others hissed at the newcomer. Noise always hummed in the patients' holding room.

Scott placed the carrier on a stainless steel countertop and glanced at Emily from her loose up-do to her grass-covered sling-pumps. She blushed under his scrutiny and the humor in his smile—she should've at least brushed the bits of grass and weed from her tawny slacks.

He retrieved a patient ID label and smiled at her. "You've been in the sun. Your freckles always pop out brightest when you've been outside. What've you been up to today?"

"Nothing much. I'm just dropping off the cat before I go to the bank." She fiddled with her purse strap. "What do you know about that house for sale up the road?"

"The ol' Farley place?" In heavy black ink, he wrote *Millie/Emily, calico stray* on the label and slapped it on top of the carrier. "It's been for sale for almost three years now. You interested?"

"Maybe." Three years? Surely, they'd be willing to negotiate a favorable price. She mentally knocked a few thousand off her opening offer. "Do you know how much they're asking for it?"

"They've been dead for a while. It belongs to the daughter now, and she lives in Oklahoma somewhere. Bet she's pretty anxious to be rid of it."

With that tidbit of information, she knocked a few more thousand off. The daughter might be open to a good deal. She grinned and resisted the urge to dance a jig. The prospects of owning a house *and* taking care of Mitchell's medical bills were looking better all the time. "I may just take it off her hands."

"You'll need a contractor. Remember Roger Norris?"

"Of course I do. He married Lauren Keller right after high school. I lost touch with them about five years ago."

"You may want to look them up again." Scott put his pen aside and rested his hands on the carrier. "Roger's the best there is in the construction industry around here. You couldn't do better than him."

Emily bit her lip. "Do you think he'd look at it with me, maybe give me an idea of what I'm in for?"

"I'm sure he would. Let me know when you go. I've been itching to see the inside of that place."

"I'll call you when I have an appointment." Anxious to talk to the realtor, Emily waggled her fingers in farewell and started for the door.

Scott's voice stopped her. "Hey, do you have plans Friday night? It's the annual end-of-summer game between Dogwood and Valley View. You still like high school baseball, don't you?"

"I do, but I can't. Too much to do. Talk to you later." She left before she could see the disappointment that always registered on his face with each rejection. Why hadn't he been as persistent ten years ago?

5

Just once, Scott wished Emily would say yes. One day, he'd simply stop asking her. He should. He should've stopped long before now.

Last year, after a ten year absence, she'd reappeared in his life clutching a trembling golden-eyed cat against her chest. She'd wrapped the cat in a towel as much to keep from getting scratched as to protect it from the rain. All Scott could see of it were its eyes and nose. Perhaps he would've seen more if he'd been able to drag his attention from the drenched woman holding it. With her dark, wet tendrils dripping rivulets down her cheeks and her hazel eyes wide with concern for her bundle, she looked more like a frightened ten-year-old than a woman over thirty—a woman he'd been in love with since they were kids. Seeing her had sucked the breath from his lungs.

Still did. Which was why he hadn't stopped asking her out.

What he wouldn't give for her to trust him. Or to return to his youth and overcome the shyness that had kept him on the outskirts of her affections in the first place. Whatever had happened in Houston changed the carefree girl he knew into this mysterious, secretive woman who still held his heart.

But he had changed, too, and he wasn't about to botch a second chance of winning her.

He closed the clinic and climbed into his truck for

a quick trip to the feed and grain store. Ahead on the road, sixteen-year-old Spencer Milligan stood on his bicycle pedals and pumped like the devil was driving him. With his head and shoulders leaning over the handle bars, he was rolling at a good clip. The boy had strong legs. Scott tapped his horn, and Spencer pulled to a stop. Scott eased beside him and rolled down the passenger window.

"Hey, buddy. Why aren't you in your new car?"

The smile Spencer wore in greeting soured on his freckled face. "Dad took the keys from me. The old *three-strikes* rule."

"Uh-huh. What'd you do twice that was so much fun you had to risk a third time?"

"Stayed out after curfew." A muscle knotted in his smooth jaw. "I'm too old for a curfew."

"You're not if your daddy says you're not."

That response didn't set well with the young man.

Scott jerked his head toward the truck bed. "Put your bike in back and ride with me. The sheriff's bringing out a rescued horse today. Maybe you can help me with him."

Faster than the flick of a stallion's tail, Spencer was sitting next to Scott in the front seat. No second invitation required.

If only it was that easy with Emily.

Scott eased back into the lane. "So, you ready for the baseball game Friday night? Now that you're entering high school, you can be part of the tradition. Valley View beat us last year. We'll need you."

"Aw, they're not gonna put me in. Freshmen don't pitch when seniors are playing their last game."

"Yeah, but I'm one of the coaches for Dogwood this year. I may have a little to say about who pitches."

He shot a glance at Spencer. "Have you and your dad been throwing the ball, giving that arm a workout?"

Spencer emitted a negative grunt.

"Is he coming to the game?"

He shrugged and slumped against the passenger door. The boy had been sullen since his parents' divorce six years ago, and even more so since puberty. He'd certainly been giving his father fits. Maybe bringing Spencer along to see the horse would be good for him.

By the time Scott had bought the feed and returned to his place in the country, Sheriff Quint Bailey's rig was already backed up to the paddock gate.

Scott and Spencer strode across the yard to meet him. Bailey was a lean, chisel-jawed man who made up for his short stature with a strong, straight back. Scott stretched out his hand, shook Bailey's, and hitched a thumb toward Spencer to introduce him. Bailey nodded a greeting, but Spencer was already heading toward the trailer and the main attraction snorting inside.

"Whatcha got, Quint?" Scott asked Bailey as they walked around to the trailer gate.

"Roan mare named Scotch Bonnet. Owner's been letting her out of the pasture so she could feed on the side of the road 'cause she'd eaten all the field hay. Problem is, there ain't much hay on the side of the road, either. He got to where he'd leave her out there unhobbled. Traffic hazard."

The sheriff pulled open the back gate, which dropped with a metallic thud on the packed dirt. Inside the trailer, the horse stamped a hoof and swung her backside around to warily watch the men. She yanked her head against the rope securing her to the side of the trailer and backed away as far as her restraint would allow.

"She wild?"

"Well, she ain't tame. I don't think the owner did much with her but let her eat."

Scott caught a glimpse of slightly protruding ribs and hip bones. She wasn't seriously underweight, but noticeably so. "He wasn't paying much attention to her nutrition."

"Nope." Bailey climbed into the trailer, cooing softly at the horse, and caught the rope at her neck before untying the lead. She stamped and danced on her back legs, but didn't rear up against him. Still soothing her, Bailey brought her to the edge of the trailer.

Scott nodded to Spencer to open the paddock gate, and the sheriff walked the mare just inside the fence, where he tied her to a post. Scott studied her. Then he pressed his ear against her left side for a few moments more before stepping back. "I can't tell that she has any gastric distress, but I'll keep an eye on her for a while. Get her on a high-fat diet. See what happens."

"You want her in a stall?"

"Yeah, for now. It'll be easier to watch her there."

Spencer pushed toward him, brows raised in a hopeful look. "I'll take her. Can I take her?"

Scott grinned. "Sure."

"Just be careful," Bailey said. "She's a mite skittish."

Spencer led the horse away, clucking and cooing just as Sheriff Bailey had done.

Bailey chuckled. "Great kid. You collecting 'em these days?"

Scott held his hands up in denial. "No, no. He's a buddy's kid."

"Shame. I was hoping to dump a couple of my own on ya." Bailey jerked his head toward the pickup. "Got some papers for you to sign." He reached into the cab of his truck and pulled out a clipboard with county papers attached.

Scott clicked the ballpoint and signed his name to the top two forms, one to accept responsibility for the horse, and the other to accept the nominal stipend the county offered as compensation. He handed it back, but Bailey was watching Spencer run a brush over Scotch Bonnet's coat.

"That's gotta be good for a boy, ya know? Taking care of animals." Bailey accepted the clipboard from Scott and grinned. "You sure you don't want a couple extra kids around here?"

"Oh, someday, maybe. Wouldn't mind having a few of my own."

Bailey winked. "It'd help if you had a wife."

"Yeah." And his heart was set on Emily. He couldn't get her to say yes to a date, so a marriage proposal seemed a bit farfetched.

Bailey loaded himself into his pickup and tossed a final wave out the window as he pulled the trailer off Scott's property and onto the highway.

Scott focused his attention on the paddock where Spencer stroked the grooming brush down Scotch Bonnet's neck. The horse seemed calmer with his attention, tilting her ears toward him as if listening to Spencer's gentle voice. Which of the two was healing the other, Scott couldn't tell, but something good transpired between them.

He entered the paddock and closed the gate

behind him.

Spencer grinned at him. "She's a great horse. Are you going to keep her?"

"Only as long as it takes to get her healthy again. Then I'll have to find a home for her."

"Is there something I can do to help? Man, I'd like to help her get well."

Scott rocked on his heels. Bailey was right. Working with a horse would be good for the boy. Getting him out to the country would be another matter. Without a car, Spencer would have to pedal that bike for miles or get a ride from his dad, Parker. Of course, how he got there wasn't Scott's concern. If he wanted to bad enough, he'd figure out a way.

"I could use your help. On one condition—no, two." He held up a finger. "First, your dad has to agree to it."

"Aw, man! He's never going to let me."

"Won't know if you don't ask."

Spencer stroked the horse's nose and shook his head. "I'll try. What's the other condition?"

"You show up for baseball practice and play in the game Friday."

"You really think they'll put me in?"

"Won't know if you're not there."

Spencer grinned. "All right, I get it. I'll be there."

"Even if your dad says no about the horse?"

"That wasn't part of the deal."

"No, but it still stands. You won't know if you can play Friday night if you don't show up."

"Yeah." Spencer shoved his hand out. "Deal."

Scott shook with him. "Deal. Now c'mon and help me unload the truck. We've got a horse to feed."

6

Friday afternoon, Emily stood on the fractured walkway in front of the Queen Anne and waited for Roger. The sunset shadows from the ancient oaks gave the place an eeriness, reminding her of a Hollywood haunted house. In the breeze and the shade, the unkempt rambling roses looked like huge, pink spiders, deliriously spinning their webs.

"Looks haunted." Scott's voice behind her made her jump. She hadn't heard his truck pull up to the curb.

"I was just thinking the same thing. It didn't look this foreboding earlier."

"It's going to need a lot of work. What do you want to fix first?"

"You mean *besides* the roof?" She pointed to the balcony. "I'd want that safe enough to sit up there and have my morning coffee."

She glanced at him just in time to see his focus shift from her to the second floor. The idea that he'd been studying her again created a stir in the pit of her stomach that she battled away.

A white truck drove up behind them, and Emily turned to greet it. Roger Norris shoved his vehicle into park and killed the engine. She hadn't seen him since high school, when he was a running back for the Snarling Bulldogs. He was once the catch of the county with ebony hair, tanned skin, startling cobalt-blue eyes, and a straight, regal nose. Add to that his rippling muscles and long legs, and it was a wonder girls hadn't swooned whenever he strutted past them.

That was then.

As he walked toward them, she noticed his distinct limp, receding hairline, and love handles drooping over his waistband.

But his eyes were still startling.

"Hello, princess!" He wrapped her in a bear hug, smooched her cheek, then held her back at arm's length. "Lauren's on the warpath. According to Scott, you've been back over a year now, and she's ticked you haven't called her." He shot a warning at Scott. "Not to mention ticked at him for not telling her sooner."

"She's pretty mad, huh?" In the ten years she'd been gone, Emily had kept up with Lauren for only the first five. After that, her business had boomed, her charity functions consumed her time, Wade Coulter entered her life—and everything else fell by the wayside. She had lost touch with everyone in Dogwood, especially after her parents died.

Now, after years of silence, seeing Lauren again would be awkward. A friend since mud pies and teeter-totters, Lauren would undoubtedly demand the details of what had happened in Houston.

Even now, Emily couldn't talk about it—something she should've thought of before calling Lauren's husband to work for her. Like a fibbing preschooler, she mentally crossed her fingers behind her back. "I'll try and get by to see her."

"Make it soon, will ya? I don't want her on my back about you." Roger laughed and then slapped Scott on the shoulder. "How ya doin', Doc?"

"Better than gravy on a biscuit." Scott shook his hand. "You?"

"I'm the sausage in the gravy, bud, the sausage in the gravy." He returned his wide smile to Emily. "You got the key?"

She handed it over and followed him to the porch with Scott at her side.

Roger held a hand up to keep them from advancing.

"Let me check these steps and the porch boards before y'all come up here."

Within moments, he deemed it safe and wrestled with the lock, muttering about rust and lubricants. The door finally moaned open, catching quickly on a warped floorboard, and a wave of dusty air greeted them from inside. They squeezed through the narrow opening.

Emily peered past Roger to the wood-paneled reception hall. A graceful stairway swept up from the entry. To the left of the stairs was the high-ceilinged parlor, to the right, a long, narrow dining room. She ignored the peeling wallpaper, musty curtains, thick dust, spider webs, and scraped hardwood floors. She visualized the rooms as they could be instead of as they were—and loved the picture. "I just have to have this house!"

"You haven't seen the rest of it yet," Roger warned. "May not be worth the money."

"Did you find out what the asking price is?" Scott brushed his hand along the banister, and a dull cherry wood emerged from under the dust.

"Yes," Emily said. "It's not too bad." Actually, it was great, but she still hoped to negotiate it down.

They moved from the dining room into the

kitchen, and Emily winced. The ancient appliances told her the room hadn't been updated in decades.

Scott tested the drawers, finding several that stuck, while Roger checked under the stainless steel sink.

"That pipe's about to rust through. It'll have to be replaced."

Emily sighed as she looked at the faded gold linoleum. "It's not the only thing."

****

After spending as much time with Emily as she would allow, Scott followed the farm-to-market road from the Victorian, past his clinic, and around another dusty curve to his modest farmhouse. It didn't compare to what Emily planned to purchase, but the electricity worked, the water ran, and the window unit ACs kept the place cool. Add a dozen acres of prime pastureland rimmed with a creek shaded by oaks and hickories, and a man could ask for nothing better.

Who was he kidding? Of *course*, he could ask for something better! A good woman to spend his life with and a crop of kids calling him Daddy and wrapping him around their pinkies. Problem was, the only woman he wanted to call "wife" was Emily, and she kept rejecting his invitations. She'd turned him down again this evening. He hadn't asked her out for anything fancy—or even anything that would take much time, only a quick soda before the game tonight.

One of these days, he'd just quit asking.

He hefted a fifty-pound bag of high-cal horse feed from the back of his truck and hauled it to the paddock, where he loaded a metal bucket with a little over three pounds of the feed pellets. He entered

Scotch Bonnet's stall, careful to close the gate behind him. She'd bolted the first time he'd gone in.

She stretched her muzzle toward the bucket. Scott fisted a few of the pellets and stretched his hand to her, opening his palm in the hopes she'd eat from it. She didn't, but she didn't back away this time, either. He poured the pellets into her feed bin and backed out of the stall. The girl had a good appetite, and her system seemed to handle the increase in food without too much strain—at least, as far as he could tell without the proper medical equipment.

How great it would be to have an equine clinic. He sighed. Maybe someday—like when he'd paid off his college loan.

He gave Scotch Bonnet a final pat and headed toward the back door of his two-bedroom farmhouse. He had just enough time to fill a jug with water before the ball game. As he climbed the back porch steps, the phone in the kitchen rang. He clomped across the ancient hardwood floor and grabbed it.

The hesitant voice of Spencer Milligan answered his greeting. "Mom's gotta work late tonight, and I need a ride to the game. Can you come get me?"

"Sure. You still under that three-strikes penalty?"

"Yeah. For another week." Spencer spit out the word *week* as if it burned his tongue. "Cuts into my freedom, ya know?"

"Well, soon as you learn your lesson, you'll get your freedom back, right?"

Silence seethed over the line. Apparently Spencer and his dad hadn't come to terms yet. The family matter wasn't Scott's concern, but as a coach of the team, the game was. "I'll see you in five minutes."

7

Late Monday evening, Emily slipped out of her shoes, left them by her apartment door, then headed to the kitchen for some ice water. The food bank where she volunteered had been hectic all afternoon, and the people unusually short-tempered.

Record heat indexes were keeping everyone edgy, and the air conditioner had struggled to cool the building. Each time the door opened, the battle was lost. The coolness of her own little home never felt so good.

She grabbed the TV remote and stretched out with a contented sigh on an overstuffed sofa. The cats were tended, the day was done, and she had nothing more to do than catch a movie. She rubbed one foot with the other and allowed her mind to go blank as Parker Milligan explained in a compassionate voice how faithful his insurance company was in times of trouble. As images of house fires swept across the screen, Emily made a mental note to contact him if she bought the Queen Anne.

Just as the tension drained from her shoulders, the phone rang and tightened them again. She retrieved the cordless from the oak coffee table.

"Hello," she said and then grimaced. Her voice sounded as annoyed as she felt at being interrupted.

"Rough day?" Connor asked over the line.

"No...no." She smiled. "Well, yeah. Just a little

stressful. Nothing serious."

"I have some news that'll brighten you up. I got the Sawyer boy all set. He'll be airlifted to Dallas tomorrow."

"Oh, that does brighten my day! How did you manage it?"

"I was surprised how amenable the hospital was. We don't have an idea of how much the boy's bills will be, but the Dogwood Medical Center's administration assured me they'd be willing to work with me. They're handling the negotiations with the Dallas hospital, too, and so far, things seem to be riding under a green light."

"I'd love to run into the parents. They seemed so hopeless before."

"Well, they're not hopeless now. At least, not where money is concerned."

"Thank you so much, Connor. I just knew you could arrange something. You're the best!"

"I'm not through yet." He paused, and she thought she'd burst with anticipation before he spoke again. "You're one step away from being a homeowner."

"Homeowner? They accepted my offer?" Emily's nerves sizzled.

"Got the call from Oklahoma this afternoon."

She jumped to her feet. "How soon can you get the papers ready?"

"Afraid she'll back out?"

"No. Just anxious to get started. Can you have them ready tomorrow? When will the closing be?"

"Ms. Farley's attorney is drawing up the papers. I can ask him to put a rush on it, but I can't guarantee when he'll get to it."

"I don't know if I can wait."

"You don't have much choice." He chuckled, but then his voice turned serious. "Both of your accounts are going to take some pretty serious hits in the next few days."

"I know. I won't touch the charities account again until all of Mitchell's bills are paid."

"I'm holding you to that promise. What about your personal account?"

"I'll be fine for the next few months. The fact Ms. Farley accepted my offer left me with a couple thousand over what I anticipated. I really thought she would negotiate more."

"She seemed ready to get rid of that old house."

"I'm glad. Now I can pay for some repairs." And she couldn't wait to implement a few of her plans. After a few more moments of small talk, she told Connor goodbye and disconnected.

A smile curved her lips. She sat for a moment and savored the word: *Homeowner*. She'd never owned a house before. In Houston, she'd been too dedicated to Deck the Walls and her charity work to spend time in her tiny apartment, much less look for a larger place. Now she'd not only found a house, she'd found the one of her dreams—once she finished with it, anyway. She needed to retain Roger and his crew so they could start the renovation as soon as the paperwork was done.

Well, no. First, she needed to contact Parker Milligan for an insurance quote. She may have enough money for the down payment and a few renovations, but she'd need financing, and every mortgage institution she'd ever heard of required insurance on the collateral.

According to the clock, it was too late. Parker's office probably closed an hour ago. He'd have to be first on the list tomorrow, but surely Roger wouldn't mind a call at home.

She dialed, and a woman answered.

"Lauren? Uh...hi." She cringed. Why hadn't she realized Lauren might answer the phone?

"Emily?" Lauren's voice registered high in disbelief, as if Emily were a talking Chihuahua. "It's been awhile."

"I know. I'm sorry. Roger said you were mad at me."

"I don't think *mad* is the right word. More like...*perplexed*." Lauren was silent for a moment. "Mama died two years ago."

Emily brought a hand to her lips and sagged in her chair. She didn't even know Mrs. Keller had been sick. Lauren had comforted Emily when her parents died. It pained Emily that she hadn't been there to return the favor. "I'm so sorry."

"Yeah, well...I needed you then."

"I wish you had called."

"I hadn't heard from you in years. What was I supposed to say? *Hi Em, how ya doin'? Mama's dead.*" She expelled a tired breath. "I understood when you and Wade were dating. New business, new boyfriend. No time. I kept thinking I'd be getting a wedding invitation. But you've been back over a year now. No wedding, no Wade, and no comment. I don't even know what happened between you two."

In the silence that followed, Emily realized Lauren wanted an explanation. But she couldn't provide one. She couldn't tell her of the flash-fire romance that ended in shame and near bankruptcy. There was no sanitized version of the events she could express to her questioning friends. Not in Houston, where they had watched her life unfold on the six o'clock news. And certainly not here, where she'd have to explain from the beginning for anyone to understand.

"I shouldn't have lost touch with you," she said. "I shouldn't have left you to face your mother's death alone. I'm so sorry."

"Yeah, well..." Lauren vented a light snort. "You owe me five years' worth of girl talk."

"Does that mean I'm forgiven?"

"That remains to be seen."

8

Scott rolled the push-mower back into his mother's one-car garage and wiped his sweaty forehead on his arm. August heat was bad enough, but the humidity made it outright unbearable. Mowing the small, quarter-acre lot of his childhood home left him dehydrated.

A fact Rita Barlow must've anticipated. She slammed out of the house with a dishrag in one hand and bottled water in the other, and shoved the bottle at him. "You look dry. Drink this before you crumble into dust."

Scott downed half of it in one gulp. "Dinner ready?"

"Just 'bout. You got enough time to clean up while I'm setting the table."

His mother led the way to the door of her tiny, red-brick house, but Scott paused on the stoop to take off his grassy sneakers and finish the other half of the water. The yard looked good, though the flowerbeds held a few weeds and promised to be his after-supper chore. He'd taken care of this lawn since he was six years old and barely tall enough to push the mower.

His father had abandoned them before Scott uttered his first words, leaving his mother to fill the roles of both parents. As Scott grew, he'd taken over the jobs his father should've been there to do.

He'd asked about his dad once when he was

eleven or twelve.

"You're dad's a rambler, honey, a vagabond. It's my sin for not seein' it beforehand."

At an early age, Scott had vowed not to be like his daddy. He'd been away just long enough to get his doctorate in Veterinary Medicine and then ran back home. And here he'd stay.

"You comin'?" his mother called from the kitchen window. "I swear, this chicken's gonna grow feathers and start to cluckin' before you get yourself in here!"

Smiling, Scott shook his head. "I'm coming."

Washed and feeling a bit fresher, he sat to a dinner of fried chicken, homemade rolls, fresh green beans, and roasted new potatoes. The steam was still rising from the chicken's crusty coat, so there was no danger of a miraculous poultry resurrection occurring tonight. He took his mother's hand and bowed his head.

"Father, thank You for this food and for the jobs that helped pay for it. Bless Mom with good health—"

"—and Scotty with a wife."

"In the name of our Lord, Jesus Christ, amen." Scott rushed the words and then raised his brows at his mother. "Mom, I'll get a wife in good time, in *God's* time."

"Don't hurt none for me to want to hurry His time a little." She passed the chicken platter. "How're things goin' with Emily?"

Scott sighed over his drumstick. "Not so hot. She keeps turning me down."

"Well, Carol is back in town. Did ya know that? And she's pretty as a spring flower. Still single, I hear."

"That's good to know. Can I have the potatoes?"

The chipped bowl passed from hand to hand. "She's going to set up shop in one of the old stores downtown. A little boutique of Texas things to sell to tourists."

"Um-hm."

"You can stuff your face and listen at the same time, you know."

"I *am* listening. And it's the same old chatter every week. I'll get married when it's time."

"Past time, if you ask me," she muttered. "So, how'd the ball game go Friday? Y'all win?"

"Yeah. Valley View played tough, but we got them."

"And how'd the Milligan boy do?"

"Good. He got seven strike-outs." Scott rose from the table to refill his tea glass and then poured some in his mother's, too. "He was burning that ball across the plate. Guess he had some anger to work out."

"His parents splitting up the way they did prob'ly caused the bulk of that anger. Saw Melissa in the grocery store yesterday with that new man of hers. After six years, you'd think she'd marry that man instead of livin' in sin like she is." His mother's mouth puckered, deepening the wrinkles on her upper lip. "Seems to me she should've moved away rather than flaunt herself in town the way she does. I bet poor Parker just hates running into them two and hearin' 'bout their antics. I don't see how he bears it."

"All I know is that Spencer's been a handful. Parker's trying to maintain discipline, but it's gotta be tough when they live in separate homes."

"Well, he's a good boy, and he's got you to look up to. You're good for him." She cast a sidelong glance. "Just think how great you'd be with your own kids."

Scott speared green beans and shoved them in his mouth.

"You know, I'm not getting any younger. I'd like some grandkids before I get too old to play with them."

"Um-hm." A pineapple upside-down cake sat cooling on the counter, with its red cherries winking at Scott as if to invite him over.

"I can get Carol's number if you'd like."

He pushed his chair back and headed for dessert.

"Or Pat's. She's still single. And I know how you are with brunettes."

"Just one brunette, Mom." Just Emily.

****

The message light was flashing on Scott's phone when he returned home. A glance at the caller ID told him Roger had called while Scott was at his mom's, but when he listened to the voice mail, it was Lauren's soft alto on the recording.

"You're forgiven," was all she said.

Forgiven for what?

Scott glanced at the clock. It was just eight-thirty, well within the range of "decent hours" to return a phone call.

Lauren answered.

"Thanks for forgiving me. What did I do?"

"I figured that'd get your attention." She giggled. "Emily called tonight."

"Did you two make up?"

"Sure. I can't stay mad at her long. Why didn't you ever tell me she was back?"

"At first I thought she was just planning to surprise you, and I didn't want to blow it for her. But the longer it took, the more I wondered if she didn't have some other reason for not calling you." He moved his medical kit off his recliner and sank into the cushion. "She didn't tell you what went on in Houston, did she?"

"Not a word." Lauren's sigh reflected all the frustration Scott had felt for a year. "Has she ever told you anything?"

"Nope. Whatever happened must've cut deep. Sometimes I'm with her and she's just like the girl we grew up with. And sometimes..." Sometimes pain shadowed her expression, and it ripped his heart out. He wanted to soothe her, protect her. "Sometimes, she's just different."

"Well, I'll get to the bottom of it eventually. She's coming over for supper Saturday night and—hey! Why don't you to come, too? I could get my two favorite single friends here at the same time."

"You cooking?"

"No, you old stink bait, I'm not cooking. And I resent that tone in your voice!" Judging by the laugh in hers, the resentment was only slight. "Roger's going to put some burgers on the pit."

"In that case, I'll see you Saturday. You don't have to ask me twice."

Lauren snorted. "I bet I'd have to if *I* was cooking."

"Don't tell her I'm coming. Let's just surprise her."

With her promise, Scott got off the line and grinned. This was as close to a date with Emily as he could get. Maybe it would soften her toward a real date.

9

"Hey, lady, what's the net for?"

I look behind me to see who's talking. He's a cute little thing. Red hair and freckles. No more than eight, probably. "Walk with me and I'll tell ya."

I limp across the hospital park, my hand on his shoulder. This late in the summer, the park's one of few places in town still green and lush. Guess the umbrella limbs of the giant oaks protect it from all this heat. The leaves are looking a bit wilted, though.

We settle at a picnic table, and I hand him my net.

"Feel that?" I ask.

"Feel what?"

"The power." I gawk in mock-disbelief, as if he should've noticed it right off. "Electrifying, isn't it?"

"I don't feel nothing." He ran his hands up and down the pole and around the net. "I don't feel nothing at all."

"Ah, well. Maybe I'm the only one who can feel it." I take the net back and shake it like vibrant energy shot up my arm at the touch. "It's strong today. Ready for the hunt."

"What do ya hunt with it?"

"Vicious creatures. Wild. See that?" I point to a place on the handle where the brown paint had scratched off when I dropped it last week. It had fallen against a chain link fence, and the scratch marks look like a lion slashed it with its claws. "This net's the only thing that saved me from a ferocious monster. He was bigger than a tiger. All fur and muscle. Claws longer than your hand, sharper than kitchen knives. His eyes were yellow and red, like hot coals. And his teeth! His teeth would've chomped me in half if not for this net."

The boy's dark blue eyes grow wide; his little cherry lips form an O.

I lower my voice. "And do you know what happened when he sank his teeth into my net?"

"No," he whispered. "What happened?"

"Presto, bang-o! He turned into a kitten!"

"Wow!" I hadn't thought his eyes could get any wider, but sure enough, they do. "Can I hold it again?"

I hand it to him. "Can you feel it yet?"

"I think I can." He caresses it like it's a royal scepter. "I do! I feel it!"

He's more likely to be *hearing* than feeling. A helicopter is coming, the props thrumming the air with a steady beat that grows louder as it approaches. We watch the chopper land on the hospital roof, its red cross visible even from here, between the leaves and branches.

He stares up at it. "What's going on?"

"I reckon someone's getting a ride."

"Where to?"

"I bet he's going to the heart of Texas. A land of health and healing. More miraculous than my net."

"Wow."

In a matter of minutes, the whirlybird thunders back into the heavens. The rapid thumping strums the air as it flies away until it's just a low hum in the distance.

"Wow." He stares through the tree limbs as if he could see the dot in the sky fly all the way to Dallas.

How fun it must be to be young. Everything's new. Each day promises an adventure. Bet he didn't think when he woke up this bright Tuesday morning that he'd be holding a wondrous, cat-transforming net by afternoon.

Even the faintest whisper of the chopper is gone from my ears now, but he's still looking in the direction it went.

"What's your name, young man?"

"Justin." He shifts his attention back to me. Those wide, blue eyes and that bright red hair. He's all the inspiration I need for the day. "Justin Ryman."

"Nice to meet you, Justin Ryman." I stick out my hand. "I'm Millie."

He takes my hand and shakes it good and firm, like his daddy had taught him right. "What's your last name, Millie?"

"No last name. Just Millie."

"How come you don't have a last name?"

"Wielders of the Special Net don't have 'em." I wink and lean down closer to him, as if I've got a big secret to share. "Millie's not my real name, either. We aren't allowed to tell our real names."

His lips form that O again. He's so cute! I could tell him stories all day.

A series of *thunk-thunk* sounds pulls our attention to the sidewalk behind us. Two boys, just a bit older than Justin, are riding skateboards over the concrete walkway.

"Hey, Allen! Watch this!" One of the kids jumps, somehow making his skateboard pop up, over, and back on its wheels. Then he lands on the board and keeps skating.

"Cool," Allen says. "How'd ya do that?"

My little friend stands and watches, longing written all over his face.

"Justin!" A woman's voice pierces his concentration, and he turns back toward the hospital. The woman comes out from a service entrance and swipes what looks like a hair net off her head. "Justin!"

"Here, Mom!" He hands me my net. "I gotta go."

He takes off in a dead run toward his mom and then stops halfway. "Will I see you again, Millie?"

I smile. "You never know."

10

Saturday evening, Emily pulled away from her parking space behind The Litter Box and turned down the red bricks of Avenue A, heading for Roger and Lauren's house. She stopped at an intersection and watched Justin Ryman, in knee and elbow pads, gather speed on his skateboard and weave a serpentine trail down the sidewalk. His gape-toothed grin drew a smile from her. She'd promised not to get into either account to help people, but she never promised she wouldn't buy a kid a skateboard.

Ten minutes later, her tires crunched the gravel in Lauren's driveway. She switched off the engine and studied their house. Tri-gabled French eclectic with a decorative oval window in an oak-stained door, and an arched entry. An upper-middle class home surrounded by similar homes, all stuck too close together, with wooden privacy fences dividing yard from yard. Outside their home, trimmed boxwoods nestled under low windows, and petunias surrounded an ornamental maple in the front.

Inside, a dear friend she'd neglected held an offer of forgiveness.

Emily took a quick glance in the rearview mirror to check her makeup, sucked in a fortifying breath, and climbed out of the car. Their phone conversation had been promising, but actually seeing Lauren could prove awkward. She walked down the concrete path to the front door, flexed her nervous fingers before she pressed the bell, then stood back to wait.

Lauren greeted her with a smile and a warm hug, and the years sluiced away.

Emily's heart filled like a barrel in the rain. She took in Lauren's cut-offs and cotton sleeveless top, her blonde hair tied back in a ponytail, and her bare feet sporting vivid red polish, and was transported back to high school. Only Lauren's laugh crinkles around her eyes tattled her age.

"You look great," Emily said.

"So do you." Lauren gave her another quick hug before turning aside so Emily could enter. "Excuse the mess."

Inside, shoes of various sizes were strewn around the floor in the spacious family room, school books and a baseball mitt covered the coffee table, and a golf bag snuggled against the bookcase. The news blared from the TV in competition with the heavy thump of music emanating from upstairs.

Lauren grabbed a full laundry basket from the loveseat and again apologized for the mess. "With teenagers, it's hard to be Martha Stewart." She snatched the remote and muted the news, while yelling up the stairs, "Michelle, turn that *down!*"

"Aw, Mom!" a female voice responded. But the music softened a bit.

"It's fine, really." In truth, Emily loved it. It was just the way Lauren's childhood home had been when they were growing up. A comfortable place for teenagers to come and hang out. "Actually, I'm a bit jealous. It gets pretty quiet around my place."

"Quiet?" Lauren's brows scrunched. "What's that? Got a definition?"

Emily laughed as she dropped her purse onto a russet microfiber recliner and kicked off her shoes, just as she had when they were kids. "Put me to work."

She followed Lauren into the kitchen and grinned at the sight of Roger standing at the counter, wrist deep in hamburger meat. He wore a *Kiss the Cook* bib apron over denim cut-offs and a Snarling Bulldogs baseball shirt.

"Hey, princess." He twisted so she would be sure to see the apron. "You must obey the bib."

"If you don't mind getting lipstick prints."

"Just add 'em to my collection." He jutted his cheek toward her.

Propping a hand on his shoulder, she stood on tiptoe to give him a peck and then reached to rub the lipstick off.

He twisted his head away. "Uh-uh. That's my trophy."

Lauren dropped the basket in the adjacent laundry room and then returned to slap her husband's shoulder. "I thought *my* kiss was your trophy."

"It wore off."

She refreshed it with an audible smack on his lips.

A twinge of jealousy snaked through Emily's veins. She'd wanted a family, had thought she'd have one with Wade. But then he'd played her for the fool she was.

She clenched her jaw and shoved the thoughts aside. This was not the time to reevaluate the past.

Fresh lettuce, tomatoes, and onions rested on the countertop. Emily picked up a knife. "Want me to slice those?"

Lauren handed her a cutting board, then grabbed the lettuce and carried it to the sink. "Tell me your plans for the house."

With effort, Emily restrained herself from bouncing on her toes like an excited poodle while she told Lauren her dreams. She wrapped up her list of renovations, then said, "I want to return it to its original state. It must've been grand in its day."

"It's not worth looking at now." Roger slapped a patty onto a platter and dug a handful of meat from the bowl to form another. "But I bet it will be grand again by the time we're finished with it."

The doorbell chimed, the phone rang, and the back door slammed—all the noises of an active household.

"I'll get it," Michelle called from upstairs.

"I'm home!" This from a young man of maybe sixteen rounding the corner into the kitchen. With his jet hair and athletic build, Trey Norris looked identical to his father twenty years ago.

The doorbell sang again, and Lauren gave her son's backside a playful swat. "Go get the door."

Trey walked away with the lumbering stride of a confident teenager. "He has grown like Jack's beanstalk since the last time I saw him."

"I swear, he shot up three feet overnight when he was twelve and hasn't quit growing since." Lauren pulled down a plate for Emily's sliced tomatoes and nudged the onion closer to her. Emily peeled it and began slicing.

The front door closed, and Trey's laughter rang from the other room. His heavy footfalls were matched by another pair as he returned to the kitchen.

"Trey is a chip off the ol' block," Roger said. "Except he prefers baseball over football."

"Much to your dismay," Scott said.

At the sound of Scott's voice, Emily got rattled and

missed her cut; the knife grazed the onion and sent it skittering from her grasp. She flicked a glance over her shoulder to see Scott knuckling Trey's head.

"You're no running back, but you're a good first baseman, aren't you?"

"The best." Trey escaped Scott's assault and went to the fridge for a soda. "How long before dinner?"

"Forty-five minutes." Roger shaped the last of the burgers.

"Say hello to Miss Emily," Lauren said.

"Hello, Miss Emily," Scott and Trey chimed in unison.

Emily caught the gleam in Scott's eyes just before he popped a corn chip in his mouth. He certainly seemed at home. Was he as surprised to see her as she was to see him?

He clapped Roger on the back. "What can I do, buddy?"

"Grab me a soda, will ya?"

"Sure deal." Scott turned toward the refrigerator and then stopped in his tracks. "Why, Miss Emily, I do believe you're barefoot."

Emily's cheeks grew hot, and she covered one foot with the other. "What, you've never seen my feet before?"

"It's been years since I've seen you so casual. I like it."

Now positive her face was a brilliant red, Emily concentrated on her onion. No way could she think of a snappy comeback with him looking at her like that.

"Mom, can I go to Allie's?" Michelle called from upstairs.

"Yes, but come down here and say hi to Miss Emily first."

Michelle appeared in the kitchen. The fifteen-year-old had inherited her mother's blonde hair and her father's brilliant blue eyes, which she turned to Emily. "Hello." She flashed a smile and then addressed her mother. "Can I go now?"

"Sure, go on." Lauren watched Michelle bounce away and then rolled her head toward Emily with a heavy sigh. "My youngest. *So* polite."

****

Emily's pulse throbbed with the rhythm of the family. She'd slipped into the activity of the kitchen as if her absence had never occurred.

But sitting in the backyard across from Scott at the picnic table, catching the flicker of his glances, feeling the warmth spread inside like dark, melting chocolate, made her wish for a more private setting with candlelight and roses and a table meant only for two.

Too often, she ignored the conversation and just watched him. The mechanics of his square jaw as he chewed. The dip of a dark strand over his forehead. The way his laughter invigorated his eyes.

He caught her staring, and in one silent instant, while Lauren and Roger laughed with their son, Scott's lips slid into that smile meant only for her. Her breath caught, her heart stopped, just as if she was sixteen again.

She flushed and reached for a potato chip. Romance was reserved for the movies. She'd learned that lesson from Wade.

Roger leaned back from the table and patted his stomach. "This ain't a thirty-eight inch belt around here. No sirree, Bob. It's the fence circling a ground beef graveyard."

"It isn't thirty-eight inches either way you look at it." Lauren goosed his side. "You've expanded another two."

"Didn't either. Belt shrunk."

Trey grabbed a pickle, rose from the table, rattled off where he was going so quickly Emily missed it, and disappeared in a whirlwind.

"Kinda leaves ya feeling tired, doesn't he?" Roger asked.

"Tired and old." Scott shook his head. "Were we ever like that?"

"Of course not!" Emily raised her eyebrows in feigned horror. "We were perfect, always thoughtful and polite, always cautious and deliberate with our actions, always more interested in studying than dating."

"Uh-huh. And what planet are you from?" Lauren rose from the table and began gathering the paper plates. "We were *exactly* like that. We were normal kids."

"Define *normal*." Emily lifted the platter holding the last two hamburger patties and the plate of leftover tomatoes, and followed Lauren into the kitchen.

"If I know those guys, they'll disappear, and we won't see them again until after everything's cleaned up." Lauren pushed the plates into a plastic trash bag and then faced Emily with her fists on her hips. "That means it's time for you to tell me what happened with Wade."

Emily's throat constricted as if Lauren had clamped her hands around it. The choke hold would've been preferable. She lowered the platters to the countertop. "He's in prison."

"What?" Lauren stepped closer. "What did he do? Did he hurt you?"

Emily wrapped her arms across her chest and shook her bowed head. No one but Connor knew what had happened, and he knew only the business end of it. She had never voiced the rest. And couldn't, even now.

Especially now. If Scott overheard her, whether she was ready for dating again would be moot. He wouldn't want her. "Please, Lauren, let it go."

Lauren hesitated, her lips tight. She rubbed Emily's shoulder. "No, honey, I don't think so. If I know you, you've been holding all this in—"

Roger entered with an empty soda can for the recycle bin, and Emily twisted quickly to the sink to appear busy with the few dishes there.

"Didn't you make a chocolate cake?" Roger poked around the dirty bowls and half-empty bags of chips on countertop, looking for the dessert.

"It's over there on the island." Lauren grabbed the plastic wrap and covered the leftover meat. "I thought we'd have it later. You can't possibly still be hungry."

He threw his hands up in a *not guilty* plea. "It's not for me. You know Scott. We'll have to call the excavators to see where his bottomless pit ends."

"Don't blame your sweet tooth on me." Scott joined them in the kitchen. "Besides, if I had a *bottomless* pit, excavation would be useless."

"Yeah, yeah." Roger cut two slabs of cake and plopped them unceremoniously on paper plates. The men pulled out chairs at the kitchen table, and Lauren wagged her finger at them.

"No. No way. Unless you intend to help clean up—and I doubt it—this is a women-only zone. Girl talk goes a whole lot better without men around." She pointed toward the living room. "Now, git!"

"Guess I know when I'm not wanted." Roger's gleaming eyes belied his sullen expression. "C'mon, buddy. Let's go catch the baseball game."

"I'm on your tail."

Once they were gone, Lauren flipped the water off and held out a dish towel for Emily. "Let's talk."

11

"Wade was a con artist," Emily whispered. Talking about him humiliated her. She grabbed a paper napkin from the porcelain holder on the table and began to twist it. "I never saw it coming, never realized how much he was milking out of the foundation."

"The Harris County Charity Foundation? I don't understand. How did he get involved with it?"

"He worked his way into it." Emily took a deep breath and let it out in a rush. "When we met at the auction for the Children's Hospital, he said he was checking out the foundation to see how we conducted business, what kind of turnout we'd have, things like that. He said he'd been charged by his church leadership to raise funds for an orphanage in Nueva Laredo, just across the border in Mexico. He wanted to enlist our help but said he knew he'd have to become known in the right circles first so folks could trust him." Her lips quirked into a wry smile. "You should've seen him. He had this clean-cut look about him that made him seem honest. I never realized."

"He sounded like a keeper. I thought you two were ready to walk down the aisle."

Heat rose in her cheeks, but she pressed on. "We hit all the churches in the county during the two years we dated. He would speak at each one, show pictures and everything. A portion of the offering went to help those poor children in Mexico. At least that's what everyone thought."

"There was no orphanage?"

Emily shook her head. Telling this to her friend, hearing her own words aloud, she felt like such a fool. "But he had proven himself well enough that the foundation decided to have a fund raiser for this bogus orphanage."

"How did he get caught?"

"He was recognized by a Texas Ranger, who was a member of one of the churches we visited. Apparently, Wade Coulter's real name is Pete Murray. He was wanted all over the state." She clenched the napkin in her fist. "They arrested us at the dinner gala the foundation held for the orphanage."

Lauren's brow furrowed. "*Us?* They arrested you, too?"

Emily's tears puddled on the table as that night three years ago played out like a slide show in her mind. Waltzing with Wade under the twinkling ballroom lights, warming when he told her he loved her, daydreaming about their future together. The commotion as men in cowboy hats and western boots shoved through two hundred revelers, shouting at Wade. At her. The handcuffs. The flash bulbs. The TV cameras. The microphones.

The jail.

A hand covered hers, and she met Lauren's steady gaze.

"He's in prison. You're not. They must've found out you weren't involved."

Emily nodded and used her tattered napkin to dry her cheeks and nose. "It took a bit of doing. Almost half of the down payment for Deck the Walls went to pay my legal fees. I hated selling my business, but I couldn't stay in Houston."

"You were exonerated, weren't you? No one could possibly believe you had anything to do with it."

"I'm sure some didn't. I testified against him—everything came out in the trial. But..." Being linked with Wade had destroyed her reputation. She could still hear the whispers, *She's that woman the con-man worked with. I don't care what anybody says, I still think she was in on it.* Once, she'd written a personal check to a favorite charity in Houston, only to have it returned. *No, thank you. Please don't contact us again.* The handwriting had been Penny Wenchel's—a friend and co-chair on many of the same fund-raising committees Emily had served on. She shook her head. Exoneration hadn't saved her credibility. "I couldn't stay."

"Ready or not, here we come." Roger barreled into the kitchen and rattled an empty soda can. "Need another one."

Behind him, Scott chuckled. He tossed the paper plates and jerked a thumb at Roger. "You won't get much work out of him tomorrow."

"Why not?" Emily smiled and hoped it wasn't too evident she'd been crying.

"He'll be sleep-deprived. After five caffeine-laden sodas, he'll be spending the night wide awake."

"Don't you worry about me. I'll be fresh as a daisy." Roger stuck his head in the fridge and brought out another soda, grinning until he saw Lauren's face.

"If you're not helping to clean the kitchen, get out of it."

Roger glanced around. "I can't tell that you've been working on it."

Lauren glared and pointed over her shoulder

toward the living room.

He stole a kiss. "I'm going. I'm going."

****

At the end of the evening, Emily hugged Lauren good-bye, blew a kiss to Roger, and walked with Scott to her car. "You seem right at home with the Norrises."

"Yeah, Lauren worries about me being a bachelor and all. Like it's a violation of nature, and hiding under her wing will stave off evil spirits."

"That sounds like Lauren."

"She's probably watching us now, you know."

"Why?" Emily looked back at the house, and the living room curtain dropped.

"Like I said, being a bachelor is a violation of nature."

"You mean she's trying to fix us up?"

"Yep." Scott opened the car door for her and leaned against its frame as she slid behind the wheel. "I know how we can ease her meddling heart."

"How?"

"Come to church with me in the morning."

Emily studied her keys, running her finger over their jagged edges. Maybe if Lauren hadn't confronted her about Wade, she would've considered Scott's offer. But the whole Houston experience was still raw, still just under the surface like an almost-healed wound that both itched and ached. Discussing it tonight reopened the wound—and she hadn't even told Lauren everything. What remained locked in her heart was the very thing she couldn't imagine Scott forgiving if he knew.

"Don't tell me you've stopped going to church."

He crouched near her, leaning against the car. "You used to be the one insisting our group went every time the doors were opened."

"I don't go so much anymore." After what happened in Houston, she couldn't go back to church, not even here, almost two hundred miles away. She glimpsed Scott's knitted brows, and with a forced smile, looked him in the eyes. "Maybe some other time. In the morning, I want to go back to the house and start planning."

"Sure." Confusion creased Scott's forehead, and he rose. "Maybe I'll see you around the clinic."

"Of course." This time her smile was genuine. "Next time Millie catches a cat."

She started her engine and pulled from the drive. And waved at Lauren in the living room window.

****

Scott watched Emily's taillights disappear before turning and stalking back to the house. He knocked and then poked his head in the door. "Mind if I come in?"

Lauren, still kneeling on the sofa cushion under the window, blushed blood red at getting caught spying. But she recovered quickly. Clambering off the couch, she confronted him. "Well?"

"Well, what?"

"You know very well *what*." She crossed her arms. "Did you ask her out or not?"

Roger dismissed her with a flick of his hand. "Leave him alone about that, you ol' busybody. He'll ask her when he's ready."

"Actually, I've *been* ready. I've asked her out

several times, but she always says no." He shoved his hands in his front pockets and rocked on his heels. "I just asked her if she'd go to church with me in the morning."

Lauren clapped her hands. "What did she say?"

"No. She said no. But it's the way she looked that's getting me—like I'd invited her to her own execution." He slumped on the sofa cushion Lauren had just vacated. "I don't understand. Did she talk to you? I saw that she'd been crying when you two were in the kitchen. Did she tell you anything?"

"Yeah, we talked."

Scott waited, but it was Roger who prompted her. "Well, what did she say?"

Lauren flipped her hands out. "You know I can't tell you that. It's the code among best friends that we don't go telling each other's secrets."

Blowing out a breath, Scott dropped his elbows to his knees and his head into his hands.

Lauren perched on the sofa arm and rubbed his shoulders. "I will tell you this. She didn't do anything wrong, but knowing her, she's feeling like she committed some unpardonable sin. Maybe she's just not ready for church yet. Why don't you take her somewhere else?"

"Yeah. Seems like I read something..." Roger retrieved the newspaper from beside his recliner and flipped it open. "Here. This is it."

He folded it to the place and handed it to Scott, jabbing at the page. "Try this."

Scott read the ad in the Entertainment section and bolted upright. "This is perfect!"

12

Think of anything other than elephants. Try not to picture a purple elephant. No pink and purple elephants should cross your mind. Why would you even want to see pink and purple polka-dotted elephants? Just don't think about them.

But you did, didn't you?

Same thing happens to me every time I tell myself not to look down.

Concentrate on that mewing kitten just one more limb out of reach. Try to stretch to that terrified orange-splotched Manx and get her out of the tree.

Don't look down!

Just because there's a hiatus on using the charities account doesn't mean there's a hiatus on cat-catching. Folks are always looking for a cuddly pet—two more were adopted just last week. All I have to do is catch 'em and love on 'em until they're cuddly again. No one wants a feral cat.

Right now, I can't tell whether that Manx is wild or just scared—like I am.

My legs clamp around the limb I'm straddling, and I wrap an arm around a sturdy branch while my other hand keeps a firm clasp on my net, which I'm too chicken to extend to the cat. And that's all it would take. Just stretch out and drape the net over her. Then she'd go berserk, and I'd fall out of the tree and land on my keister right smack in the middle of the fire ant mound beneath me.

A whiff of smoke tickles my nose, and the urge to sneeze hits. I let out a whoppin' *Ah-choo!* and the kitten gets a bolt of courage, leaps from the tree, and darts away in a colorful blur. Now I'm stuck on this limb with a net and no prey. At least I'm in a good place to find the source of the smoke.

I wrap both arms around the branch and swivel a bit to peek over my shoulder. Sirens are blaring. The whole sky over the downtown area is covered in a billowing gray cloud.

Dear Father in Heaven, not the diner!

My pounding heart drives me into action. I toss my net beyond the fire ants and scoot backward on the limb until I'm up against the tree trunk. After one huge stabilizing breath, I swing down to the ground. I don't land on my keister and nothing's broken, so I grab my tote and net and hightail it up the street to town. "Hightail" being relative, of course. Turtles would giggle at my hobbling gait.

The street changes from dun concrete to red brick, marking the entry to the town square, and I rest against the pale pink stucco of the Jarrott's Pharmacy building. Always liked that pink building. Looks great against the red street.

Says the woman dressed in green and blue.

I catch my breath, walk to the front of the pharmacy, and turn the corner. There's the diner, its white storefront and blue canopy hazy under the smoke, but it's all right. The fire seems to be beyond it. At the corner opposite mine, Annie is standing with her arm around Clara, the diner's owner. Some of the other merchants hover nearby. They have their backs to me, watching the fire trucks screeching to a halt on the street behind the diner. I limp over and prop a hand on Annie's shoulder for support.

"Any idea who's house it is?" I ask.

"Homer and Eloise's place."

Clara's fingers are splayed across her mouth, and deep creases etch in her ancient face. Homer Peritte is her brother.

"I don't know what they'll do," she says from behind her fingers. "They're on a fixed income, and with Eloise's condition..."

Several years ago, when Eloise's hands were paining her something awful, she finally went to the doctor. Rheumatoid arthritis, he'd said, and put her on steroids for a good while. The medicine caused her bones to become so fragile, she broke a hip a few years ago and has been in a wheelchair since. Last winter, she cracked a rib just by coughing.

The city of Dogwood suffered when she lost the use of her hands. She could no longer crochet baby blankets to donate to the maternity ward or lap quilts for the nursing home. The police and fire departments still keep her afghan throws in their vehicles for when they find someone in shock or just plain cold, but the comforters will never be replaced unless someone else takes up the challenge.

Such a sweet, giving lady...and now this.

The police have blocked the street and are doing their best to avert the curious, but we wander up to the yellow sawhorse barriers just the same. We're not the only ones. Folks line both sides of the street as if some parade was featuring zebras instead of cop cars.

One young man wanders away, shoving his hands in the pockets of his jacket. He wasn't wearing the hood—kids call a jacket like that a hoodie—but why he's wearing it in August beats me. Even the coldest of cold-natured folks don't need a jacket in August.

Down the street, Homer and Eloise are a safe distance from their home, thank the Lord. From beside her, Homer leans into his wife's wheelchair, holding her the best he can. Both of their crinkled faces contort as they watch the beast devour a lifetime of memories. Eloise's bent, gnarled hands cover her face, and she slumps in her chair, her narrow shoulders shaking.

My own tears fall as I watch the flames licking the sky.

I can't take it anymore. In spite of the hiatus, I need to *do* something.

****

Distant sirens made Scott look over his shoulder as he climbed from his truck in front of the clinic. A black, roiling cloud rose from the downtown area. His chest clamped around his heart. The smoke looked awfully close to The Litter Box—and Emily. Could her apartment be on fire?

He raised a foot to the running board of his truck, ready to climb back in and speed to town, but a sedan pulled in beside him. From the passenger side, a blue-eyed blonde, about twelve years old, gave him a tearful glance. Her mother got out, her own face red with signs of crying. "Barkley was attacked by another dog. Please, please see if you can help him."

Scott turned and watched the smoke trail toward them on the wings of a high-altitude breeze. He traced the line back to its source, and again his heart clutched as he pictured how near the fire seemed to Emily's place.

"Please?" The child's plea wrenched him in two.

With another glance over his shoulder, he closed his truck door and opened the car door for the young girl. "Let's see what I can do."

A rat terrier wrapped in a bloody green towel panted on the girl's lap, its eyes dull with pain. "So this is Barkley, huh? What's your name?"

"Ashley." She sniffed, and fresh tears rolled down her cheeks. "Can you fix him?"

"I can sure try." He lifted the towel-wrapped package from her lap and motioned for them to follow him into the clinic and to an examination room, where he laid the whimpering bundle on a stainless table and called for his nurse.

Gently uncovering his patient from the towel, Scott examined the extent of its wounds—several lacerations, one of which was a four inch gash at the dog's throat.

His nurse, Tammy Gaston, appeared through the side door and smiled at Ashley and her mother, who had introduced herself as Janet Morrison. Tammy looked at the injured dog. "Poor thing."

Scott took Tammy aside. "Start an IV, okay? Let's see if we can eliminate some of his pain."

He motioned for Janet and Ashley to join him at the door to the exam room. "It'd be best if you wait outside for a bit." He ushered them into the lobby. "Dani will take care of you."

He glanced out the clinic's glass-paneled entry doors toward town and clenched his jaw. The smoke hadn't diminished, it rose and curled and traveled the high wind as if led by some winged devil. If only he knew Emily was safe. But a tearful child sniffing from a waiting-room chair spurred him to return to work.

On his way back to the examination room, he stopped by Dani's desk. "Call The Litter Box for me, would you?"

"You don't think—"

"I don't know yet."

A few minutes later, as he examined Barkley more closely—discovering the dog also had a disjointed hip—Dani poked her head into the room. "No response."

His stomach twisted. Where was Emily?

"Do you want me to try again?"

"Yes—no." Once he got involved with the dog, he wouldn't be able to take the phone. "I'll call when I'm through here."

After ninety minutes of intensive work on the dog's wounds, Scott summoned Ashley and her mother. He rested a hand on Ashley's thin shoulder. "He's going to be fine. He lost a bit of blood and his hip is going to be sore for a while, but he's going to be all right. He's unconscious right now, and I'd like to keep him overnight, but when we release him, he'll have to wear a cone around his neck." Tammy lifted a translucent plastic cone to show them. "This will keep him from chewing on the stitches."

With a nod, Scott left the rest of the instructions for Tammy to give and slipped out of the room.

Dani called to him. "Porki's next. Room two."

Scott groaned. The Vietnamese pot-bellied pig had a tendency to eat things that caused gas. He was undoubtedly there for some gastro-intestinal ailment, and his effluvia would make examination a challenge. The room itself would be out of commission for the rest of the day so it could air out. "Be there in a minute."

He landed in his worn leather desk chair and dialed The Litter Box. Five rings, no answer. After another five, just in case Emily was in the refuge instead of her apartment, he tried her cell. Still no answer. With a huff, he rocked the chair, making it squeal. *No answer* didn't mean *no problem*. But it didn't mean something was wrong either. *Lord, please don't let anything be wrong.*

****

"You can't do anything about it this time, Emily." Connor rested his forearms on his polished mahogany desk and interlocked his beefy fingers. "Aside from your basic living expenses, you have a mortgage now. Renovations to finance. The Sawyer boy's hospital bills. You can't do all that *and* help the Perittes—not to the extent you have in mind."

He was right. With all her plans, her funds would be tighter than the lid on a pickle jar until her next installment. And his list of her expenses didn't include the mortgage on The Litter Box. But there had to be a way. "I know I haven't gone through the entire down payment on Deck the Walls. Surely I can spare some of it."

"It's invested. You can't touch it without hefty penalties and taxes."

She rose from the padded client's chair to gaze out the dingy windows. The office occupied a corner in the top floor of the tallest building in town which, in a city of just over thirty thousand, stood only six stories high. Still, from the corner windows, she could see much of the town below, sprawled like a lazy snake sunning along the railroad tracks. Not a block away, the charred sacrilege that was once a beautiful old Georgian home profaned the town's serenity. Wisps of smoke from still-glowing embers whispered of violence.

Homer Peritte had been her high school history teacher. Eloise had been her grandmother's closest friend. The thought of being unable to help them scorched Emily's throat as surely as the tongues of that fiery monster had scorched the Perittes' possessions. There had to be something she could do.

She turned to face Connor. "What about the CDs? Won't a few come due soon?"

"Those are a minor asset—personal emergencies only. Besides, the Perittes are going to need more than you have in those CDs." He joined her, his brows lifted, giving his bulldog face a sympathetic countenance. "Skateboards are one thing, Em, but you simply don't have enough to help the Perittes."

Emily slumped against the credenza under the window, her strength sapped as if she'd spent the day rebuilding the house herself.

"You're acting as if it's all on your shoulders. They have insurance. They have more friends in this town than they realize. Everyone will want to help them—" His face brightened. *"That's* what you could do. Organize a fundraiser. You're good at it. Then we'll see what funds are available and maybe you could supplement some of what's needed."

"I can do that. I know of several ways to raise money." She snatched her purse off the chair, planted a kiss on his plump, ruddy cheek, and headed for the door. "I can't wait to get started."

"Hang on. Don't go yet." Connor lifted his briefcase and opened it on his desk. "Did you see today's paper?"

"No, not yet. Why?"

He withdrew a newspaper, found the page he wanted, and creased it to a quarter of its size. His face was grim as he handed it to her. "Look at this."

On page three, on the inside column above the fold, a personal ad glared in bold print from its flowery border.

The Sawyer family would like to extend their heartfelt appreciation to the benevolent person who made our son's surgery possible. Due to your generosity, Mitchell will have a fighting chance to beat this cancer. No words can express how deeply grateful we are.

"Oh, that's sweet. But why are you worried about it?"

"I just thought you should see it. I know how you like to keep your activities a secret."

She frowned. "But this doesn't expose me, does it?"

"Not by itself, but Paul Goodrich, the reporter who first wrote about the Sawyer boy, thinks it'll make a great follow-up story to find the benefactor."

"He can't find me, can he?"

"Not through me. Not through my office." Connor leaned forward and crossed his arms on his desk. "But I think you and Millie need to be careful for a while."

"Millie? Why would anyone think she's the benefactor? She certainly doesn't look the part."

"Well, maybe you're right. I doubt anyone will make the connection. I just thought I'd tell you. Goodrich is very good at his job."

"I'll be careful. Thanks for the warning." She strapped her purse over her shoulder and rose to leave. "Meanwhile, you be thinking of how much you'll contribute to the fundraiser. And make it good."

With a quick smile at Kellie, Emily walked through the secretary's office and out the law firm's door, mentally planning the fundraiser for Homer and Eloise. Should she do a raffle, or would an auction be best? Or both. Both would be good. And a dinner.

A thought stopped her in her tracks just outside the elevator—this was how it started in Houston.

One auction. One *successful* auction. Then another, then a few charity balls and functions, then she'd been sucked into the scene. The publicity. The mountainous stacks of solicitations.

Wade.

And now a news hound was after her. What if he discovered who she was? If she ended up in the paper, could Wade find her? He was up for parole soon, and he hadn't been too happy when she'd testified against him. What if he got out? What if he found her?

13

The doors opened and slid closed before Emily could stop them. She poked the button on the wall again and stepped back to wait.

Anonymity was vital. She couldn't be at the forefront of a fundraiser. Media coverage was both inevitable and invaluable for a successful event. Just one picture of her in the paper or on a local station could somehow get back to Wade.

No. She couldn't risk it. Connor was right. The couple had insurance and tons of friends and family, children and grandchildren. Someone would be willing to take them in and help them back on their feet. Sure, it would be a hardship for them for a while, until the insurance check came, and they'd probably have to leave town to stay with their son and daughter-in-law, unless they could find a place here, but they'd be all right.

The elevator doors opened, and she stepped in for the ride down.

The most a fundraiser could do was speed up the couple's recovery, maybe let them get a jump-start on rebuilding before the insurance check arrived. They'd get by. They didn't really *need* Emily's help. She should just quietly work on her own house and stay out of the limelight.

On the first floor, her heels clacked across the gray marble as she strode to the exit. She shoved open the door and took a quick breath. Her lungs filled with the charred air.

Ever since she'd returned to Dogwood, she'd helped people she didn't even know. How could she *not* help the Perittes?

She reached the curb and unlocked her car. She should solicit Lauren's help. If they worked on it together, Lauren could handle the public and the media. Besides, thinking of all this rationally—which she should've been doing all along—the only way Paul Goodrich could discover her identity was through Connor, and he'd promised to keep her secret.

She settled in the front seat and phoned Lauren, getting only her voicemail. "Hey, kiddo, it's me. Give me a call."

The more she thought about it, the less threatened she felt. Between Connor's promise and Lauren's help, she should be able to pull this off without a single flash-bulb moment. As for Paul Goodrich—*humph!* She had better things to worry about, like buying the insurance for her new house.

****

After she'd arranged with Parker Milligan to insure the Queen Anne, she unlocked the front door with a sense of reverence. This was *her* house. Her home. The Queen Anne belonged to her.

Excitement bubbled like the healing waters of an artesian well. Refurbishing her own home would be the springboard to her new career: rescuing other houses of historical design from decay and ruin. She'd be working again. After the buyers paid off their mortgage on Deck the Walls and her most popular wallpaper designs were no longer in vogue and drawing royalties, she'd have no income. Returning to work was crucial, and before-and-after pictures of her new home would be proof to the world of her talent.

Well, not the world, but proof to enough people to keep her working.

A horn blared, and she jerked around to see Scott's pickup park behind her convertible. He stepped from the truck and pocketed his keys. Dressed in jeans and a blue chambray shirt, he exuded masculinity as he waded through the weeds to the sidewalk.

Emily's blood pulsed. She hadn't seen him since Saturday night. "Hey, Scott. What are you doing here?"

"I was heading into town to look for you." He was near enough, she could see worry lines crinkling his forehead. "Was that your apartment on fire this morning?"

"No, it was the Perittes' house. Burned to the ground."

"Ouch. They all right?"

"Shaken, but uninjured."

"That's a relief. But I'm really glad it wasn't your place." He smiled, and her nerves flittered like hummingbirds on spring flowers. He pointed up at the second floor. "Won't be too long before I'll be waving to you on the balcony."

"It'll be long enough before you see me up there. You saw how much damage there was."

He looked her over, no doubt taking in the worn jeans and paint-stained work shirt. "Is that what you're doing here now? Planning to fix it all by yourself?"

"I wish." She led him into the entry and dropped her purse by the door, casting a critical eye around the grand hall. "I'm looking for things I *can* fix myself. I don't think I could just sit back and supervise while Roger and his crew did all the work."

"So, the lady loves tools."

"Some of them." She ran her hand over the cherry-wood banister that escorted the stairs up from the entry. Smooth as tree bark. "Palm sanders come to mind."

"I think we can fix that." He put his weight on the bottom stair and then climbed the next few steps. "We can fix those squeaks, too."

"*We?*"

"Sure. I'm good for more than just destroying the sex lives of cats."

"Millie and I are certainly glad you're good at that." She followed him up the stairs, pausing to finger a loose strip of wallpaper. Terra Verde Arabesque on an eggshell background. She lifted the paper and looked at the backing. Silk screened by machine. Circa 1920. Not old enough to be original to the house, but too old for her to leave on the walls. She'd have to—

"Em? Emily?" Three steps above her, Scott leaned against the wall with his arms crossed. "Did you hear me?"

Her cheeks grew hot. She felt like she'd been caught daydreaming in class. "No, sorry. What did you say?"

"I asked if Millie was going to move in here with you."

"Oh. Uh...no. No, she'll probably stay in the apartment. You know, close to the cats."

"Where did you meet her?"

"Houston." She brushed past him and continued up another step.

He stopped her with a gentle hand on her shoulder. "Do you think you'll ever be able to tell me what happened there?"

The stair she stood on was warped and so worn it dipped in the middle. She shifted her weight, and the step squealed like a rusty hinge—like her nerves whenever he asked about Houston.

"We really do need to fix these stairs." She pulled away and continued upward. A trickle of sweat trailed down her back. "First thing I'll do is get the water and power on. No way I can work in this house without at least a fan."

"Maybe the air conditioner still works."

"Wouldn't *that* be heaven?"

An old pop song chimed from her cell phone. She scrambled down the steps to the front door and dug the phone from her purse. It was Lauren. "Hey, ladybug. You got my message."

"A bit late, sorry." Brakes squealed in the background. Lauren must have been in her car. "What's up?"

Emily stole a glance at Scott, who was testing another step. Then she slipped into the dining room for privacy. "Did you hear about the fire in town today?"

"The Perittes' house? I heard about it. Awful, isn't it?"

"Yeah. I want to hold a benefit auction for them. Interested?"

"Oh, that's a great idea. I'd love to do something to help." A siren shrilled in the background and grew louder as it neared Lauren's car. She kept silent until it passed. "Another fire truck. No telling where that one's going. So, do you want to come out Saturday?"

"Sure. What time?"

"Shoot for early afternoon."

"That works, but there's one thing. Don't mention this to anyone until we have a chance to talk." She poked her head into the grand hall and caught sight of Scott on the second-floor landing. "I have something I want to discuss with you, and I can't right now."

"Where are you?"

"At the house. Scott and I are looking for ways to keep my money from padding Roger's pockets."

"Scott's with you? I won't keep you then. Say yes. See ya Saturday."

"Say yes to what?" But Lauren had already disconnected. Emily folded her phone and stepped into the foyer to peer up at Scott. "That was Lauren. What am I supposed to say yes to?"

Looking like the shy teenager he once was, he shoved his hands in his pockets. "Going to the community theater with me Saturday night."

She tilted her head. She'd already said no to him so many times she'd lost count, and she still wasn't sure whether she was ready to date. But he looked so cute standing there, braving another rejection, that she found it difficult to turn him down. "Yes. I'd love to."

****

Scott's knees almost buckled. "Excuse me? Did you just say yes?"

Emily laughed and nodded, and he felt he'd grown three feet. Restraining from crowing like a rooster, he mustered all the dignity he could summon and smiled as he went down the stairs with a studied nonchalance. "Good. Seven work for you?"

Her eyes sparkled like sun-blessed crystal. "That

works."

"Good." Suddenly, the suave, confident, man-about-town persona he'd slipped into dropped to his ankles like over-sized britches. What was he supposed to do now that she'd accepted? What should he say? Was there a—a *protocol* for this? "Should I—uh...should I pick you up here or at your apartment?"

Humor teased her lips, and he realized how foolish his question was. But she was gracious. "The apartment would be best."

"Good, good." He rocked on his heels. "So, seven o'clock at your apartment."

"Right."

"Right." More silence, more heel rocking. Finally, he made a show of looking at his watch, even though he had no place to be. He just needed to find a double-sized root beer float to drown this shyness he thought he'd outgrown. "I'd better be going. I'll see you at seven Saturday night."

"We'll have a great time."

He nodded, gave her a little wave and then sprinted to his truck. She'd said yes!—and he'd acted like an idiot. He charged up the engine and squealed his tires as he raced from the house.

True, he'd been shy as a kid. But he'd outgrown it, hadn't he? Learned to deal with it. He'd even dated in college. Sure, he may have gotten a late start at it, but he'd finally gotten up the nerve to ask someone out. Several someones in fact, not that he was bragging.

Up on the left of Central Avenue was the carhop restaurant, just one block away from the turnoff to his mom's house. At sixteen, when he'd gotten his first set of wheels—an ancient blue sedan—he used to stop at the place on his way home and wash away the day's humiliations with root beer floats. Fortunately, he'd had a high metabolism and was skinny all through school. Since his metabolism was still high, he wasn't worried about ordering one now to settle his nerves.

The street light turned red. While the truck idled, he watched a carhop on skates carry a brown paper package and two giant sodas to a late model convertible.

Once, in high school, Emily had pulled her new hatchback into the space right next to his rust-spotted car. The lid to his float wasn't on good, and he'd fumbled the drink, drenching the front of his shirt with root beer about the same time Lauren, sitting in Emily's passenger seat, shouted a greeting out her window.

When Emily leaned forward to wave at him, he'd wanted to drop through the floorboards and slither away. He'd hated that she'd seen him looking like the gawky teenager he was then. That was the night before auditions for the high school play and...

The play!

An idea formed in his mind, and when the light turned green, he zipped past the restaurant and turned left a block away, heading toward his mother's—and the things he kept stored in her attic.

14

Someone's sitting at my table, not that I mind. It's not like I usually come into the diner at this time of day. I'm rarely here for breakfast, just the occasional lunch. And, besides, there's more than one air conditioner vent in this place.

The diner is layered from right to left. Red plastic booths at the window on the right, deli-style tables next, then the bar stools around the counter, and finally the kitchen. The only thing that doesn't fit into any of the rows is the glass-front counter, filled with candies and topped with a cash register, perched right next to the front door. But what's important to me is the grate-covered vents in the ceiling. It's already hot this morning.

I limp back to the last booth, slide my net in, and plant myself directly under a blast of cool air.

"Mornin', Millie," Annie says. "You're here early."

"Had a hankerin' for pancakes." And a twenty dollar bill, crisp and fresh, burning a hole in my pocket. It's seldom I treat myself to a meal, and breakfast is my favorite. I grab the folded menu propped between the bowl of sugar packets and the salt and pepper shakers. Gotta love this fare—fried everything. Clara doesn't believe in letting the spoons get greasy all by themselves. "I'm hungry this morning. Slap on some sausage and eggs-over-easy with the pancakes."

"You are hungry! I don't think I've ever seen you eat so much. Anything to drink?"

"Water. No—milk. I feel like splurging." I glance behind the counter and then check the register. "Where's Clara?"

"She's been coming in late the past couple of days since the fire. Guess having Homer and Eloise at her house throws her schedule off."

"So she's putting them up for a while?"

"Until they decide where to go, I guess."

Someone calls Annie, and she gives me a smile before slipping off to another table. I look around at the other diners clinking silverware against plates. Blue collars, pink collars, business suits. Wherever they fit on the social ladder, folks still get hungry. People who wouldn't get invited to join the local country club sit right close to those who would keep them out. That's what I love about this place. Highbrow meets redneck in the only downtown diner open for breakfast.

In the next booth, a thirtyish blond man munches on a toast wedge and talks with his mouth full. "According to the CEO's assistant, they just got a letter with a certified check that was supposed to be the first of several."

The older man sitting across from him, with his back to me, lowers his coffee cup. "Did she say who the letter was from?"

"Some attorney. Uh—" Blondie flips open a notepad. "Matthews. Connor Matthews, Attorney-at-Law."

I pop a hand to my chest. If my heart wasn't so strong, I'd be in cardiac arrest right now. Those two must work for the paper. Is Blondie Paul Goodrich? The brown-haired guy must be the editor. I glance around the diner and try not to seem like I'm listening, but my gaze keeps snapping back like nails to a magnet.

"So, this Matthews guy is footing the bill, right?"

"Nope, we don't know who's paying for all this. Matthews represents someone who 'wished to remain anonymous,' according to the letter."

"She let you see this letter?"

"No, and this is the strange part. She said even if it didn't breach confidentiality, she couldn't show it to me. Instructions were to shred it." Blondie slapped the table. "Can you beat that?" His cell rings, and he grabs it from his pocket. "Goodrich...yeah, he's here...we're on it."

"What's going on?"

"Another fire a few blocks over. We gotta roll." He shoved a piece of bacon in his mouth and rounded up his pen and notepad while the other man tossed twenty-five dollars on the table.

"That makes three now," the dark-haired guy said as he headed out the door.

"They say this one's goin' up fast..."

The door closes behind them, and I take a moment to breathe. My head's so jumbled I don't know what to think. Ol' Connor's smart. Shred the letter. That was brilliant! At the same time, though, I worry about the fact there's another house burning.

There's no sign of smoke out the window. Wind must be blowing the other way. The Wednesday morning traffic thins long enough for me to see a silver and white kitty licking something on the sidewalk across the street. Pretty thing. Lucky for him I'm too hungry to go after him. I'll park myself on the courthouse lawn later and see if I can find him again.

"They've got another fire, huh?" Annie approaches with my milk and a steaming plate that makes my mouth water.

"That's what I heard. They were newspapermen, weren't they? Was one Paul Goodrich?"

"Yeah, he comes in from time to time. The other one's Kevin Favente, the editor." She plops down some extra napkins for me. "You hear about the second fire yesterday?"

"I heard the siren. Who got hit?"

"The Chapmans."

My heart wilts. Al and Lorraine Chapman own Chapman's Home Improvement Center. Right after Hurricane Rita ripped through our area, they discounted their prices so folks could repair their homes. Good Christian people. "I sure hate hearing that."

"Me, too." She twiddles her pencil. "Newspaper's calling it arson."

I hover my knife over the little single-serving butter tub. "Do they know that for sure?"

She nodded. "They quoted the fire chief. Said the city's calling for an investigator from the FBI or something. Those beautiful old homes. It's sad."

"It's a sin. Someone has no respect for antiquity. No love of beauty." I shake my head and slather butter all over my pancakes. "How are the plans for your barbecue restaurant coming along?"

Her face lights up bright enough to guide ships from sea. "We're buying the lot this afternoon. Just a block from here. Oh, Millie, I wish there was a way to thank whoever sent us the funds for this. Kyle said there was no return address..."

You bet there was no return address on that

envelope. That's what keeps an anonymous benefactor anonymous.

She gets called away again. I douse my pancakes with syrup and start scarfing them down with the sausage and eggs like I hadn't eaten in a month. After I finish, feeling fuller than a tick on a fat cat, I reach for the ticket.

Six dollars and fifty cents? Highway robbery! You'd think those were the golden eggs the goose laid.

I dig the twenty out of my pocket and hobble up to the counter to pay the bill and then back again to leave a seven dollar tip for Annie. Leaves me with six and a half. More than enough.

Wonder if I can still find that pretty silver cat.

15

Silver grumbled from his cage in the passenger seat as Emily pulled into Lauren's driveway Saturday afternoon. Lauren waved at her from the front yard where she stood watering the pansies with a garden hose.

Emily switched off her engine and climbed out, hoisting the pet carrier with her. "I hope you don't mind, but I brought a friend with me. I had to pick him up before the clinic closed and hated to drive back into town."

Lauren twisted the nozzle on the hose to shut off the spray and strode to the car to peek at the drowsy cat. Emily could've sworn bright red cartoon hearts throbbed from her friend's eyes. "Oh, he is just beautiful."

"Isn't he? He's neutered and vaccinated and up for adoption, if you're interested."

Lauren laughed. "Oh, I'm interested. Just let me check with the boss first. Come on, let's get him inside."

"I'm glad you don't mind. It's a bit hot out here for a groggy cat. He's suffered enough for a while."

"I wish you had told me you were going to the clinic. I would've asked you to bring Scott." Lauren stopped beside the house to turn off the faucet and then winked at Emily. "I would've put him to work helping Roger with the honey-dos."

"He had a full waiting room. He told me to tell you thanks, by the way."

"For what?"

"He said you'd know." Emily pinned her with a mock glare. "But I'm sure it has something to do with our plans for tonight."

"Oh. He's welcome." Lauren waggled her eyebrows. "And so are you."

Emily playfully slapped her shoulder.

They walked inside, and Lauren pointed to a place beside the TV for Silver. Emily glanced at the dopey-eyed cat. Once his cage was still, he could drift back into oblivion until the anesthesia wore off. She lowered the carrier to the floor.

"It's quiet in here. Where is everyone?"

"The kids are making the most of their Saturday at a neighbor's pool." Lauren dropped to her knees beside the coffee table and started stacking dominoes from a recent game back into the box. "I shooed Roger over to Chapman's Home Improvement Center so he could get what he needs to *finally* fix that leaky shower. He should be gone for a good while."

"Awful about the Chapmans' home, isn't it?"

Lauren nodded gravely. "The fire truck that passed me the other day was going there."

"And there was another fire just Wednesday—Cal and Markie Wallace."

"I wish they'd catch this guy."

"Me, too." Emily kicked off her shoes and knelt across from Lauren. She stacked the ace-deuce and double six in the box. "Do you think we'll get enough out of an auction to help all three victims?"

"I don't know. In a town this size, the money sources can either dry up quick or rally in the face of adversity."

"Let's just hope they rally."

Lauren ripped the score page off a pad of paper and wadded it and then tore off several sheets and slid them to Emily along with a pen. "What are you planning to donate?"

"I don't have much anymore." Emily considered the irony of hosting a benefit while being so cash poor herself. "Cats, I guess."

"Oh, sure. I bet they'll fetch a good price." With her chin in one hand, she tapped her pen on the table with the other. "We need to come up with a hefty plan to squeeze some money from our local rich folks."

"Yeah, about that." Emily stole a glance at her friend from under her brows. "I need you to take full credit for this fundraiser."

The pen stopped tapping. "That doesn't make sense. I don't know the first thing about raising money like this."

"I know. I'll be right here to help you all the way. I just need to be behind the scenes."

Lauren squinted at her. "What's up?"

"Nothing, really. It's just...well, these kinds of events attract the media. And we need the media. The more hype we can get, the more funds we're likely to raise."

"But you don't want your face in the public, right? Is this about Wade?"

Emily nodded and frowned at her cuticles. "You should've seen the look he was giving me while I testified against him. Pure hate." She shuddered at the memory. "I don't want him to know where I am."

"He can't do anything to you. He's in prison."

"Yes, but he's eligible for parole in a few months."

Emily sighed. "Charity fraud is a white-collar crime and his sentence wasn't that stiff. He may not be the kind who would hurt me, but—"

"But we aren't going to take that chance." A quizzical look crossed Lauren's face, and she tilted her head. "Wouldn't he guess you came home? Doesn't he know where you're from?"

"No, he doesn't." She sighed. "We rarely talked about me—something else that should've clued me in to what a jerk he was. We talked about the orphanage and about him. All of it turned out to be lies, of course. I was an idiot."

"No. You were a woman in love." Lauren reached for Emily's hand and rubbed her knuckles. "It's a shame. I know how much you loved working with charities and organizing fundraisers. It's like he took something from you. Took from you the one thing you love doing. What do you do now?" She smirked. "Write a check like the rest of us whenever someone wants money?"

"Oh, no. I fell into that trap in Houston, and it's one thing I'm glad to have left there. Haven't you ever noticed how many more solicitations you get once you start that?" Emily smiled. "No, I have my ways. I help who I want to help. I just do it anonymously."

With raised brows, Lauren looked at her curiously, but shrugged when Emily didn't say more. "All right, then. I'll handle all the public stuff. You just show me what to do."

The back door slammed, and Roger stumped into view with a sack in his hand, which he left by the door. "Wow. So much beauty in one place." He leaned down to kiss his wife and tossed a smile at Emily.

"That didn't take you long," Lauren said.

"Knew just what I wanted and just where it was. The king of home repairs knows all." He chuckled at Lauren's smirk and then peeked into the carrier. "Great cat. Can we keep him?"

Lauren let out a *whoop!* and stretched her arms toward him. "I was hoping you'd want to."

He returned and bent to accept her hug. "Have the town's do-gooders been doing good, or have you two been gossiping the entire time?"

"We haven't even started the gossiping yet." A mischievous gleam appeared in Lauren's eyes, and she pinned it on Roger. "You know, you could be a do-gooder, too."

He looked like a trapped fox. "Oh, no you don't. You're not going to have me picking out floral arrangements and linen napkins."

"Of course not. Last time you did that, the flowers were orange plastic and the napkins were chartreuse." She winked at Emily. "No, I want you to donate your services to be auctioned off."

"No flowers and napkins?"

"Nope."

"What will you give me in exchange?"

"What do you have in mind?" Lauren's voice was low and sexy, a suggestive spark filled her tone.

He squatted next to her and rubbed circles on her back. Nuzzling her hair, he muttered, "Help me fix the shower leak."

She pushed him, and he fell over backwards, laughing. "Hey, it was worth a shot."

Using Lauren's shoulder to haul himself up, he looked at Emily. "What about you? Want to help?"

"No, no. Not me. I'm not that much of a do-gooder. Besides, we'd better get to business before I have to scoot." She grabbed the blank pages off the table and tamped them down into a neat bundle.

"Not staying for supper?" Roger gave her an impish grin. "You got a hot date?"

Emily felt heat rise to her cheeks at the knowing look on Lauren's face.

Lauren winked at Roger. "She finally said yes to Scott."

16

Standing before the mirror, Emily smiled at her reflection and slid her hands down the smooth navy satin of a floor-length split skirt. The last time she'd worn this had been at the grand opening party for Deck the Walls seven years ago, and it still fit. Her satisfaction waned when she caught sight of her bare toes peeking out from under the hem. Finding her shoes should've been the first thing she did. No telling where they were. Her skirt swished against her legs as she rushed to her closet, butterfly sleeves billowing.

She didn't have an ounce of the confidence she'd felt when Scott asked her out, but she had no valid reason to be this nervous. This was *Scott*—her lifelong friend, her secret crush since sixth grade, her cats' veterinarian—for goodness sake! At one time, having him ask her out would've caused her heart to float. Maybe it would still be light as eiderdown in the breeze if it wasn't so busy hammering its imprint into her ribs.

Inside her modest walk-in closet, she dropped to her hands and knees to dig through shoes piled loosely on the floor. She had a classy pair of string sandals to wear with this outfit, but they were hidden among the sneakers and loafers her current lifestyle demanded. She found a smooth pebble resting on the floor and slipped it back into a pair of tennis shoes and then caught sight of the sandals in the back of the closet and grabbed them.

With both feet strapped precariously into the spike-heeled sandals, she stumbled back to her full-length mirror and caught sight of the dust on her shins and the cockeyed angle of her bugle-beaded neckline. She brushed and straightened and glared at her reflection. Even after everything she'd been through the past few years, *ninny* was a word she would never have applied to herself. Until this moment.

The doorbell clanged, and she slapped a hand over her startled heart. She blew a breath through her cheeks and then sucked in another. And another, until her nerves calmed and her senses returned.

This really was ridiculous.

Ninny.

With a final glare at her reflection, she headed downstairs and to the door, shooing cats with their shedding fur away from her skirt.

In his navy suit, striped tie, and crisp white shirt, Scott was a striking man. The breeze brushed his hair alluringly against his forehead as he held out a bouquet of Shasta daisies and baby's breath. "Still your favorites?"

Surprise bubbled like champagne as she filled her arms with the flowers. "Yes, they are. Thank you for remembering. They're beautiful." She sank her nose into the petals and then waved him in with a smile. "Just let me put these in water."

"Don't you want to know what this is?" He stepped inside and held out a small, flat package wrapped in green paper and a white bow.

"That's sweet, Scott, but you didn't have to get me anything. The flowers are more than enough." The rectangular gift was light and thin as a pancake. "What is it?"

"Open it."

She handed the flowers back to him to hold and then slid her nail along the tape on the bottom of the present. The paper fell away, revealing the age-yellowed program of a high school play.

She caressed the pamphlet and flipped through it, remembering the names of her classmates. "I can't believe you kept this all these years."

"That's what we're going to see tonight." His expression softened. "Of all our high school plays, this is the only one we starred in together."

"I remember. Playing a role was always so much fun. I could be whoever I wanted to be, do things I wouldn't ordinarily do."

"Tell me about it." He slid his hands in his pockets and rocked on his heels. "As long as I could be someone else, I wasn't shy. Stepping into character helped me survive college."

Emily glanced at him, giving him a sly smile. "Too bad you never exercised what you'd learned *before* college."

He laughed. "It took me all those years to perfect it, and by the time I got back, you were already gone."

Gone. To Houston. To her downfall.

She reached for the daisies. "I need to put these in water."

Upstairs in her kitchen, she stared absently at the vases stored in the cabinet over the refrigerator. Almost two years had passed since Wade received his prison sentence, and at least a year since she returned home for a fresh start. Would the pain of her life in Houston *ever* become a distant memory?

She shook her head. She should've broken her date

with Scott. She just wasn't ready.

But she saw no way out. He was standing downstairs waiting for her—probably surrounded by cats—and she needed to get moving or they'd be late. She glanced back to the table where she'd laid the program and the flowers.

He'd remembered. After all these years, he'd remembered.

Smiling to herself, she grabbed a clear, pot-bellied vase and filled it with water. Softly humming, she quickly arranged the flowers.

****

Good thing Lauren had reminded Scott of Emily's favorite flowers. She had beamed when she saw the huge bouquet he brought. But the look of surprise on her face when he gave her the program made his chest swell. Tonight would be great. He just knew it. He'd seen the sadness cloud her expression and worried she would change her mind about going, but she was cornered now.

If she crawfished out of going to the play, she still had to face him alone in the refuge. If nothing else, they could sit on the stairs while he cajoled her into talking to him. Earlier, as he drove to her apartment, he'd made a pact with himself not to bring up Houston or question her about what happened there, but if she backed out of their date, all bets were off. He'd grill her like a T-bone on a hot fire until he gained some understanding of what had happened to the girl he'd loved most of his life.

He spied Daisy peeking from the round entry of a gray, carpet-covered box and stooped to coax her out.

The fact that Emily would take care of the cats endeared her to him even more. She'd always been sensitive to both people and animals, kind-hearted and giving. Maybe someone in Houston had taken advantage of her generous nature. He balled his fist at the idea of anyone hurting her. She'd been wounded so deeply, there were times he didn't recognize her at all, as if her personality had been altered. And he didn't know how to help.

Perhaps it was best he didn't know who had caused her pain. He'd hunt the man down and serve him up as dog food.

Daisy eased out of the box and took a few tentative steps toward him, and he softened. She came within reach to allow him to pet her, and his anger melted entirely. He asked the Lord for forgiveness for wanting vengeance on whoever had hurt Emily. *But, please, Father, show me how to help her.*

Upstairs, her apartment door opened and closed, and she descended into his view. Excitement tightened his stomach, as it always did when he saw her. She smiled at him, and his breath rushed out in relief. She hadn't changed her mind.

Whatever had made him react with all the cool of a pimply-faced teenager when she'd accepted this date was long gone. He met her at the bottom of the stairs and extended a smile and an escort's arm.

****

After the play, Scott turned into a parking space outside Zabaglione's. Emily's heart jumped. She'd always wanted to eat here. The restaurant sat hidden off Main Street behind a black wrought-iron fence, a tidy courtyard, and a cracked red-brick façade, half covered with ivy. The *Roma* setting made the place a draw for tourists in the area, a prime location for married couples' date nights, and a popular choice before the prom. And it was expensive.

"If you're trying to impress me, you've succeeded."

"Enjoy it." Scott unlatched his seatbelt. "If we were still kids, our date would've been a cheap movie and a one-topping pizza."

He exited the truck, circled it to let her out and then guided her through the gate and the herb-scented courtyard with his hand resting gently on the small of her back. Every molecule in her body focused on the warmth of his touch.

A fragrant blanket of Italian spices wrapped them the moment they entered the restaurant. The hostess led them to a quiet corner booth with a white linen tablecloth and a tapered candle dripping wax on a fat-bellied wine bottle. The waitress brought two glasses of ice water and the menus.

After they'd placed their orders, Scott leaned toward her. "Did you enjoy the play?"

"Oh, yes. I'm enjoying the whole evening." She glanced at him from beneath her lashes.

"I like being with you. I wish you had said yes when I first asked you out." He seemed to see only her, his smile was intended for no one else.

The setting reminded her of her daydream at Lauren's house—candlelight, a table for two, the warm, delicious feeling of being alone in the universe with Scott.

For a moment, he studied his water glass, frowning at some unseen infraction. When he focused on her again, the smoky light of desire had dimmed, replaced with bright interest. "I think what you and Lauren are planning for the fire victims is great."

"She told you about that?" She cringed inwardly. Although Roger's knowing was unavoidable, she hadn't wanted anyone else to find out, not even Scott. "What did she tell you?"

"Just that you're helping her plan a fundraiser and you two are collecting goods for an auction. How can I help?"

At least Lauren hadn't told him the whole story. Emily crossed her arms on the table and leaned forward with a smile teasing her lips. "You can donate your services."

"Oh, yeah, that's good. I can see the slogan now." He held his hand up as if picturing a banner on a distant wall. *"Help the fire victims! Spay or neuter your pet today!"*

Emily laughed. She followed his gesturing hand but snagged sight of a man two tables over.

Paul Goodrich.

She stared at the handsome journalist leaning intimately close to the dark-haired beauty next to him. As the woman slipped a strand of hair behind her ear, her diamond wedding set caught the light in a dazzling show of fire and ice. Her laughter rang across the room, and Goodrich beamed as if proud to have brought it from her lips.

He looked harmless now, not at all like a villain intent on exposing Emily, wrecking her privacy, and possibly setting her up for an assassination attempt by a con artist. He was just another man in love.

The waitress brought their meals, and Emily jerked her attention from her would-be nemesis. At least he wasn't on the prowl. Tonight, she was safe to enjoy Scott's company.

But she couldn't help keeping a wary eye on the other table.

****

Jealousy circled like a vulture in Scott's mind, but when he caught the look on Emily's face as she stole glances at the man nearby, he realized her attention was tinged not with interest, but discomfort—or even fear. Again, he battled his desire to yank her history in Houston out of her and settle his curiosity once and for all. But he decided to simply regain her attention instead.

"I'd be glad to fix a pet or two."

"What? Oh, wow! That's so generous! Your donations will really help." Her cheeks flushed cherry red. She cut into her chicken picatta and was apparently content now to keep her mind on this table. "We need so many more. I just hope we can make enough money to benefit all three families."

"Three? I knew about the Perittes and the Chapmans. Who's the third?"

"Cal and Markie Wallace. Their house was hit Wednesday morning."

"Man, that's rough. I really hope they catch the arsonist."

"So do I." Her brow furrowed. "I know the Perittes are staying with Clara, and I found out the Wallaces are with their son and daughter-in-law. I wonder where the Chapmans landed?"

"They don't have family here. Right now they're in the motel over by the highway." He shook his head.

"Sad situation. No telling how long they'll have to stay in the motel before their house is rebuilt. Maybe a friend will take them in or they can rent a place for a while. At least they can get the building supplies at their store."

Again, Emily's focus swiveled to the other table. Something about that man—or maybe the woman beside him?—worried her. Scott couldn't take it any longer. "Is everything all right? Do you know that couple?"

"No. I've never met them." Her hand shook, her fork clattered against her plate. "I was just—I mean— did you see the diamonds in her wedding ring? They're astounding!"

Diamonds? He didn't buy it. Something else was going on in her head, but he turned to look just the same and caught sight of the couple rising from the table to leave. Good. With them gone, he could have Emily all to himself again.

****

Full and satisfied from dinner, Scott escorted Emily to the door at The Litter Box. Other than her distraction with the other couple at the restaurant, the evening had been perfect, and he wasn't sure he wanted it to end.

She must've felt the same way. Instead of reaching into her purse for her key, she turned and leaned back against the door. "I had a great time. Thanks for everything."

"I had a great time, too." He toyed with a silky strand of her hair. "We're having a picnic at the church tomorrow after service. Want to come?"

Panic rose in her eyes as soon as he got the words out. "Scott—"

"I'm not asking you to come to the service, just the picnic after." He stopped playing with her hair to trace her jawline with his finger. "I mean, think about it—Mom's fried chicken and applesauce pound cake. How bad can it be?"

"Well—"

Lowering his head, he brushed his lips lightly against hers. "Say yes."

"Convince me." She tilted her head, inviting another kiss.

He lingered this time, tasting her sweetness, pulling her closer. "Say yes."

"Once more."

Again, he kissed her and felt her hands slide up his back. He'd waited for this all of his life...and he'd have to wait a bit longer, or his actions would be beyond his control. "Say yes."

"Yes." Her voice was breathless, her eyes still closed, her lips slightly parted.

He drew a sharp breath at the invitation offered. If he played his cards right, he'd see this vision every night forever, with her as his wife. But this wasn't the time. He swept his thumb lightly along her cheek. "I'll see you tomorrow."

"Tomorrow," she whispered dreamily, and a soft smile rested on her lips. "I'll see you tomorrow."

As she let herself in, he shoved his hands in his pockets to keep from reaching for her. She waved her fingers and closed the door. With his heart about to explode, he turned and jogged toward his truck as if by moving faster, he could make tomorrow come sooner.

17

I feel like an undercover agent hiding in the shadows. It's too early on a Sunday for anyone to be up and about, but I'm not leaving my place among these cedars until I'm sure. Last time I did this, I was sneaking a skateboard into Justin's backyard. Got right up to the steps before the dog next door started barking his fool head off. Fortunately, there aren't any dogs near Clara's place.

She has a single story, low-roofed house in a style popular back in the sixties. It's still dark inside—well, it's dark outside, too. The front door has a square-cut window in it. Sometimes the framing board's loose on windows like that; maybe I can slip the envelope between the wood and the glass. She'd be sure to see it then. But if it won't fit there, maybe I can jam it between the door and the frame. Maybe I'd have to ring the doorbell to make sure she sees it. Can't have it just sitting there.

It's not much, just five hundred. Just enough to help with the added expenses of having two extra mouths to feed, two more showers to drain the water heater—that sort of thing.

One more glance up the street and at the surrounding homes and then I slip out from among the trees and ease up the sidewalk. A garage door opens somewhere behind me, and I skitter behind a blackjack hickory and peek around its broad trunk. Across the street, two doors down, a dad and his son are hitching a boat trailer to a pickup. I can see them pretty good by the glow of the garage light.

They get the boat ready and jump into the cab of the truck. Dad fires up the motor and rolls down the driveway. The garage door lowers, and the headlights of his rig sweep toward me. I duck behind the tree to wait until the fishermen pass and then step from my hiding place. Since I've already trampled Clara's lawn, there's no point in heading back to the sidewalk. It's just a few more steps in the grass until I'm on the front walk.

A light flips on in the house.

I rush to the door, jam the envelope in the window framing, and hurry back to the cedars to watch what happens.

Clara steps out and grabs the envelope as if she'd seen me put it there. She looks both ways from her front walk, scratches her sleep-matted hair, and opens the envelope. She gawks at the contents, and I stifle a giggle. I love watching folks open their surprises, but I hope she didn't see me. Can't be anonymous if someone knows who you are.

After she goes back inside, I start walking. I have two more stops to make before the sun sets fire to the day. May have to get the car for the trip out to the highway. I'll never beat the sun if I walk.

****

Finding the Wallaces at their kids' house took up more time than I'd hoped, so I had no choice but to get the car to run to the motel on the highway. The sun's up and beaming when I pull into the circle drive in front of the lobby. I grab the last envelope and make sure it's good and sealed before heading inside. The girl behind the counter—Hayley, according to her name tag, and she can't possibly be a day over twelve—gives me a bleary-eyed greeting and a tired smile like she'd been up all night. And she probably was. The night shift has gotta be killer on the body, even one that young.

"Are Al and Loraine Chapman here?"

"Yes, they are. I don't even have to look up their room number anymore. They've been getting lots of calls and visitors. They must be popular folks, ya know?" Her lips droop a bit. "'Course, it's just awful, isn't it? Their house burning down and all? Did you know about that?"

I nod in the bare breath of space she gives me to respond and start to hand over the envelope for her to leave for them when she kicks her tongue into action again.

"I guess their friends don't have anywhere to visit 'em but here. And that's kinda sad, ya know? I mean, there isn't a lot of space in that motel room. Of course, the Chapmans *could* go visit folks in their homes, but for some reason everyone seems to come over here."

"That's good. I'm glad they've had visitors. Could you—"

"Well, I guess folks mainly come over here to take 'em out to eat or bring 'em food or something. Not that I notice. I don't pry, ya know? I just know things. Just see what's going on."

"Of course you do—"

"And that journalist, Paul Goodrich? He came up last night, but they were out. He said he'd catch 'em sometime today." She leans toward me like she's sharing a secret. "Isn't he just the hottest man you've ever seen? I know he's married and all, but..."

Just hearing his name smacks my heart to a dead stop. I admit he's a looker, but mostly, he's a threat, and the way this gal's talkin' I'll still be here trying to hand over the envelope when he shows up. Can't have that!

I reach across the counter and lay a hand on hers. "Excuse me, I just need to leave this for the Chapmans. Can you make sure they get it?"

"Oh, sure. But I bet they're up. Want me to ring their room and have them come—"

"No, no. Just give it to them when you see them, please?"

I'm heading to the door when she calls out, "Who should I say this is from?"

Those sliding doors couldn't close behind me fast enough.

****

Emily leaned against her closet door and stared at the array of clothing inside. Soon, Scott would be there to pick her up, and she wasn't ready. Preparing for her date today wasn't as simple as it had been last night; dressing up for a play was standard etiquette. But a church picnic, when you hadn't attended the services, was a bit trickier. Should she dress for church as everyone else had? Or should she dress for a dinner on the grounds? She had twenty minutes to make up her mind and get ready.

She decided on a flowing ankle-length skirt and an ivory poet blouse, which she buttoned in front of the mirror. With her flat sandals, the overall effect was reminiscent of a 1920s America the artist Monet would've loved. She shoved her fingers into her scalp and shook her hair until the dark curls cascaded around her face.

Yes, indeed. Monet would've been pleased. All she needed was a lacy parasol. She twisted in front of the mirror. Her skirt swirled softly around her legs and sighed, *Romance.*

She grinned at her reflection. Maybe romance was just what she needed in this new life she was being forced to create. Scott's kiss last night had certainly reminded her of what she'd been missing. And this time, it felt *right*, different from how she'd felt with Wade. Or maybe her memory of their relationship was distorted by the results.

But it was different with Scott. She shook her head at their life-long courtship—or lack of one. A second date between them was an incredible forward step in their relationship. And that second date was just moments away.

She slipped her keys and lipstick into a white crocheted bag and headed downstairs to wait. Either he was late, or she'd dressed in record time. She glanced at her watch. He wasn't late.

Bulldog, a fat tabby, curled around her leg, and she sat on the bottom step to rub his chin. She wasn't nervous like she had been before their date last night. She was...excited. Why was that? Why had she been so convinced last night that it was too early to date, yet this afternoon she could hardly wait for Scott to ring her doorbell?

A car door slammed outside, and she leapt to see if it was him, catching a glimpse of his pickup through the storefront windows. She opened the door just as the bell chimed.

Scott had loosened his red herringbone tie and unbuttoned the top button of his white broadcloth shirt, giving him a casual Friday-at-five appeal. His hair wisped his brow with flair, and his eyes sparked when he saw her. He looked her over, curled hair to coral toenails, and gave her a roguish movie-star smile.

She relished his appreciation, feeling prettier in her picnic casuals than her evening satin from last night.

"Ready?" He offered his arm.

She nodded and rested her hand on his sleeve.

He opened the truck door for her and slipped his Bible from the passenger seat to the dashboard before helping her in.

The sight of the brown leather book with its gold lettering pricked a hole in the ballooning perfection of the day. The *church* part of church picnic hit her like a judge's gavel, and she found herself wishing for a dowdy sweater to take cover in. Although she wouldn't technically be going to church, the reality of being in the presence of so many of her old friends made her nerves shudder. What if someone knew about her past in Houston? She couldn't risk Scott finding out.

"You all right?" Scott waited to close her door.

The hem of her skirt dangled outside the truck. She slipped it in and gave him a nervous smile. "Yeah. Sure. I was just thinking..." There had to be a way to avoid this—or maybe postpone it until she could regain her wits. "Shouldn't I make a casserole or something? I mean, I really hate to go empty-handed. Maybe I should make something?"

He laughed and shut her in. Like a warden

slamming the cell door. Through the open window, he said, "Don't worry. Between my mom and Lauren alone, there will be enough food to go around."

As he rounded to the driver's side, she felt her muscles relax at the reminder that Lauren and her family would be there. The church wasn't exactly an enemy camp, but it still felt nice to have an ally.

****

Located two miles outside of town, the double-spired, white frame church looked just as Emily remembered, but the elms sheltering it seemed shorter than when she'd climbed them as a child.

The surrounding lawn hosted a game of tag, and young kids dressed in the bright yellows and blues of summer chased each other among the weeds.

Scott parked on the grass behind the church and peered through the windshield at the picnic tables. To the right of the tables, Lauren raised to her knees on her spread blanket and waved like a soccer fan.

"There they are." Emily pointed and then laughed at Lauren's gestures. "I think that means we're supposed to get our plates before we join them."

"Sounds like a plan." Scott yanked off his tie and draped it around the rearview mirror before getting out of the truck.

Emily cast a glance at all the other faces looking their way and drew a sharp breath. She lowered the visor, as much to hide as to check in the mirror, and gave herself a placid smile—the smile she should've practiced *before* returning to the church home of her childhood. Maybe only a few of the members would remember her. Anonymity. She craved it. As long as no one knew her, she wouldn't have to answer questions. She squeezed her eyes shut.

Please, God. Strike them all with memory loss.

Scott helped her from the truck and escorted her between the cars parked on the turf. As they crossed toward the buffet tables, he rubbed her hand, and she realized she'd been clenching his arm like a drenched rat on a river raft.

He lowered his lips to her ear. "Relax, would you? With all this food out here, no one's going to bite *you*."

"I know. You're right." She pressed a hand against her stomach.

He drew her to a stop in front of him. "But you're still nervous."

Tucking her lower lip between her teeth, she nodded.

"There aren't that many people here you don't know. It's not like I'm dragging you into a ring of strangers."

"I know. That's just it." She peeked at the picnickers from the corner of her eye. "Running into folks I know one or two at a time is one thing. But everyone, all at once? I'm not sure I'm ready."

"Tell you what." He draped his arm across her shoulders. "If someone gets too inquisitive, you just give me the nod. I'll ride up on my white steed and rescue you."

"Your white steed or your red truck?"

"Whichever is closest." He gave her a gentle nudge toward the crowd. "You'll be fine."

She laughed and let him guide her to the buffet. Maybe his mom's chicken would settle the buzzards circling in her stomach.

****

"It wasn't as bad as I thought it'd be." Emily settled her skirt around her legs on Lauren's blanket and grabbed a sandwich from the plate of finger food she'd managed to score between comments from old friends.

Good to see you ranked most frequent, right before the nerve-stretching, *So nice to have you back,* to which she simply smiled. She wasn't about to explain that she wasn't "back," wasn't going to add hypocrisy to her list of sins. The question that had made her wish for the white horse, though, was *When will we see you in church?* She hadn't known how to respond, especially since Scott's mother was the one who'd asked. Emily had mentally crossed her fingers: *Soon.*

"You should've been back long before now." Lauren shook a fried chicken wing at her. "We're not ogres, you know."

"Speak for yourself." Roger popped a fist to his chest and belched.

His wife withered him with a glare. "Nice. Really nice."

Scott took a swig from his soda and then turned his attention to Emily. "I saw Millie walking about early this morning. You kick her out of the apartment?"

Lauren looked from Scott to Emily. "Who's Millie?"

He'd seen her? Emily was certain she'd been careful. "She's...a friend. From Houston. And, no, I didn't kick her out."

"I've seen her around, but I keep waiting for you to introduce me to her formally." Scott turned to the others. "Millie's kept me in business with cats since she came to town."

"I don't understand." Lauren wiped her hands on a paper napkin and focused on Emily. "I thought you were the one with the cat mission."

"She helps."

"Yeah." Scott smirked. "She's the one who does the actual catching."

"All right, fine." Emily conceded the minor point. "I help *her*. She does all the work."

"You'll have to bring her over some time. I'd love to meet her." Lauren's gaze shifted. She nudged Roger and pointed at something behind Emily. "Trey and Carla are cute together, don't you think?"

Finally. The subject landed on someone else for a change. Emily turned to look. The two walked shoulder to shoulder with their heads tilted toward each other as if exchanging lovers' secrets. They did look cute together.

"Yeah, cuter than pet store puppies." Roger hefted himself up with a grunt. "Reckon there's another chicken leg over there?"

"Let's hope there's at least two." Scott rose with only a smidgen more grace and then propped his arm on Roger's shoulder. "C'mon old buddy. I'll hobble over there with you."

Lauren watched them leave. Then she scooted closer to Emily. "Now spill it."

"Spill what?"

"Don't be dense." Lauren slapped her shoulder. "How'd it go last night?"

Heat rose to Emily's cheeks. "It was great. We had a wonderful time."

Lauren clapped her hands. "I knew you would!

Whatever took you so long? Admit it"—she pointed at Emily and gleamed with victory—"you like him, don't you?"

Of course, she liked him. She'd always liked him. But he'd seen Millie and was curious about her—and, what was worse, he made Lauren curious about her, too. Emily couldn't let either of them know the truth about Millie.

The truth about Millie. The truth about herself. So many secrets to keep from those who loved her. But would anyone love her still if they knew what she'd hidden in her heart?

18

Scott reached across the truck's console for Emily's hand, and she hesitated just an instant before wrapping her fingers around his. By the time they left the picnic, the sun was sinking below the horizon. She was tired from the heat, full from multiple trips through the buffet line to nibble on leftovers, and happy about spending the day with friends—some of whom she hadn't seen since she'd left for college. She simply wanted to enjoy Scott's company a little longer. She'd worry about his curiosity later.

He squeezed her hand. "You have a good time?"

"Once I got over my nerves." And no one seemed to know about her past, a plus in itself.

"Who do you think changed the most since the last time you were here?"

"Oh, that's easy—Camille Beauchamp. Last time I saw her, she was a chubby, pimple-faced kid with braces on her teeth. Puberty wasn't kind to her." Now, she was a stylish brunette with no sign of the teenager Emily had known.

"I knew you'd say that." A grin split his face. "Guess what she's doing now?"

"No clue."

"She's a dermatologist, married to a dentist. They live in Tyler."

"Good for her!" Some of the school kids had been cruel to Camille, even some of the church group were unkind.

"The best revenge is to live well."

"And it sounds like she did just that." Emily mulled the thought over. She wasn't particularly interested in revenge. Wade had ruined her reputation in Harris County, and there was little she could do about it. Revenge against him certainly wouldn't put her back in the good graces of Houston society. But living well—*living* instead of hiding! The thought was so appealing that for a moment, she'd forgotten the consequences of not protecting her anonymity.

Scott slowed to turn left toward her apartment but came to a complete stop when the wail of a siren pierced the air. Flashing red lights passed in a blur from the direction of The Litter Box and continued for several more blocks to their right.

Emily's lips tightened. Another fire. Another family victimized. Another set of memories and treasures consumed by the monster's insatiable appetite.

Shaking his head, Scott turned the truck toward Emily's home. "I can't believe this guy is still at it. I thought the city was bringing in the FBI."

A young man in a gray hoodie passed under the street light, and Emily was struck with a vague sense of recognition. He climbed into a small car in the shadow of an elm. The area was so dark, Emily couldn't identify the make, much less the color, of the vehicle.

"Here we are." Scott parked in front of Emily's apartment, and her heart quivered in her chest. If the walk to her door was like last night...

He helped her from the truck and draped an arm around her shoulders, an arm he didn't remove once they'd reached the door. Instead, he turned her to face him. In the soft glow of the street lamp, his intention was clear. She caught her breath and watched through half-closed eyes as his lips drew nearer to hers. His arms were firm and secure around her, his kiss gentle and probing, and for one tender moment, she floated on gilded clouds. Her body ached in protest when he broke the spell and rested his forehead against hers.

When he spoke, his voice was husky. "I'd better get moving. Dani's off tonight, and the animals need to be fed."

Unable to trust her own voice, Emily nodded.

"I'll call you later."

Again she bobbed her head, but as he turned to go, she found her tongue. "I had a great time. Thanks for taking me."

He smiled and then strode to his truck.

She watched him drive away. Then she let herself into her apartment. Leaning back against the door, she brushed her fingers across her lips. If living well was the best revenge, kissing Scott Barlow was living well.

****

With the last of his canine patients back inside from their nighttime romp in the yard, Scott flicked out the lights in the clinic, locked the door, and returned to his pickup. An orange glow pulsed in the distance near Dogwood's historical district. Another home had gone up in smoke. Lauren and Emily would have another family to add to their list for the benefit funds.

Emily.

He hadn't thought about her in—what? Five whole minutes? And thinking of her now brought an ache to his chest. He missed her. He'd still be with her if Dani hadn't taken the night off, leaving him responsible for the animals. Probably for the best, though. If he was still with Emily, he couldn't promise he'd stop with the kissing. Just that one soft moment had been enough to heat him through winter—and they had a long way to go before winter.

He pointed his truck toward home. When he arrived, he pulled into his usual spot beside the house. Spencer Milligan's gray car was parked near the barn, still ticking off its heat. Scott strolled across the yard to the paddock, where the young man stroked a grooming brush along Scotch Bonnet's neck.

"Hey, Dr. Barlow." Spencer grinned over the horse's back. "Bonnet's doing good, isn't she? Is she better?"

"She's on the mend. Gained about forty pounds since I got her." Scott propped a foot against the lower rail of the paddock fence and crossed his arms over the top. "You and that horse get along fine. You reckon your dad'll let you have her?"

Spencer snorted. "No. Of course not."

"Won't know unless you ask."

"Dad hasn't been too good at saying yes to anything lately. Especially not to me."

"Too bad. That horse takes to you. You two go well together."

"I know." The young man's face lit up. "What if I just buy her anyway and keep her here? Dad wouldn't have to know, and I'll be glad to take care of her. What do you think? Would that work?"

"Can't do that, son. I don't have enough stalls to board her and the sick horses, too. I can keep her in the pasture for a while, but I'll have to find a home for her." Scott rubbed the stubble on his chin. "Besides, I won't be a part of going against your father. If he says no, it'll have to be no."

Spencer flung the brush toward the barn and stalked to the fence, glowering at Scott with an anger deeper than Scott had ever seen in him before. "Y'all stick together, don't you? Everyone your age. Your generation. You think you have a right to tell people what they can and can't do. Where do you get off, huh? Where do you get the right?" He balled his fists and stood wide-legged, geared for a fight.

Scotch Bonnet tossed her head and skittered away to the far fence, but the horse's fear didn't register with Spencer. He was focused on Scott.

Scott's heart pounded against his ribs as he tried to think of how to calm the boy. The last thing he wanted was a skirmish with a kid. He lowered his foot off the rail so he could stand steady, never diverting his attention from Spencer's glare. "Spence, I don't claim to have a right to tell you what to do. But I also don't have the right to go against your father's wishes. This is between you and him."

For a moment, the only sounds were Bonnet's hoof pawing the packed earth and Spencer's breath heaving from his lungs.

Scott didn't know what else to say to Spencer to settle him, but the boy was riling a nervous horse, and Scott needed to get him out of the paddock.

"Come on, buddy. I bet I've got some of Mom's left-over chicken and apple cake. Maybe even a meat loaf. She came by yesterday and stocked my fridge with far more than I'll ever eat by myself. Why don't you come on in and we'll have us a little snack. What do you say?"

Slowly, Spencer's hands relaxed and the anger melted from his expression. "I've got to put the groomin' kit up."

"Don't worry about that now. Let's eat. My stomach's just about growling." After a day-long picnic, Scott was far from hungry, but he got Spencer out of the paddock and safely on the other side. Scott ruffled his hair and, with a hand on his shoulder, walked to the back door.

The soft spot Scott had for Spencer was probably derived from his own abandonment. But Spencer was lucky. Parker was still around, still loved him.

But whenever parents split, the kids had it rough.

Scott knew that first hand.

19

Breakfast was so good last week that I figure a Monday morning repeat would be better than dew on dandelions. A young man comes out of the diner and holds the door open for me. With my net in one hand and a newspaper in the other, I smile my thank you at him and hobble inside.

Annie and Clara have their heads together over a paper on the countertop. They look up as I approach, and I give them a little wave. "Mornin', you two. Annie, just give me what I had last time."

"Sure thing, Millie." She whispers something to Clara, and Clara whispers back. Both grin at me.

I find my booth and drop my net on the seat, sliding in beside it. Then I spread my own paper out flat on the table.

The fire yesterday was the Wellingtons' Tudor manor. Burned almost to the ground. The fire chief says the arsonist used an accelerant this time, but doesn't say what kind.

"Milk, Millie?" Annie calls from the counter. She's got a sweet smile this morning. Clara's smiling at me, too. Both of them are grinning like cream-thievin' cats. Like they've got a secret.

"Milk sounds good." The way they're looking at me makes me squirm.

I flip the page in the newspaper and catch the headline: "Mysterious Benefactor Strikes Again," by

Paul Goodrich.

Annie brings my glass of milk and then taps the article with her finger. "Clara got some cash yesterday, too." She says with a knowing look. "She caught a glimpse of someone with gray hair darting away from her window."

Uh-oh. My pulse is pounding so hard in my ears that all I hear is the rush of blood, but I keep my cool. "You don't say? I wonder who it was?"

Annie's smile broadens. "Don't know, but I bet it's the same person who brought Kyle to me from Waco."

"Now, wouldn't that be something!"

"Wouldn't it?" She winks. "I'll get your breakfast. You need anything right now?"

I shake my head, and she grins again before heading toward the kitchen. Has she figured it out? Have both of them figured it out?

I give myself a little shake. Nothing I can do about it if they have. I smooth out the paper and give it a look. The article isn't much. Mentions the Chapmans getting an envelope of cash. Don't know who told him, them or that chatty Hayley. I'm positive he didn't see me over there, but the fact that Clara may have seen me—and Scott did see me out somewhere—means I gotta be more careful.

In the article, there's a bit about the Sawyer boy—he came through his surgery fine—thank you, Lord—and some farfetched speculation about where the funds came from that doesn't even come close to the truth. Which is good. Let that ol' buzzard bait speculate.

The bell on the door jingles and Goodrich himself walks in with that editor of his. They nod to me as they sit in the booth just in front of mine.

Annie comes over to the next table. "Can I get you gentlemen some coffee?"

They place an order aside from their coffee request and then sink into a conversation they must've started before they came in. Before long, Paul's voice rises and crests on a wave of frustration. "I don't even know where to start looking. The Sawyers didn't have any idea who's paying for all this. They got the message from the hospital's CEO and didn't bother to ask questions about where the funds came from."

"Someone who's got that kind of money shouldn't be hard to find." Kevin sounds like a boss in no mood for excuses. "It's not like Dogwood's the Who's Who of the rich and famous. Take a look around and see if you can't figure it out."

"You're acting like I haven't been trying." Paul's brows scrunch over his nose. "He's not likely to be wearing a neon sign."

Kevin says something too low for me to hear, and Paul's lips droop at the remark.

"You're pushing pretty hard for something that doesn't amount to anything more than a human interest story."

"Folks will want to know who the soft touch is around here." Kevin jabs a finger across the table. "And I want you to find out. Soon, before this story cools off."

Soft touch? They want to know who the *soft touch* is? The story should be about God's love. Or miracles granted through God's generosity. Or at the very least, one human's concern for all of humanity.

Soft touch?

I squint my eyes shut and picture a line of con artists stretched out to the horizon, all rubbing their hands together like the evil, mustache-twisting villains in silent movies. I picture Wade Coulter lying in wait, ready to get his revenge.

Before I know what I'm doing, I've got my fists planted on the table and I'm halfway out of my seat. "Leave her alone!"

Kevin turns and stares at me.

I scoot out of the booth, knocking over my milk and bumping into Annie. She drops my breakfast with an echoing clatter of dishes and silverware. Oozy eggs-over-easy slip into the milk I spilled all over the floor.

I lock my gaze on Kevin. "You don't know what you're doing!"

"What do you know about her?" Paul twists in his seat. He looks like a hound on the scent. "Who is she? Where can I find her?"

My heart thumps hard as a treed 'coon's with each question he barks at me. What have I done? Everyone is staring, forks and coffee cups suspended in their paths toward parted lips.

Clara circles the counter and heads toward me.

Annie reaches out for me, but I whirl away.

Kevin's almost to his feet.

"Leave her alone!" I surge toward the front door like a dog's on my tail.

Behind me, Clara's voice is stern. "Not before you pay your tab, young man."

I shoot a glance over my shoulder as I push out of the diner. Clara and Annie are blocking the two men from catching me. Bless their sweet souls.

I forgot my net. It's still in the booth. I don't know whether to go back for it or to let it be. I turn to go to the diner, but then I turn the other way again. I can't seem to move one way or the other. I'm standing on the sidewalk with my fingers over my mouth, trying to get my brain to work.

After a deep breath, I decide to go home. I'll go back for my net after they leave.

Paul pushes out the door and looks down the street opposite my direction, and Kevin is right behind him. Neither one has my net. Maybe they don't know it's still in the seat.

Paul spots me and nudges his boss. "There she is!"

He starts in my direction, and that's all it takes to kick my feet into gear. There aren't enough folks on the sidewalk to dodge around, no one to hide behind, and the stores aren't open for another hour, so I can't dart into any of them. Best I can do is an off-balanced trot on a sore foot.

"Hey, lady! Hey!" Paul is a few short feet behind me. "We just want to talk. Why are you running?"

A red pickup pulls over just ahead of me and the passenger door swings open.

"Millie! Jump in!"

I don't ask questions. I make a beeline for the truck and scramble into the seat without even looking at the driver until I slam the door on those evil buzzards.

"Are you all right? What's going on?" It's Scott Barlow, of all people.

I can't worry about that now. "Just drive!"

He pulls away from the curb and slides back into traffic. "Who are those guys?"

"Reporters." I'm huffing like I just ran a marathon and don't recognize my own voice. I keep my head turned toward the right rearview mirror. The two guys are watching us drive away. Paul's got a notepad. Bet he's getting Scott's plate number.

"What do they want with you?"

I clamp my mouth shut. Gotta keep my wits about me. This whole thing is just bizarre, and I've never thought out what would happen in a situation like this before. I never thought I'd *be* in a situation like this. What a mess I left for Annie to clean up! What on earth got into me? Never in my life have I panicked like that—and I hope I never do it again.

The news hounds disappear into the diner, but I keep my head turned to the side window. For all I know, I look like a crazed old woman. I don't want Scott to see me like this.

"Millie? Do you know what they want?"

He's rescuing me. I've got to answer him—can't be rude—but the less he knows, the better. "They think I know something."

"About what?"

"About someone in town." Nip it. Nip it right now. No more questions. "Can you just take me home?"

Scott circles the town square, backtracking to the old Woolworth's building. Seems like we hit every red light.

I want my net. I want those men to leave me alone. I want all this to go away. The closer we get to The Litter Box, the antsier I am to hide in my apartment. I've got to think of a way out of this mess, and sitting in the truck with Scott doesn't make it easier. When he pulls up in front of my home, I jump and run.

Didn't even dawn on me to thank him for the ride.

****

Emily splashed cool water on her face. Her heart was still racing over what had happened to Millie.

What a mess. There was no way Millie could be anonymous now. Paul Goodrich would be all over her like a kitten on catnip every time she went out. And Scott! Emily cringed, not even wanting to think of how close a call that had been.

She needed to get the entire ordeal out of her mind. She'd bought a house. And not just any house, but the one of her dreams, the launching pad of her new career, the project that would keep her busy and out of sight for many months to come—a thought that carried far more weight now than ever before.

Time for Millie to retire.

20

Things were rolling now. The electrician just left; he had checked the wiring and declared it old, but safe enough. She'd made an appointment with him to rewire the place at a later date.

A plumber was on his way to make the bathrooms functional again, and Roger's crew would begin renovations later in the week.

The safest place for her to work and still be out of their way was the parlor. Fists on her hips, she eyed the room. The ancient gold-flocked wallpaper was cracked and pealing. Spider webs decorated the stained crown molding, and dust caked the baseboards. All the woodwork, including the window frames and the paneling that climbed a third of the way up the walls, needed revitalizing with a good dose of tung oil.

But without electricity, which wouldn't be turned on until later in the day, the room was too dark to work in. She tried to move the heavy drapes aside, but they crumbled at the touch. For her to be able to see what she was doing, they would have to go.

She moved a six-foot ladder Roger had left for her, propped it in front of one of the four windows, and climbed to muscle the rose velvet valance off the wall. The heavy rod and material dropped in a heap below her, and she cautiously stepped down, coughing as she eased into the cloud of dry-rot and the throat-clogging mustiness of antiquity.

One done, three to go.

With her lip between her teeth, she stood back and considered taking down the lace sheers. Of course, they'd probably crumble at the touch too, and the room was stuffy enough after the first valance. Besides, if the window was bare, the afternoon sun would make the parlor too hot for work.

She moved the ladder over a few feet, climbed it, and wrestled another fleur de lis-tipped rod from its perch and then sent it and its heavy velvet load cascading down. By the final window, her arms were quivering with fatigue as she struggled to work the last cantankerous rod off its hook. Amazing what a lack of exercise could do to a girl's biceps. She freed the rod with a final jerk and lost her balance. The valance sank, the ladder crashed to the left, she fell backward and landed with a breath-wrenching thud on the unforgiving hardwood floor.

"Emily!" Heavy footfalls echoed through the room, bringing Scott to her side. "Are you all right?"

She wheezed in one breath and desperately gulped for another. The room spun like an off-kilter carousel. Closing her eyes didn't stop the spin.

"Is anything broken?" Scott probed her ribs with a confident gentleness he must have used on injured animals in his clinic. "Can you move your feet?"

She wiggled her tennis shoes and drew an easier breath to answer him. "I'm fine, really. Nothing broken. Just a little dizzy."

"Got the wind knocked out of you, huh?"

"Yeah." But there was no pain when she breathed. Thank the Lord she hadn't broken a rib. She cracked open an eyelid and looked at Scott. "What are you doing here? Aren't you supposed to be de-worming dogs or something?"

"I've been trying to call you. Can you sit up?" He held her arm, slid a hand under her back for support, and helped her ease into a sitting position. "Still dizzy?"

She rolled her head on her shoulders and rubbed her neck. "No, I think I'm all right. When did you call?"

"I tried most of the morning. I was going to spend my lunch break driving to The Litter Box when I saw your car here."

"I turned off my phone and must've forgotten to turn it back on." Her fingers found a tender spot on the back of her head. She was in for one doozy of a knot. "So, what's so important you were willing to ride halfway to town?"

He sat back on his heels and draped his arms over his knees. "I'm worried about Millie. Did she tell you what happened?"

"Yeah, I know about it."

"Good. Then will you tell me?" He flipped his hands out. "All she said was the men after her were journalists wanting information about someone she knows. I assume that 'someone' is you."

Emily turned her head. "Yes."

"Is this about Houston?"

"In a way."

Air shot through Scott's teeth with an audible hiss. "Why can't you tell me what you've told her?"

"I didn't *tell* her anything. She just knows." The frustrations of the morning hiked Emily's temper and tumbled out in her tone. She took a breath and reeled herself in before continuing. "Millie was there with me.

She lived it with me."

"Lived *what* with you?"

"Stop! Just stop asking me, Scott. I'm not ready to share this with you. Can't you understand? Can't we just enjoy each other and let this go?"

A blend of pain and sorrow flickered across his face, but he nodded. He stood, helping her up as he did. The motion caused her head to throb for a moment, but the pain eased as soon as her feet were steady under her.

"Mom called this morning and told me to invite you over Friday night. She said she'd make your favorite cheesecake."

"Double chocolate almond swirl?" Only the best cheesecake on the planet, prepared by the world's best baker.

The heaviness of their previous conversation hung in the air and mingled with the settling dust, but she didn't want it to come between them now that they'd finally advanced their relationship.

Judging from the hope apparent on his face, he didn't either.

"What time?" she asked.

"Seven OK?"

"Seven's fine."

"Good. Now, how 'bout lunch? Have you eaten?"

"Not yet."

If he hadn't mentioned his mother's cheesecake, she would've done just fine skipping lunch. Now she felt like she hadn't eaten in a week.

"Want to run to town with me?"

She looked down at her work clothes, already coated with dust and bits of velvet. "Like this? I don't think so."

"How about I just go to the deli and get us both a sandwich?"

"That's a plan. Make mine a meatball sub."

He gave her a quick kiss and ran out the door. While he was gone, she bundled the drapes and hauled them to the front yard to be carried off later.

Every time he asked about Houston, her stomach knotted. Guilt, no doubt. If they were to continue in a relationship, she should tell him what had happened. Fairness dictated it. He had a right to know if the woman he dated was marked for murder by an angry con-artist—if she was. But the rest of it? She shuddered at the thought.

Maybe she'd never have to tell him.

By the time he returned, toting two plain brown paper sacks and a couple of sodas, she had cleared the disturbing thoughts from her mind and the downed drapes from the parlor floor. She was struggling to raise a window as he entered.

"Hey, let me help you with that." He put down their lunch and came to her side. With a couple of well-placed whacks along the frame, he managed to get the window up with relative ease, and a breeze rustled the dry lace sheers.

"How'd you do that?"

"It wasn't too hard, just loosened it up a bit." As he looked at her, his smile slipped. His gaze changed. Softer, darker. Desire smoldering in their depths. He rested his hand along the side of her neck and with his thumb, rubbed what must've been a smudge off her cheek. "Someday, you'll trust me enough to talk to me."

Before she could even think of a response, he smothered her lips with his own. His arms slid down her back and pulled her to him as he deepened a kiss she was all too hungry for. She felt his muscles under her hands and loved the raw power in them. Right now, she'd tell him anything...

Someone cleared his throat at the parlor's arched entry, and Scott and Emily jumped apart like two teenagers caught by their parents.

The stranger, with "Jason's Plumbing" stitched on the pocket of his blue coveralls, shuffled his feet and grinned at them. "Hate to break y'all up, but if you'd just point me to the bathroom, I'll be out of your hair and you can get back to it."

Emily's face burned with what must've been the reddest blush in the spectrum.

Scott, bless him, took charge and led the plumber down the hall to the first floor bath, while telling him of the other two upstairs.

Not knowing what to do with herself, Emily paced in the parlor until he returned.

Scott stood in front of her and rubbed her arms. "You all right?"

"Oh, sure. Mortified, but all right."

"Nothing to be mortified about." He gave her a light peck. "I've got a one o'clock appointment with a black lab and her sore tooth, so I'd better go. See you Friday. Don't back out!"

****

Scott took a bite of his sub-club sandwich in one hand and steered with the other. Sheriff Bailey had warned him against eating while driving more than once. But most times, if Scott wanted lunch, this was the only way. At least he didn't have a cell phone at his ear.

Emily was making him nuts. How long did he have to wait before she'd open up to him? How many times did he have to prove himself trustworthy?

The idea of asking Millie about Houston had popped into his head an instant before she'd jumped from the truck. Next time he saw her, he wouldn't think twice about it. In fact, he had stopped at the cat refuge on his way to the deli, but if she'd been inside she hadn't answered, and an extra trip around the downtown area hadn't awarded him with a glimpse of the gray-haired eccentric.

His first introduction to Millie left him even more curious. In spite of her limp and her hair color, she looked younger than she appeared from a distance. But she'd only afforded him the occasional glance at her face before they'd arrived at the refuge and she'd taken off like a cat up a tree. He knew Millie was a bit secretive—like Emily—but he never realized just how much.

And it all tied back to Houston somehow.

He was almost tempted to find out who the reporters were who were chasing her and pump them for what they knew. But if doing so would hurt Emily, he couldn't risk it. He'd waited too long for her.

At the clinic, he shoved the last bite of sandwich in his mouth and wadded the paper. Parker Milligan's maroon SUV sat in the parking lot, meaning Chica, the Labrador Retriever, was waiting to get her tooth fixed. He grabbed his soda and went inside.

Parker stood and thrust a hand toward him in greeting. "Dani already took Chica back, but I wanted to talk to you before I left."

"Sure. Come to my office."

Scott cleared a box of medicine samples off a straight-back chair and nodded for Parker to sit. "What can I do for you?"

"You're already doing it." A muscle twitched in his jaw. "Spencer told me about the horse and being at your place last night. He really looks up to you."

"I'm sure he looks up to you, too."

"No, not the same way. I'm his dad, and at his age, I'm just the natural enemy. He's got so much anger in him these days. Probably because Melissa and I split up, but there's more to it than that, and I just can't get to the root of it. Do you know?"

"I wish I could help. You're right about him being angry. It doesn't take much to spark his temper these days. Guess that's what makes him so good at baseball."

"Yeah, well, now that the season's over, he doesn't have much of an outlet. Do you think having that horse will help him?"

Scott squelched his excitement, not wanting to appear overeager. He didn't want to push Parker into a decision. "Animals help all the way around. They have a calming effect on folks, and owning a horse will give Spencer a sense of responsibility, something he'll have to take care of on a daily basis—something to look forward to every afternoon."

Parker nodded and rubbed his forehead as he thought. "This is going to cost some serious money, isn't it?"

"The horse herself is free. She's a rescue. But her hay and stall won't be cheap, and I can't keep her stabled at my place after she's healthy again. I just don't have the funds."

"She's healthy aside from being a bit

underweight?"

"Seems to be."

Parker's jaw worked as he stared out the window.

"Take your time and think about this," Scott said. "I'll keep her for another week or two, so you don't have to make up your mind right now." This wasn't a decision to be made in a day.

"Thanks." Parker stood and extended his hand. "Don't tell Spencer I'm considering it. I'd hate to get his hopes up."

Scott agreed and shook the man's hand. Had his own father ever agonized over him this way? Probably not, but he'd like to think so.

21

Next morning, Emily was in a booth by eight-fifteen. The Down Home Diner hopped with the early crowd of hungry citizens. At the table in front of her, four silver-haired men drank coffee and laughed at each other's jokes. Loners clad in business attire sat at the deli tables and the counter, all with coffee mugs in one hand and books, reports, or newspapers in the other. Emily shook open her own morning paper and smiled at the waitress as she poured the coffee.

"You ready to order?"

"Not yet. I'm waiting for someone."

"Well, I'm Annie. Call me when you're ready." She turned to the next table.

The cowbell on the door clanked. Emily watched someone she didn't know enter and then glimpsed Millie's fish net propped against the wall behind the cash register. Thank goodness Paul Goodrich didn't have it—and she couldn't risk him getting it. He'd hold it for ransom. *Sure I'll give you the net, just answer one little question.* Or two, or ten. No, she couldn't risk it. She'd grab the net before she left.

She sipped her coffee and flipped through the paper. The police and fire chief still hadn't discovered who was burning all the houses and couldn't draw a connection between the victims to determine a motive. But they did know the fires had been started with a highly volatile accelerant. At this point, they were offering a five thousand dollar reward for productive tips. What a blessing no one had been injured in any of these blazes. Surely, a witness would step forward with information before the arsonist hurt someone.

She flipped to the society page and caught sight of a chatty article with Goodrich's byline.

Who is Dogwood's Cat Lady?

In light of several recent reports of exceptional generosity, The Dogwood Daily has been in search of the mysterious benefactor. One recent encounter with a resident known only as "Millie" raised the question: Just who is our local cat lady?

A familiar sight around town, Millie catches strays for The Litter Box, a non-profit cat refuge owned by All Creatures, Inc., a tightly held private corporation with a membership more secretive than a cat's night out.

Could Millie be the founder of this animal charity? Does her generosity stop at cats? Although she recently refused an interview, it would be interesting to discover the truth: Does our cat lady have angel's wings?

The nerve of those people! What was their obsession with a few good deeds? Was generosity so uncommon these days that a giver had to be hounded by the press? Didn't laws exist to protect people from nosy reporters?

Emily's purchase of the old Woolworth's building was a matter of public record. How thankful she was now that Connor had possessed the foresight to incorporate her and protect her privacy. Only he and his secretary knew of her connection to "the tightly held corporation."

The front bell rang again, and Lauren breezed in with her briefcase in hand. She scanned the diner until she saw Emily, then waded through the tables to the booth in the back corner.

"Glad you got my call to meet me here. I have so many errands to run for Rog and the kids, I'm not going to have time to breathe today." She dropped her briefcase and purse onto the seat across from Emily and slid in beside them. "Am I late?"

"No, I was early."

Annie brought another cup and the coffeepot. "Morning. You two know what you want, or do you need some time?"

"I know what I want." Emily glanced at Lauren. "Do you?"

"I haven't eaten here in ages." Lauren grabbed a menu off the table. "What are you having?"

"Pancakes, eggs-over-easy, and sausage. Breakfast of champions."

"Breakfast of truck drivers, you mean."

"Long may they roll." Emily raised her mug in salute and sipped.

After a moment, Lauren ordered and, as Annie left the table, opened her briefcase. "I have two ads ready for the printer." She pulled them out and slid them across the table. "Which do you like best?"

"Oh, I'd forgotten how talented you are." Using computer graphics, Lauren had developed similar advertisements for the benefit auction, prominently featuring the Perittes' former home and an auctioneer's gavel, with various items for auction hodge-podged in the background. Color schemes and lettering were the only differences. Emily pointed to one with the fluid gold lettering on an emerald green banner. "I like this one the best."

"You do? I really like the Tuscany red best."

Block print lettering in vivid, cobalt blue boldly announced the auction on the red ad, but the green was still Emily's favorite.

Annie returned with their plates and looked over Emily's shoulder. "Wow, those are good."

"Be the tie-breaker and help us decide." Lauren swiveled the two pages so Annie could see better. "Which one do you like best?"

"This is for Homer and Eloise? Does Clara know?" Before they could stop her, Annie shouted for her boss.

Emily's jaw tightened, but she forced herself to relax. People would inevitably discover her help in the fundraiser. As long as her picture didn't wind up in the local paper, she would be safe.

"Well, look who's graced my humble diner!" Wiping her hands with her apron, Clara emerged from the kitchen and joined them. "You two just don't come around often enough." The ads caught her attention, and she picked up the green one. "What's all this?"

"Lauren's planning an auction for the arson victims." The words tumbled from Emily's mouth before Lauren could respond. "Maybe you'd be willing to post an ad in your window."

"Once we decide which we're using," Lauren added.

"I really like this red one." Clara's crinkled cheeks flushed, and her eyes rimmed with tears. "But whichever one you choose, bring a few by, and I'll put them up myself. I'll even donate a half-dozen dinner specials to the highest bidder."

Lauren lit up as if Clara had offered the Crown Jewels of England. "How generous! Thank you."

"No, it's generous of you." She turned to Annie. "Their breakfast is on the house."

Emily opened her mouth to protest, but Clara waved her off as she headed back to the kitchen. "Least I can do."

"Looks like you made her day." Annie crumbled their bill into a wad. "Let me know if you need anything."

"I guess we did make her day. Did you see her tear up?" Lauren leaned over the steam of her Denver omelet. "So, have you had any more dates with Scott?"

"No, no dates. But I'm supposed to have dinner with him and his mom Friday night."

"He's taking you home to meet his mother? How sweet." Lauren's eyebrows waggled.

"I've already met his mother. Don't make anything more of this than what it is. A dinner with old friends." Emily huffed in exasperation.

"'Old friends.' Well, one of them is. The other is what they call a *love interest*."

"Would you stop? There's—" Emily caught sight of Paul Goodrich outside the door. He was late; he should've had his caffeine fix long ago.

"You and Scott have a lot in common." Lauren sliced into her omelet and forked up a mouthful. "You always have. I used to get so aggravated with his shyness."

"I always thought it was kind of sweet." Emily dragged her gaze away from the reporter, who made himself at home at the counter. Since he didn't know who owned All Creatures, Inc., he didn't really pose a threat. She shouldn't give him a second thought—

wouldn't give him a second thought. She took a bite of her syrup-soggy pancakes. "Watching his ears grow red when he got flustered. It was so cute!"

"Not when it kept him from asking you out," Lauren mumbled around her eggs. "You two should've been together a long time ago."

"You'll have to design some business coupons, you know."

"Changing the subject?"

"If I don't, you'll keep at it until you've planned the wedding."

"You know me too well." Lauren looked at her watch and then downed another bite of her omelet, chewed fast, and grabbed a sip of coffee. "I have to run. I'll draft coupons for the diner later so Clara can see them."

"Clara's not the only one." Emily rested the fork and shot her a victory grin. "Scott's donating five spay or neuter procedures."

"Oh, that will be fun to illustrate. The auction is really shaping up now, isn't it?" Lauren looked as gleeful as a kid on a bike. "Come over tonight and let's do some serious work."

"Are you planning another surprise date with Scott?"

"You know me. I'm the mastermind of devious plans."

"Award-winning. What time?"

"Seven thirty?"

"That works." And it wouldn't hurt her feelings at all if Scott showed up.

They left a tip for Annie and rose to leave. As they slipped to the front, the reporter idly stirred his coffee while chatting on his cell phone. He might not pose a threat, but Emily couldn't wait to get clear of him. Being in the same room with him threatened to bring up her newly consumed breakfast.

"I'll see you tonight." Lauren gave Emily a quick hug. The cowbell chimed as she exited, and Emily glanced back to see if Goodrich heard. He didn't turn, but still she hesitated, eyeing the fish net. Maybe she should grab it and run.

"I told you no charge." Clara appeared from the kitchen.

"I appreciate it." Emily stole another peek behind her.

Goodrich was concentrating on his breakfast.

She lowered her voice. "I thought I'd take Millie her net."

"Good idea." Clara reached for it and passed it across the counter. "I tried taking it by, but I kept missing her."

"Thanks. I'll make sure she gets it."

"Excuse me. You know Millie?"

Emily turned and bumped into the reporter. She backed away and collided with the diner's front door.

"I'm Paul Goodrich, *Dogwood Daily News*." He stuck out his hand.

Emily's face tightened with wariness. She hesitated before taking the proffered hand. "I know who you are."

He drew her away from the door. "What can you tell me about Millie? Do you know her last name?"

"Why don't you ask her?"

"She's not an easy lady to catch." His smile wore on her nerves—carefully applied, showing just the right amount of straight, white teeth, and as sincere as a politician's pledge. "I was hoping you could help me out."

"Sorry. Anything you want to know, you'll have to ask her." She shot him an icy glare. "Now if you'll excuse me, I'll be on my way."

He reached into his shirt pocket for a business card. "Maybe you can have her call me. I really would like to ask her a few questions."

For an instant, she considered leaving without accepting his card but changed her mind. It would've been rude, and as far as Paul Goodrich knew, she didn't have a reason to be rude to him. She took it and slipped it into her purse. "I'll see she gets it."

****

At Chapman's Home Improvement Center, Emily parked and threw Millie's net into the trunk. The last thing she needed was someone else questioning her about the cat lady. Just one busybody's call to Paul Goodrich could make her life miserable. Perhaps the thought hinted of paranoia, but she wasn't about to risk being the focus of his attention again.

Inside the store, she grabbed a cart, wheeled it past a display for home winterizing, and hunted supplies to strip the wallpaper in her parlor. Soon, with her basket full of the things she needed, and some she didn't, she headed toward the checkout stands.

"I can get you right here," said a freckle-faced teen—Spencer Milligan, according to his name tag.

She pushed the cart to his register. "Are you related to Parker Milligan?"

"My dad. You know him?"

"Just bought my homeowner's policy from him." As he checked her things, she pulled her credit card from her wallet. "Do you know where I can rent a floor sander?"

"We've got the top of the line sanders." He scanned the last item and then accepted her card and studied it. "We can even deliver it to you, Ms. Taylor."

"Well, I'm not ready for it quite yet, but it's good to know I can get it from here when I am." She signed, slipped her card back in her purse, and smiled. "Time for me to get to work."

As she loaded her car, the clean air of a norther brushed her cheeks, and the sun winked from behind wispy clouds—a perfect day to raise the windows on the old house and begin her work. A quick run to her apartment to change clothes, and she'd be ready to strip some walls and whatever else she had time for before heading for Lauren's this evening. She cranked her engine and pulled out of her parking place.

Fifteen minutes later, she parked at the curb in front of The Litter Box, and a black sedan pulled up behind her. Paul Goodrich emerged from inside. She frowned. He was everywhere these days. She should gun her motor and race away, leave him in her dust. But she hesitated just a moment too long. He rapped on her window and then moved aside so she could open her door.

"What a pleasure to run into you again." His smile appeared genuine, but as she allowed him to help her from her seat, she gritted her teeth at the humor in his voice.

"Have you been following me all morning, or were you just waiting here?"

Spreading his hands in innocence, he broadened his smile. "Pure coincidence, I promise. You're here to deliver Millie's net? Why don't I walk you to the door?"

Before he could touch her again, she squirmed away to open the trunk. He mustn't learn she lived here, she'd never have a moment's peace. Yet, here she was—trapped. What could she do but allow him to escort her? She clamped her hand around the net and without a backward glance, marched down the sidewalk toward the entrance and pressed the doorbell.

Paul stopped beside her, shoulder to shoulder. His very presence made her muscles tighten across her back.

"This is a public place, isn't it? An adoption agency for cats?" He tried the door, found it locked, and then peered through the crack in the curtains on the storefront window. Emily would have to pin that shut. After pressing the bell again, he hammered his fist on the door.

"She's obviously not home," Emily said.

"Give her a minute longer. She's crippled, you know. Has that limp."

"Yes, I know."

"Do you know how she got it?"

"She's not home." Emily turned on her heel and strode back toward her car.

Paul matched her pace, hands in his pockets as if he was taking a casual stroll. "You know, strikes me funny you haven't even asked what I want to talk to her about. Aren't you the least bit curious?"

"I try to mind my own business." She shoved the net back into her car and slammed the trunk. "Perhaps you should do the same. Excuse me." She brushed past him and slid into the driver's seat.

"I wouldn't make a good reporter if I minded my

own business." He slipped up behind her, closed the car door, and flashed a good-natured grin at her through the side window. "I'll catch her before long, and you can read all about it in the society page."

Seething, Emily pulled away from the curb. Would he stake out the place until he got what he wanted? What was she supposed to do if she couldn't get into her own apartment?

22

From the stop sign a block away, Emily glanced left toward The Litter Box. Paul's black car was still parked at the curb. Good grief. Had he been there all day?

She'd had to buy some used clothes from the thrift store just so she could work in her house. Now, she was sweaty and dirty and smelled of wallpaper stripper. She wanted—no, she *needed* a shower, and she didn't want to have to fight him off to get one.

Her lips tightened, and she pulled forward. Instead of turning toward her apartment, she drove around the block and came up the back way. She pulled into her usual parking place and headed to the back staircase leading to her apartment. She'd always entered the refuge from the front so she could check on the cats before going up, but the back entry would have to do today.

She tiptoed up each cast-iron step to keep the stairs from ringing and alerting Goodrich of her presence. Once on the landing, she flipped through her keys, unlocked the door, and pulled.

Nothing.

The door hadn't been opened in years, and it cantankerously refused to budge now.

She yanked again, with the same results. Finally, she put down her purse, planted a foot against the wall next to the doorframe, and tugged with all the force she could muster. The abrasive squeal of the rusty hinges sent shivers racing down her back and set her teeth on edge. She shot a glance over her shoulder and scanned the parking lot. The entire staff of *The Dogwood Daily News* must have heard the shrill grating of metal on metal.

When no reporters materialized with cameras and notepads, she ventured another pull on the door and opened it wide enough to enter. Finally, with it closed securely behind her, she leaned back against it and released a heavy sigh. She might as well keep some lubricating oil handy. Now that the snooping journalist was staking out her place, she'd be using this door more often.

After a quick bite and a shower, she changed into a clean pair of jeans and ran downstairs through the refuge to peek out the window. No black car. The man did have his limit after all, and it apparently hit around supper time.

Still, all the way to Lauren's house, Emily couldn't help but to check the rearview mirror, and once there, she surveyed the street before pulling into the driveway. Scott tapped on her car window. She'd been so intent on watching out for Paul, she hadn't even noticed him approach. Climbing from the driver's seat, she offered a smile.

He leaned in for a quick kiss. Then with his arm around her waist, he guided her toward the house. "What were you looking around for? You hiding from someone?"

"That blasted reporter. He's been hanging out at the apartment, trying to get an interview with Millie."

"Got you feeling a bit paranoid?"

"A bit."

"Then it won't make you feel any better to hear that he called me."

Emily stopped in her tracks. "What?"

"Yeah. I don't know how he associated me with Millie, but he had a ton of questions."

A knot formed in Emily's stomach, and she pressed her hand against it. "What did you say?"

Scott shrugged. "What's there to say? I don't know anything."

Roger appeared in the doorway with a soda in hand. "You two gonna hang out here and talk, or are ya comin' in where the work is?"

"Neither." Scott dipped Emily in the classic pose of a dramatic kiss and then smacked her lips good and loud before letting her up again. "We're gonna start some neighborhood gossip."

Giggling, Emily tugged down the front of her shirt and patted her hair back in place. "Right now, I can't afford any gossip. Why don't we get to work?"

Inside, the kitchen table had been stripped of its napkin holder and salt and pepper shakers and redressed with a thick stack of Tuscany-red flyers and matching envelopes. A stamp dispenser and a few sheets of computer-generated mailing labels completed the ensemble.

"Sweet tea or soda?" Lauren asked. Her hair was swept up on the back of her head, giving her a sophisticated look undermined by cut-off jeans and a pink pull-over.

"Tea," Scott said. "What's with the do?"

Lauren patted the knot protruding from her crown. "Michelle wanted to fix my hair for me. Not bad, huh?"

"Not good, either," Roger grumbled.

Lauren poked him in the ribs.

"I think it looks great." Emily slipped past her and grabbed a couple of glasses from the cabinet. "A little formal for envelope-stuffing, but nice."

Lauren dodged Roger's swat to her backside and skittered to the fridge for the tea pitcher. Watching the two of them together made Emily wistful. They always seemed to have fun and enjoy each other. As she filled the glasses with ice, she slipped a peek at Scott, who had nabbed a tortilla chip on the kitchen island and was dousing it in salsa while Roger chatted about some baseball game. Scott had exhibited his playful side more often since they'd started dating, and she loved it. Would it continue after they were married?

Would they get married?

The thought sent delicious shivers down her spine.

Was he over his shyness enough to propose?

Even that silly kiss on the front porch had sufficiently started her blood simmering in her veins. A white gown, a set of vows, and a soft, romantic honeymoon night—

An ice cube fell and slid across the floor, and Emily mentally smacked herself back to reality.

Lauren scooped up the ice and tossed it in the sink. "You're as bad as I am. Can't fill a glass without at least one cube landing on the floor."

"May as well throw it down. You know it's going to fall anyway." Scott took a glass from Emily with a gentle touch of his hand that sent tingles up her arm. The idea of marrying that man grew more powerful by the minute. The warmth she felt now had little to do with virginal purity.

"Who's ready to work?" Lauren filled her glass with tea and headed for the table. "We've got a lot of foldin', stuffin', and stickin' to do."

"About a hundred times." Roger pulled out a chair near the stamps. "These jobbers are self-adhesive. I reckon this is the perfect job for me."

"You're not getting off that easy." Lauren divided the envelopes and mailing labels between him and Scott. "These are self-adhesive, too. Wouldn't want you to strain your tongue."

Roger poked his out at her, and she laughed as she lowered herself in the chair next to him. Emily sat across from Lauren, next to Scott, and began folding the flyers into thirds. But before the crew was good and started, Scott's cell beeped.

"Hey, Dani, What's up?...uh-huh." He rose from his seat. "Yeah...Where am I going?...tell him I'm on my way." He snapped his phone shut, and Emily's heart plummeted. "Sorry folks, I've got an emergency. Blue heeler caught in a barbed wire fence."

"Oh, the poor thing," Lauren said. "Can you save it?"

"Won't know until I see him." He laid a hand on Emily's shoulder. "Walk me out?"

With her hand in his, Emily walked with him to his pickup. This wasn't how she'd planned the evening when Lauren had told her he would be coming. Of course, daydreaming about their wedding hadn't been in the plans either. That was a bonus.

When they reached his truck, Scott turned and ran his hands up and down her arms. "Sorry about this."

"It's an emergency. You have to go."

"Call you later?"

"Sure." She stepped closer and rested her hands on his shirt. "You can call me anytime."

He wrapped his arms around her waist, pulling

her closer still, and bowed to meet her lips. The kiss he gave her was guaranteed to cause neighborhood gossip, but she didn't care. Her hands savored his muscular chest and snaked around his neck so her fingers could curl in his hair. Her knees were threatening to melt just as he pulled away.

He took a deep breath and relaxed his hold on her. "Bad night for an emergency."

She nodded. "But you can't let that poor dog suffer."

"Nope." He rested his forehead against hers. "Want to join me for the Wednesday night youth group tomorrow? We can go out to dinner right after."

The question startled her, and her fingers stilled from twirling a lock of his hair. She hadn't thought of returning to church since the picnic, but perhaps she could. No one seemed to know of her past. But her nerves still stretched taut at the thought. Members of her own church in Houston had been so cruel. She just wasn't sure she was ready...

Before she could think of a response, he tilted her chin to study her face. "Maybe lunch would be better?"

A sigh of relief escaped her lips, and she smiled. "No place fancy, though. I'll be working on the house again tomorrow."

"No place fancy." He kissed her, unlocked his truck, and climbed in. With a parting wave, he took off.

Emily waved back, watched his taillights round the corner, and then touched warm fingers to swollen lips. She sighed at the emptiness his absence caused, marveled at the understanding he'd exhibited.

He'd never stopped asking her to church, but he hadn't pushed either. Such patience.

Maybe she should propose to him.

23

Inside the cat refuge, Emily peeked between the curtains covering the storefront windows. Sure enough. Goodrich's sedan sat across the street, sparkling in the early morning sunlight. He held a newspaper in front of his face like a dime-novel detective.

After a belly rub for Bulldog, Emily climbed the inside stairs to her apartment. With everything going on—the auction, her house, that newshound-on-the-scent downstairs—retiring Millie had been a smart move. She just didn't feel quirky and colorful. She felt...harried—unless she thought about Scott. Then she felt like a love-sick teenager. Right now, nothing in her life allowed room for the little eccentric lady's wanderings.

She grabbed her purse, crossed the living room to the back door, then headed out to the stairs behind the building—where Paul Goodrich leaned against the rail with his hands in his pockets and that exasperating smile slapped across his face.

"Good morning. How's Millie today?"

"She's fine."

"You give her the net?"

"Of course."

"Reckon she has a minute to talk to me?"

Emily glanced at the door. "She's still resting. She wanted to sleep in this morning." His *I don't buy it* smirk unnerved her, but she raised her chin. "Perhaps if you called in advance instead of hanging out here like some deranged stalker, you'd have a better chance of catching her."

"Sure. Got her number?"

"Look it up!" She sidestepped around him and darted down the stairs with him on her heels.

"Can't very well look it up if I don't know her last name." In a dance that was becoming far too familiar, he raced to open her car door. "You don't seem to like me very much. I'm just doing my job, you know."

"So far, your job has involved stalking my friend and harassing me. I'm amazed you'd consider that endearing." She jammed her key into the ignition and yanked the door out of his grasp to slam it shut. With barely a glance to check for traffic, she spun out of her parking place and shot into the street.

Whether or not he was doing his job, he was a nuisance. Surely he could find something in Dogwood more interesting than a little old lady.

At the post office, Emily loaded her arms with the bundles of flyers she'd left in the car overnight and dropped them into an out-going mail slot. She stopped at her box and opened it. Inside were the usual circulars, the latest edition of a popular cat magazine, and an official-looking letter from her attorney in Houston. Her hands shook as she ripped open the envelope.

"This is to inform you of the upcoming parole hearing of Peter Michael Murray, aka Wade Robert Coulter, set for 9:00 AM, Monday, September 12..."

In two weeks? How could he be scheduled for a hearing so soon? His sentence had been far lighter than Emily had expected, but still she thought the time he was required to serve would be longer than this.

Clutching the mail to her chest, she darted from the post office. Back in her car, she dug her phone from her bag and called Connor.

"Maybe they're crediting him with time served," Connor said. "If he's been a model prisoner, they could be cutting him a break."

"What if that 'model prisoner' comes after me?"

"Calm down. You're getting ahead of yourself. We don't know that he'll be released after this hearing."

"But he'll be released someday, either on parole or after serving out his sentence. What if he comes after me then?"

"Look, I searched your name on the Internet once and had a hard time finding anything current. Even your birth certificate lists your birthplace as Lufkin instead of Dogwood, and your real estate is under the name of All Creatures, Inc. So are your utilities. And your phone number is unlisted. If you're sure you never told him where your hometown is, he's not going to find you easily."

She was sure. At least she thought she was.

Wade's ego had rarely allowed discussion beyond himself and the money he needed to raise.

What on earth had she seen in him?

****

Scott examined the blue heeler as it slept off the anesthesia. The dog was lucky to be alive after ripping open his belly in a battle against the sharp wire, but even surgery didn't guarantee he'd stay that way. Scott would've euthanized the animal if not for the owner's pleas to save him. Hours of surgery, a good cleansing of the innards, and a healthy dose of the strongest antibiotic available in veterinary medicine might save the dog's life, but what pushed survival more in his favor had been the prayer Scott and the owner had intoned after all was done. Scott had no doubt the Creator cared for all His creations.

He checked the IV in the dog's foreleg before moving on to the feline side of the practice. Quite some time had passed since one of Millie's captives occupied a spot back here.

Had she lost her touch? He hadn't seen her around town lately. As private as she was, no doubt Paul Goodrich had spooked her, especially if he was hanging around near the apartment, as Emily said.

When Scott talked to him, the reporter had shown interest in Millie as the town's anonymous benefactor—a surprise, since nothing about her indicated an ability to dole out large sums of money on a whim. She had no place of her own. Her feet were her only apparent means of transportation. Her clothes were dirt cheap.

Between Emily and Millie, Scott would've bet on Emily as the more likely benefactor, but since she just bought the old Farley place, she probably didn't have the funds to spread all over town.

Thoughts of Emily's excitement over her new house brought a smile to his lips. Thoughts of her in general made him smile. She had offered the slightest pout when he had to leave Lauren's house last night, just enough to make him want to think twice about answering the emergency call. The kiss she'd given him when she walked him to the truck left him craving for more. He wouldn't mind a lifetime supply.

A mewling, tiger-striped kitten propped her front

paws against the wire caging her. Scott retrieved her and absently stroked her silky belly.

Although he'd been growing deeper in love with Emily with every date, the fact she never opened up about the years she was gone still gnawed at him. What had changed her? He'd been careful not to ask about Houston, but the longer they dated, the more difficult silence became. Everything he'd learned about her had come in dribs and drabs during the year since she'd returned, and it wasn't much.

Each answer seemed to result in more questions. But all the questions fell into two categories: What happened in Houston? And why had she stopped going to church?

There was a third question which was gaining prominence in his mind: Would he ever be able to get her to return to worship services?

How great it would be to have her with him, to be able to escort her to their seats, drape his arm around her, hold her hand while they prayed together. Marrying her in that church, watching their kids be baptized in it—all the things that rang of roots and home and permanence revolved around the church he'd grown up in. They'd grown up in. What he wouldn't give to get her back in it.

He sighed. A little more time, a few more dates, and maybe she'd give in. Meantime, he could slip some questions into some of their easy moments together. Today's lunch break would count as one of those dates, but he couldn't risk questioning her because they'd be rushed. Rushed or not, any time spent with her was special.

According to his clock, he had three hours before he could see her. Three long hours.

"Sheriff Bailey's on two," Dani called from the front desk. Her informality was one of the reasons he liked her. For one so young, she had a quick mind and ran the office like an old pro, but pressing a button on the intercom to announce patients or calls wasn't her style. She found yelling down the hall far more effective.

Scott put the kitten back in her cage and jabbed the button on the phone. "Hey, Quint."

"Hey, yourself. What's your schedule like today?"

"Swamped. Why?"

"We got a bunch of horses at the Expo Center's corral. I'm calling everyone I can to take some of them. You got room for one or two?"

"What kind of shape are they in?"

"Couple of them are in serious shape. I got Doc Clifton over in Longview to take them. But the other two ain't bad, just a bit skinny, a few flesh wounds in their hide. Stuff needing constant care more than high technology."

Scott's stable only had two stalls, but Scotch Bonnet was well enough to turn loose in the pasture. "I'll take those two, then. How 'bout I pick them up after work?"

"Won't do. How 'bout now?"

"Won't do. How 'bout lunch time?"

"See ya then."

Lunch with Emily would have to be on the run, assuming she'd be interested in riding out to the arena. A quick call confirmed she would be. That old game-for-anything spirit he'd loved about her when they were young was still part of her personality. At least that hadn't changed in Houston.

****

With Emily beside him in the pickup and the trailer heavy with the weight of two scarred and skittish Appaloosas, Scott drove a farmer's forty miles per hour back to his house. He was in no hurry since his one o'clock appointment had canceled. It was twelve-thirty now. He had an hour to unload and get back to work.

"I didn't realize you were such a hand with horses," Emily said. "When did you develop a love for them?"

"I've always loved horses." He reached for her hand and was rewarded by her fingers entwining with his own. "Equine medicine fascinated me in college."

"But you have a small animal clinic. You didn't want to work on horses?"

"It's not a matter of what I want. It's what I can afford, and I can't afford the special equipment necessary for a large-animal clinic." He took a left turn off the highway onto a red-clay road. "The sheriff knows how much I can handle, so he doesn't call me for the worst cases." He parked his rig near the paddock gate and killed the engine.

Emily, dressed sensibly in jeans and tennis shoes, was a prime candidate—the only candidate—to help him unload the trailer and settle the horses in.

"You mind getting a bit dirty?"

"Not at all." She climbed from the truck and circled around to meet him at the trailer gate. "Just tell me what to do."

She worked alongside him, feeding the horses and tending their wounds. Gingerly, she applied ointment to a shoulder laceration.

"You look like you enjoy this work," Scott said.

"I think I would, given the chance to do it regularly." She smiled over the mare's withers. "You love it, too. You really ought to open a clinic."

"Maybe someday, when the money's right. For now, I'm content working with small animals." He screwed the top onto the ointment tube. "Which reminds me. How's Millie?"

Emily's concentration on her horse intensified; her lips tightened as she studied a wound along the animal's spine. "Don't you think this is infected?"

"Here, let me look."

The injury indeed looked infected—red and pus-filled. He shaved around it, washed it with a strong antibiotic soap, then covered it with the ointment. That Emily had avoided his question hadn't escaped him.

Whenever she didn't want to talk about something, she changed the subject, although she'd never done it before when he asked about Millie. Something was up, but whatever it was, she wouldn't tell him. Once she decided to keep a secret, it was kept.

Still, he wasn't giving up so easily. "So, how is Millie? I haven't seen her since she jumped from my truck."

"She's fine."

"Still hunting cats?"

"No, not so much."

"I reckon all that attention scared her some."

"A bit."

Scott ground his teeth. He could shape a horseshoe barehanded easier than he could get this woman to talk when she didn't want to. How many secrets was she holding anyway? She wouldn't talk about Houston or about why she left the church, and now she wouldn't talk about Millie.

He didn't have much time to press the issue, but come Friday night, he was going to get answers if he had to pry open her mouth and yank the words out himself.

24

"I can't believe it took Scott a year to get you over here!" In an aromatic cloud of perfume and roasted chicken, the plump, buxom Rita Barlow wrapped Emily in a hug as warm as sunshine and as comfortable as a down pillow. Then she held her at arm's length and scowled. "Shame on you. If you weren't going to come to church when you got back from Houston, you should've at least come here."

A twinge of guilt struck a nerve, and Emily offered an apologetic smile. "You're right, Mrs. Barlow, and I'm sorry I didn't."

"We're all adults now. Call me Rita." She patted Emily's shoulder. "I'm going to finish up with dinner. You two just make yourselves at home."

"Anything I can do?" Emily asked.

"I can always use a couple of extra hands."

Emily followed Rita through the dining room, where the table was stretched to its fullest size. In the kitchen, mashed potatoes, buttered corn, and English peas speckled with pearl onions steamed from what must've been Rita's best crockery. She freed a pair of roasted chickens from the oven, and the aroma of thyme and rosemary perfumed the air.

"Goodness, it looks like you're feeding half of Dogwood," Emily exclaimed.

"Nah, I'd need more chickens for that many." Rita settled the roaster on a hot pad on the countertop and pointed with her chin to a pine hutch. "Plates and glasses are over there. Flatware is in that drawer right under."

The doorbell rang, and friendly greetings erupted from the living room while Emily opened the hutch. "You planned a party, huh? How many settings do we need?"

"Six," Rita said.

The preacher, Micah Walton, clomped into the kitchen, filling the entire room with his presence. From behind his massive frame emerged Paul Goodrich and the woman he'd been with in Zabaglione's.

Emily fumbled the plates, and they clattered on the shelf—but didn't break, thank heavens. Her face was already burning; if she'd actually broken the dishes, her cheeks would've incinerated in a flash.

Scott entered behind them, and she speared him with a glare. He lifted his hands as if to say he was as surprised as she.

"Emily! Good to see you!" Micah's voice boomed and echoed in the small kitchen. He suffocated her in a hug and then rested a meaty paw on her shoulder and gently pushed her toward the journalist. "Emily Taylor, I'd like you to meet Paul and Amber Goodrich."

Paul nodded. "Actually, we've met...almost. I never caught your name." The congenial smile on his lips contradicted the journalistic interest quirking his brows. "How is Millie today?"

With nerves stretched taut, Emily straightened her spine. "I really don't know. I haven't seen her."

"Funny how no one seems to know her last name. You two must be the most secretive women in Dogwood."

The heat returned to Emily's cheeks. "Really, I—"

"I'd still like to talk to her. You gave her my card, didn't you?"

"Now, Paul." Amber Goodrich placed a hand on his arm, and her diamonds flared in the kitchen light. "We don't need to be discussing business tonight. We're guests here. How nice to meet you, Emily."

"You, too," she mumbled. Amber offered a gracious smile, and Emily's lips twitched in return. If she discovered Scott had known about this...

Micah slapped Paul on the back. "These two are looking for a new church, and I figured if I couldn't convince them to join ours based on my preaching alone, I'd draw out the secret weapon of Rita's cooking." His smile spotlighted Rita in a manner extending beyond Christian love, and she fluttered a hand at him.

Again Emily caught Scott's eye and raised a questioning brow. Again he shrugged. Typical man. Totally oblivious. Scott hadn't a clue of what Emily had seen in an instant: The widower Micah Walton was wooing Rita Barlow. Which meant he wasn't there solely to get Emily back in church. That was one worry off her mind.

Paul Goodrich, however, was another matter.

"Supper's about ready now." Rita shooed everyone out. "You all go make yourselves comfortable. Wash your hands, Scotty. And anyone else who feels they need to."

Emily stayed behind to put ice in the glasses and pour the tea. Her nerves stretched to the snapping point, but she couldn't very well sneak out and hide. Regardless of how much she wanted to. She was being silly. The word *ninny* popped into her head again, and she smiled.

Paul Goodrich didn't know anything, only that she was acquainted with Millie. And with so many others at the table, Emily could easily shift the focus off herself if he intended to pry this evening. She lifted her chin and marched into the dining room with the plates and flatware.

****

"Awful about all the fires, isn't it?" Rita passed the peas to Amber. "I just can't imagine losing my house that way."

"I know. It's terrible," Amber said. "That last one was just three doors away from us."

"Somebody ought to put a stop to it," Micah rumbled. "I thought they were bringing in some specialist from the FBI."

"They did," Paul said. "An arson investigator from the Dallas office, name of Lamont. Jillian Lamont. She's been to each of the houses now, but whatever she discovered, she's holding it close to her vest."

Rita beamed across the table at Emily. "Emily's planning a fundraiser for the victims. Auction, right?"

"Yes, but I'm just helping, Lau—"

"You're being too modest! Scotty says—"

"Been fishing lately?" Scott lifted the rolls from the table and passed them to Micah.

"Just last night, in fact. One old bass gave me quite a battle..."

As Micah recounted his victory, Emily flicked Scott a grateful smile.

Paul wore a curious look. Something in his expression made her uneasy, as if he'd latched onto a clue and was anxious to follow it. He raised a brow. "When is the auction going to be?"

She shifted in her seat. Why couldn't Micah's fish be newsworthy? "In a couple of weeks."

"I'm donating a few procedures," Scott announced.

Rita patted his hand. "That's good. You always were a generous sort."

Micah scratched his chin. "I don't know how many folks will bid on a free sermon, but maybe they'd like a fishing trip for a few kids and their parents?"

"I can contribute a wedding cake or two," Rita said.

"That is so generous. All of you." Emily's throat tightened.

Micah's love of fishing and kids was known throughout the county, and his private pond jumped with panfish. His offer could bring in quite a bit of cash. As could Scott's. Her own bank account was witness to how charitable his offer was. But Rita's cakes! Her pastries were coveted all over East Texas. The smallest of her wedding cakes was priced over seven hundred.

Emily couldn't wait to tell Lauren.

"I have a score card autographed by Arnold Palmer, the pro golfer," Paul said. "I'll be happy to add it to the items to be auctioned."

Amber clasped his arm. "Oh, honey, that would be a terrific contribution. And I could donate an autographed book!" She named the title and author with a glowing smile.

Emily gasped. "Your generosity is overwhelming."

"And well-appreciated," Micah said. "No one can

say Dogwood doesn't take care of its own. We're a good lot of folks here. Good folks."

Paul caught Emily's gaze and held it. His donation had a price tag, but she couldn't imagine what it could be. Nor did she want to.

25

Scott showed Spencer how to change the dressing on the Appaloosa's spine wound. The laceration was healing well; the skin surrounding it looked pink and healthy. Just a quarter-sized spot of gray remained in the middle.

"I asked Dad about keeping Scotch Bonnet."

Scott hid a grin. The boy didn't know his dad had already asked about the horse. "What did he say?"

"He hasn't said anything yet."

Scott rubbed his brow. Over a week had passed since he'd brought the Appaloosas to his place, and before long, paying for both them and Bonnet would be too much. He knew he'd promised Parker some time, but at the time, he hadn't anticipated boarding two more horses. "Well, I'm going to have to find a home for her soon."

Spencer's hands stopped moving. "Why? You have three horses here, and they're all doing good. I thought you said you could only handle two, but you're handling three real good. And I can help. Really! I'll come every day and help with the horses. I'll feed 'em and tend their wounds and muck the stalls. Whatever you need. And you can count that as pay for boarding Bonnet, couldn't you? Couldn't you do that?"

Scott shook his head. "How are you going to find time to do it all? School starts soon, and your work hours at Chapman's will be later in the day. It's fine now, especially since today is Saturday, but pretty soon you're going to get tired of the added responsibility on school nights."

"No, I—"

"And what about this spring when baseball season starts? You'll be on the high school team this year. You going to give that up to muck stalls?"

"I can do it. I can do all that *and* take care of the horses. You'll see. Give me a chance, will ya?"

The boy's eyes pleaded with Scott, ripping his heart out. But he had to be firm. "I'm sorry, buddy. I just can't do it. Even if you could do everything you say, I can't afford to keep a healthy horse and still take care of two injured ones."

Spencer's face splotched with red, his eyes turned stony. Without another word, he turned and stomped away.

Scott flexed his hands as Spencer's tires spun clots into the air in his eagerness to leave. The boy was always so angry these days, and having a horse—or any pet, really—might help settle him.

If only things were different and Scott could afford to keep every horse he wanted...but that just wasn't the reality of his bank account. His clinic brought in decent money, but the nature of small animal practice dictated he'd never get rich.

The best he could do for Spencer was to call the boy's father before putting an ad in the paper. Finding someone to adopt an old horse took time. Maybe it would be all the time Parker needed to make a decision.

His cell phone vibrated in his shirt pocket.

"Want to go to Jefferson with me?" Emily's voice

sang in the receiver and instantly lifted his spirits.

He grinned. "The most romantic town in Texas? You bet."

"The romantic side is nice, but so are the antique shops. I need to find some furniture for the parlor. I'm almost finished with it."

"Good enough reason to go. Be there in two seconds."

"Hold on. I'll be *there* in two seconds—wherever 'there' is. Are you at work?"

"Home. You don't want me to come get you?"

"No. I feel like driving. If I haven't been cooped up remodeling the house with Roger and his crew, I've been cooped up working on the auction with Lauren. I'm ready for a change, and a long drive will do me good."

"Well, your two seconds are up and I don't see that convertible flying down my drive. When will you be here?"

"Give me thirty minutes."

"Not one minute longer."

****

As they drove with the top down, Emily's hair whipped behind her, giving her a carefree look Scott hadn't seen in a while. He liked it.

Twenty minutes from town, mid-morning on a glorious September day, and all thoughts of Spencer sloughed away.

Scott stole another look at Emily. Her cheeks flushed in the wind, her freckles brightened under the sun's rays, and the corners of her mouth curled up with contentment. Her guard was down.

He stretched his arm across her seat back. "Hear any more from Goodrich?"

"No, thank heavens. He was really getting to be a pest."

"I bet Millie's glad he's out of the picture."

"You can say that again."

Scott studied the horizon for a moment. The opportunity to learn more about Emily had never been better. How many questions could he ask before he totally wrecked their day? More than just that one, surely.

"You know, you never did tell me about your store in Houston." He maneuvered carefully into the subject she'd been avoiding for the past year. "What was it? Deck the Halls?"

"Deck the *Walls*. Just a play on words. It was a great little store. Turned a good profit within the first two years."

"Decorating doodads?"

"Well, yes, but more than that. All kinds of imported and domestic fabrics for drapes and curtains. Upholstery fabrics. Wallpaper—many of my own design."

"Sounds impressive."

"It was. I loved it. Being an interior decorator allowed me into some of the most prominent homes in Houston and the surrounding area."

"If you loved it so much, why did you sell your business?"

Emily stiffened. "Do you hear that? It sounds like it's coming from my engine. Do you hear it?"

"Hear what?"

"That tapping. It's so faint, but I hear it. Don't you?"

No, he didn't. And he doubted it was even there. He rubbed the back of his neck. "Can't hear a thing."

"Oh, well. Maybe it's nothing." She flashed him a dazzling smile. "Where do you want to eat when we get there?" She listed a few restaurants. "I love them all."

"They're good. Any one is fine." Scott slumped in his seat and watched the trees zip by. Emily could erect a wall faster than anyone he knew.

Her hand slid down his arm and came to rest in his. An apology? He looked at her tapered fingers. Her palms were rough, and the nails were stained from the work she'd done on the old Farley place.

He gave her hand a squeeze. Apology accepted. For now. "Actually, I could go for a hamburger."

****

What a productive day it had been. Emily had found a Victorian double-end settee framed in rich walnut, a pair of matching salon chairs with needlepoint cushions, and an incredible oval coffee table mounted on an ornately carved pedestal. Each piece was a genuine antique, masterfully crafted and beautifully maintained. Of course, the price of the entire set was astronomical, but she took less than an instant to decide to buy it.

With her financial situation being as tight as it was for now, the best she could do was leave a down payment with the overjoyed merchant. Then, using the camera on her phone, she'd taken several pictures of the jacquard upholstery on the settee. She couldn't wait to design matching wallpaper. The parlor would come together nicely with the addition of the furniture.

"I can see the wheels turning in your head," Scott said from the passenger seat. "You must be planning where you're going to put all that stuff."

Emily almost jumped at his voice; she'd forgotten he was in the car with her. She emitted a giggle more appropriate for a nervous cheerleader and apologized. "You're right. That's exactly what I was doing." Her cell phone rang from somewhere in her bag, and she asked Scott to get it.

"Em's Interior Design. This is her ever-faithful servant speaking."

She swatted him and grabbed the phone.

Lauren was still laughing. "I take it you're on a date."

"Of sorts," Emily said. "We're just coming back from Jefferson. What's up?"

"Well, I have some bad news. Tracy broke her legs and one of her arms while they were on vacation."

Emily gasped. Tracy was Lauren's younger sister. Emily knew her almost as well as she knew Lauren. "What happened?"

"They were on vacation, hiking in Big Bend. She slipped and fell off a cliff. It's a wonder she's alive."

"Oh, no. I'm so sorry to hear it. How are Dave and the kids?"

"They're fine, thank heavens. Not a scratch on any of them. But I have to go to Shreveport and take care of everyone for a few weeks."

"*Weeks*?" Emily almost swerved into the next lane. "Hold on. Let me pull over." Once the car was idling on the shoulder, Emily spoke sharply to Lauren. "The auction is coming up. Surely you mean you have to leave *after* it!"

"They need me now. David's leaving on a business

trip tomorrow, and I have to help with the kids."

Emily rubbed her temple. "Of course you do. I can't believe I even said that. It was just me being selfish. I'm sorry."

"Don't apologize. I know what's on your mind. Just stay away from the cameras."

"Oh, don't worry. I will."

"But even if your picture hits the paper, it won't matter." Lauren used her most rational, reassuring voice. "Really, it's not like the population of Houston is going to care a whit about a little auction in Dogwood."

Emily signed off and closed her phone. She didn't care about the population of Houston. If her picture made the paper, and the paper posted it on their website, she could be found. Wade could find her. Easily. And if his parole was granted, he could come after her.

"What's wrong?" Scott massaged her shoulder.

For a moment, she drew comfort from the warmth of his hand and then pulled back onto the highway. As she drove, she told him Lauren's news.

"Wow," he said. "That's rough. When is she leaving?"

"I forgot to ask, but I assume tonight or first thing in the morning."

"Good thing you two have everything ready for the auction." He studied her. "You do have it ready, right? Anything you need me to do?"

"I can handle what we need to do now, but I may need you during the event." She'd need him to come between her and anyone with a camera. Only a week spanned between the day of Wade's parole hearing and the auction—an entire week for him to find her if he had a mind to. She had to stay out of the limelight until then.

What was she thinking? She had to stay out of the limelight *period*. He could come after her at any time once he was released. Never again would she volunteer to work on a charity event, or anything else that could land her picture in the paper or bring attention to herself.

She shuddered. Maybe she was being silly. A ninny. Other than at the trial, when he'd stared so hatefully at her as she testified, he'd never given her reason to believe he'd get revenge on her. He'd never tried to contact her during her last few months in Houston while she sold her business. No letters, no phone calls. No attempts at all.

Yes, maybe she was being silly.

Still..."You can be there, right? You can help?"

"Count on it."

****

Once they'd parked in Scott's graveled drive, he reached over and cupped her neck, running his thumb along the tender spot behind her ear. The porch light highlighted her hair and invited him to run his fingers through silky tresses.

She sighed. "I enjoyed the day. I'm so glad you were free to come with me."

"Wouldn't have missed it." He gently pulled her to him and savored the lips he'd been tempted by all during the day. After a long, delicious moment, he pulled back a fraction. Having to stop was a hateful, necessary duty. He breathed in her scent one more time—soap and sunshine—and then cleared his throat.

"Want to see the horses?"

"Sure." Her voice was husky. She turned off the ignition as he climbed from his seat.

The crisp evening breeze cooled the fire building within him as he walked to her side of the car. She seemed happy, relaxed, compared to the few moments after Lauren's phone call. This might be the perfect time to issue the invitation he'd been wanting to offer. He opened her car door and offered his hand. "Micah has something he wants to announce at the church tomorrow night."

"Oh?" Her eyebrow cocked and a little smile tilted her lips. "I bet I know what it is."

"You know exactly what it is. You caught on faster than I did." He slipped an arm around her slender waist and guided her toward the paddock.

"Did he talk to you first?"

"He did. Mom was with him when he told me." Scott chuckled at the memory. "I don't think I've ever seen her blush so much. Or seem so excited. It's not like Micah was asking me permission, but I would've granted it anyway. She deserves to be happy after all these years."

"When's the wedding?"

"I guess we'll find out tomorrow night when he announces." When they reached the pipe rail fence, one of the Appaloosas nearby bobbed her head and nudged his hand. He rubbed her nose to buy time and then swallowed to dampen his parched throat before asking Emily a variation of the same question she'd been saying no to since her return to Dogwood. "So, you want to come to church with me tomorrow night?"

It was her turn to swallow, and she gulped audibly. For a moment, he thought she was developing her escape plan again. She rubbed the horse's cheek. "Did Goodrich join the church?"

"Well, yes, but I'll fend him off if he comes near you." He assumed a pugilist's stance, legs spread, fists raised. "He won't get past me!"

"My hero." She laughed and shook her head. "I'll go with you. Besides, I wouldn't want to miss it!"

26

Emily sat on the padded pew, snuggled comfortably in the crook of Scott's arm. Micah was winding down his lesson for the evening—one she actually got to enjoy once she discovered Paul had missed the service. Her earlier surreptitious glances around the sanctuary in search of the Goodrichs were often met with smiles and curiosity by the regular members.

Their encouraging looks allowed thoughts of returning to church to enter Emily's mind. Many of the people in attendance here had been friends once and could be again. This wasn't Houston. She didn't run the risk of falling for another Wade Coulter—not with Scott by her side. The people she knew here would have no reason to turn on her as those in Houston had. She'd see to it.

The more she thought of it, the less she could blame her Houston friends for being suspicious of her. They'd had no way of knowing she'd been just as duped as they were. Maybe it was time for her to release that hurt and forgive them.

As she bowed her head to ask God's help, Micah bowed his and intoned the closing prayer. Then, before his "amen" died from the airwaves, he said, "Now, before y'all run off, I have an announcement to make."

He lowered his bulk down the steps from the dais and extended a hand toward the front row. "Come on up here, Miss Rita."

Scott's arm tightened around Emily's shoulders, and she glimpsed a teary smile on his face.

With his hand resting on the shoulder of a blushing Rita Barlow, Micah spoke into his wireless microphone. "It's no big secret around here that most of the extra weight I carry is from this sweet lady's good cooking. Well, I'm here to tell you that cooking isn't the only admirable quality Rita possesses. Y'all know she's a fine woman of God and a steadfast leader in this church and in the community. I've been blessed with her company for a while, and now I'm looking forward to having that blessing full time."

He paused dramatically as people murmured and exchanged knowing grins.

Rita's smile broadened, and she nudged him. "Why don't you just tell the folks you proposed to me?" Either she'd intended for her prompting to be broadcast through the speakers, or she didn't realize how sensitive the preacher's microphone was, but her question brought cheers from an overjoyed congregation.

From the back, a tenor voice yelled out over the crowd. "Well, what'd'ya say, Miz Barlow?"

Rita pressed her hands together and brought them to her smiling lips. Then she held them wide and shrugged as if to ask, *what else could I say?* "Yes. I said yes!"

The crowd vaulted to their feet and rushed to the front to congratulate the couple. Much of the cacophony echoed off the sanctuary walls until Micah remembered to turn his microphone off.

Beside Emily, Scott sniffed and brushed away tears with his free hand.

Emily wiped her own tears and leaned into him. "You know that makes you a PK."

"Preacher's kid." He chuckled. "I can't say as I mind that too much."

As the church members disbursed, Scott and Emily went to the front and exchanged hugs and back-slaps with Micah and Rita.

"I'm so happy for you," Emily said.

Rita giggled. "I feel like a kid again."

Micah moved between Emily and Scott and draped an arm around each. "When are you two going to announce?"

Emily's face flushed with enough heat to melt her makeup, but Scott seemed unfazed as he looked at her. "Soon as I can convince her it's a good idea."

Her lips parted. She didn't even know he'd been thinking about it. *Now! Ask me now! What's taking you so long?*

But Micah had already reclaimed Scott's attention. "You two make a good-looking couple." Micah squeezed her shoulders once more before releasing her. "Get on with it and we can have a double wedding."

Scott smiled at his mother. "I wouldn't want to interfere with Mom's special day."

Rita patted his hand, which rested on her shoulder. "You and Emily want to come over tonight? We're having coconut cake and coffee at the house for whoever wants it."

"I'd like to, Mom." Scott kissed her hair. "But it's Dani's week off, and I have to cover the clinic. Those dogs get ornery when they don't get to romp in the yard before bedtime."

"Well, you two have a good time."

"Thanks for the invitation." Emily gave her a hug

and then gave Micah one. "I'm so happy for you. Congratulations!"

****

With the taste of Scott's good-night kiss still sweet on her lips, Emily drove home from the clinic. She had left her car there instead of asking him to drive to her apartment in town on his clinic-duty night.

As he drove her from the church to the clinic, she'd hoped he would broach the subject of marriage again, but he concentrated instead on his mother's happiness and his admiration of Micah. He was right. He should focus on their happiness.

So should she. If she and Scott were meant to get married, they would, and Emily would be happy to wait. She didn't want to do anything that might overshadow Rita's joy.

Emily slowed near the Queen Anne. Roger and his crew had worked on the kitchen all day yesterday, and she hadn't had a chance to see what they'd done. Wouldn't hurt to take a peek at their progress.

As she pulled into the drive, her headlights flashed across the front porch—and landed on a hooded figure in the process of swinging something through her windows. Glass shattered everywhere. The figure froze where he stood and squinted into the car's twin beams before darting into the shadows, where she lost sight of him.

She sat numbly in her car with both feet mashed against the brake pedal, and her fingers clamped around the steering wheel. He looked like the person she'd seen leaving the fires. Same height, same size, same gray hoodie.

Was he the arsonist? Was that why he was here? He wasn't just breaking in, wasn't just vandalizing a vacant house—had he intended to set her new home on fire?

She bolted from her car and sprang up the porch steps. The scent of acetone stung her nose; the air was so thick with it, her eyes burned. She didn't dare open the door—just the scrape of the hinges could spark a flame—but she dashed from window to window looking for a fire. And didn't find one.

Her legs quivered under her, and her head swam; she had to sit down. She wobbled back to her car, reported the crime, and called Scott. Then she huddled in the front seat, shaking as if stranded in an ice storm.

27

Red and blue lights from fire trucks and squad cars flashed against the Queen Anne, giving it a surreal, carnival atmosphere. So many uniformed officers swarmed the place, Emily worried the rest of the county was without police protection.

The acrid smell of acetone had dissipated, thank heavens, but two apparently empty cans of it were now tagged as evidence.

She drew closer to Scott, thankful for the strength of his arm around her, and tried to concentrate on Sheriff Bailey's questions. Illuminated by the headlights of his vehicle, the man appeared to be in his late fifties. Even in his boots, he was barely an inch taller than she was and no bigger around than her thumb, but the square cut of his jaw and the deep command of his voice left her with little doubt of his authority.

"What time did you arrive at the house?"

"Not that long ago. Right after I left the clinic. Around eight?" She glanced up at Scott for confirmation; he nodded.

Bailey surveyed the surroundings. "No street lights here. Did you leave the porch light on?"

"No. I hadn't planned to come tonight."

He poised a pen over a small pad. "Tell me exactly what you saw."

Emily did.

"And your headlights landed right on him? Could you make out who he was?"

"No, I couldn't tell for certain. It happened so fast, and I just wasn't expecting—"

"But you could see him, right? You saw him?"

"I saw a figure in a gray hoodie. That's all. He was just...shadowy. Then he took off around the house. It was all so fast."

"Could you tell how tall he was, how much he weighed?"

Emily stared at the nearest pillar on the porch. The height of the post was at least ten feet, and the hooded figure probably hit just over halfway. But her imagination could have been playing tricks on her. "He wasn't real tall, and he seemed fairly slender, but I don't know. I just can't be sure."

One of the officers called to the sheriff from inside the house, and he thanked her before striding to the door.

As Emily watched him leave, a flash blinded her eyes and she squinted in pain. She opened them to the sight of Paul Goodrich standing in front of her with a concerned look on his face and a camera strapped around his neck.

"Hello, Emily. Scott." He greeted them as casually as if they'd crossed paths in the grocery store. In a sympathetic tone, he said, "Sorry about the vandalism. Is the house yours?"

Emily tightened her grip on Scott's arm. She shouldn't lie, but she couldn't answer. If Goodrich discovered she owned the house, it wouldn't take him long to discover that All Creatures, Inc. belonged to her, too, and everything would fall apart. She couldn't imagine what would happen. Didn't want to.

As if reading her thoughts, Scott edged forward and shielded her from the reporter. "How did you find out about this?"

"Police scanner. The journalist's favorite tool. Emily, did you see who broke out the windows?"

"She just caught a glimpse of him," Scott said. "Like she told Bailey, she didn't get a good look at him."

Paul turned to face the house. "Which way did he go?"

"She didn't see, but I'm sure he's long gone by now."

The deputies moved away from the front of the house, and Goodrich fingered his camera.

"I need a few more pictures before I turn this story in." He gave Emily a smile. "Looks like you prevented another fire. That'll be in the headlines."

She withered where she stood. Despite Scott's protectiveness, she'd landed in the spotlight, and the very publicity she'd sought to avoid barreled toward her like a one-ton truck.

Scott circled her in his arms again, and she sank into them gratefully. "It's bad enough he's been hounding Millie for information," he mumbled against her hair. "I don't want him hounding you, too."

A familiar figure stepped into the beams of the headlights. "Hey, lovebirds! I reckon God smiled on you today."

"Roger! Why are you here? How did—"

"I called him," Scott said. He extended his hand in greeting. "Did you bring the plywood?"

"It's in the bed of my truck. When's everyone going to clear out of here?"

"Soon, I reckon. They've already been here"—

Scott glanced at his watch—"almost an hour. Can't imagine what else they expect to find."

Emily glanced over her shoulder.

Paul had apparently finished with Sheriff Bailey and was heading back into the murky shadows he'd come from. Within moments, he paused his car at the curb beside them. "Front page news. Y'all be sure to get a paper in the morning."

Scott watched him speed away. "I know the man's just doing his job, but I'll be glad when he finds some other bone to chew."

****

Thirty minutes later, all the official vehicles disbursed, leaving only Scott, Roger, and Emily standing in the front yard.

Roger strode to his truck. "Let's get those windows boarded up. I don't want anyone stealing my equipment in there."

Scott followed him, and Emily, still a bit shaky, walked toward the pale glow of the porch. The light from a pair of sixty-watt bulbs glinted off crystalline shards of glass and the once-painted floorboards. Now the paint peeled and buckled and stuck to the bottoms of her shoes because of the acetone. The full-length, etched window to the right of the door gaped open with sharp glass teeth reflecting the light. Adjacent to it, two of the three beveled-glass bay windows snarled at their own shattered condition. Replacing those panes wouldn't be cheap. Hopefully, Parker wouldn't balk at being called upon so soon.

28

Ten o'clock Monday morning, Emily burst into Connor's office and tossed a newspaper on his desk. "Have you seen this?"

True to his word, Paul Goodrich had run her picture on the front page with the caption, "Good Samaritan Thwarts Fire Attempt." Line one of the article named Emily Taylor as the good Samaritan.

Connor adjusted his glasses over his bulbous nose and peered at the grainy photo. "It isn't a very good likeness of you, is it?"

"It's good enough." Her hand trembled as she pointed at it. "Wade will be able to find this. Able to find me. If he gets paroled today, he can come for me!"

"I was going to call before you came barging in here." He laid his glasses on his desk and leaned back. "Wade wasn't granted parole. The decision was delivered at 9:00 AM."

Emily lowered herself onto the cushion of a client chair. "Great. Now he has that many more months to build up his anger toward me."

"Or let it settle down."

"Maybe." She sighed. "Well, at least I'm safe for now."

"You're safe, period," Connor said in a stern voice. He delivered an *end-of-argument* glare.

She wanted to believe he was right, to take comfort in his words. But she couldn't. "Don't they have computers in minimum-security prisons? With this article in the paper, I'm just one web search away from discovery."

Connor studied her a moment longer as if taking stock of her fear. "Come around here. Let's just see how vulnerable you are."

As she stepped to his side of the desk, he fired up the computer and landed on his homepage. He typed her name into the search bar and hit enter. "Emily Taylor" was not an unusual name. A photographer, a golfer, even a director of some office in Washington, DC, were among the results of Connor's search, but nothing current about Emily Taylor of Deck the Walls fame, formerly of Houston, Texas.

"Maybe *The Dogwood Daily News* hasn't updated their site yet. Maybe that's why it's not on the Internet."

"Let's see." Connor navigated to the paper's website. Sure enough, her picture was on the site in full color. "You're safe, Emily. You're just being paranoid."

She offered a weak smile. Perhaps he was right. Maybe she was being paranoid. But Wade's snarl in the courtroom continued to niggle at her memory, and she could imagine it growing more evil with each day he remained locked up. Yes, she could consider herself safe, for as long as she stayed out of the camera's eye.

****

Outside the Victorian, a table saw, manned by a muscled construction worker, squealed through the silence as it sliced a one-by-four in two. The noise decibels dipped only slightly as the man tossed aside the cut boards and prepared another to hit the blade.

Emily gritted her teeth against the high pitched wail and skittered into the house, which proved unable to mute the racket from outside.

The sharp acetone odor no longer hung in the entry, but thanks to the strong chemical, whatever varnish that hadn't worn off with age now cracked and flaked beneath her feet. Because of the plywood covering the windows, the entry itself seemed shrouded in gloom. She'd talked to Parker about replacing them earlier, although she wasn't certain she wanted the new glass installed until the arsonist was caught.

She turned toward the light cascading from the bare windows in the parlor and surveyed the room with its naked walls and dull woodwork. She needed to sand off any old wallpaper glue and prep the walls for new paper, a chore she'd begin as soon as she talked to Roger.

She found him in the kitchen, yanking up floorboards from along the wall where her sink and appliances once stood. The cabinets had been ripped out. Now raw wood stood in stark contrast to the ancient wallpaper above the counter line.

Roger grunted against stubborn nails until he finally yanked up another board. He caught sight of her and sat back on his heels.

"You'd've been much better off if that arsonist had tried to set fire to the kitchen—and succeeded. See that?" He touched one of the discarded planks; it crumbled on contact. "Rotten."

Emily tsked and shook her head. "I wasn't expecting this."

"No, neither was I." He laid his hammer down and stood to stretch his back. "And I hate to say it, but this adds to the renovation cost."

"How much?"

He told her, and she winced. Now the cost for the entire project swelled way over budget—and they'd just begun. No telling what he'd find in the bathrooms or upstairs. The next payment from the sale of Deck the Walls wasn't due for a few more months. With the mortgages on the cat refuge and the Victorian, along with the payments on the furniture she'd found in Jefferson and all her other expenses, she couldn't afford hefty increases to Roger's estimate.

"You may have to stop the job after this until I get another cash infusion."

"Let's wait and see." He draped an arm around her shoulders. "It's not unusual to encounter these little surprises. You paid us a third up front. We're good for now."

Roger's assurances lifted her spirits a little.

"I hope so."

"We are. I have to get back to work." He guided her from the room. "Have you decided what colors you want in here? What appliances?"

"Not yet, but I'll know by the time you're done." Rummaging through her mind for decorating schemes always uplifted her, and within the moments it took to return to the parlor, she was humming to herself.

Hours later, Roger poked his head in. "You need to call Scott."

She grinned. "My pleasure. Any particular reason?"

He entered, ran a hand along the freshly sanded drywall, and gave a nod of approval. "I just got a call from Gary over at Fleetwood Marine. He's going to donate an aluminum bass boat for the auction. Some of this stuff we're getting is too big to keep at the house. We need a storage unit, and we'll need Scott and his truck to help us move the stuff over there."

Emily looked at the dust powdering her arms, her shirt, and undoubtedly, her hair. "I'll handle it, but I have to shower and change first."

"Get cleaned up so you can get dirty again?" With a smile, Roger looked at his watch. "It's four thirty now. Scott closes the clinic at five. What do you say we meet at my place around six?"

"Sounds like a plan."

He nodded and left the room while she brushed dust from her hands before searching her purse for her cell phone and punching in Scott's number.

****

At the storage facility, Emily appraised the contents of the mid-sized unit. She'd caught the facility manager moments before he closed the office for the day, signed the lease, and obtained the key. Now, at eight, the unit was over half-full with boxes of small items, the boat, and a new golf cart, a last-minute contribution from the local pro golf shop.

"Can you believe the generosity of the folks in this town?"

"You sound surprised. I've always thought Dogwood had some pretty special people in it." Scott wrapped his arm around her waist. "And you're pretty special for spearheading this auction."

Emily's cheeks warmed. She had given up the pretense that the auction was Lauren's brainchild, but she still felt uncomfortable taking the credit.

Roger's cell phone rang. He whipped it from its

holster on his belt and flipped it open. "Hey, babe, perfect timing." He eyed Emily and Scott. "The two lovebirds are getting mushy." Emily swatted at him, but he jumped from her reach. With a wink and a wave, he headed for his truck with the phone at his ear. "How's your sister?"

Emily watched him leave. "Have those two ever been apart?"

"Sure," Scott said. "But not for long. This extended separation will be difficult for them. Those two are proof of God's marriage mystery: *the two shall become one flesh.* They even breathe in unison." He smiled, a little wistfully, she thought. "Maybe people will be saying the same about us someday."

Her breath lodged in her throat as he lowered his lips to hers. Even as his mouth explored her own, one thought ricocheted through her brain: *He's going to propose!* She held him tighter, trying to show him how quickly she'd say yes once he uttered the words. But when he pulled away, he offered only a soft smile. "I guess we'd better get that storage unit locked up."

She swallowed her disappointment and brought out the key. Oh, well. Standing on a concrete parking lot surrounded by ugly metal buildings wasn't the most romantic place to propose marriage. When the time came, she wanted to be in a far more memorable place, like Zabaglione's with its dripping candles and soft Italian music.

He drove her home with his fingers locked around hers and his mind somewhere beyond her reach. She studied his profile from the corner of her eye, uncertain whether to interrupt his thoughts. If he was trying out different ways to propose, she definitely didn't want to interrupt him, but what if he was trying to back out of his comment?

Maybe people will be saying the same about us someday.

The words still hung in the air between them. Was he sorry he said them?

His silence continued as he escorted her up the walk, and with every step toward her front door, the timer on her heart ticked down to zero. If he didn't say something soon, she'd explode.

At the door, he cleared his throat, and her pulse skyrocketed.

"Well, goodnight." He gave her a light kiss, a brotherly kiss, and then turned to go—and her heart crashed to the cement at her feet.

Burning tears came, and it was a draw whether they or her mounting frustration caused her to fumble her keys. Frustration, humiliation, disappointment—she didn't know which to pick as the apt description of what she felt. Heat scorched her face as she finally clasped the right key and jammed it into the lock.

"Emily?"

She stilled her shaky hands but didn't look back. "Yes?"

"I love you."

His words made her turn. "What?"

Shoving his hands in his pockets, he bowed his head slightly and peered at her from beneath his brow. A shy smile tilted his lips. "I love you."

****

In a flash, the distance between them disappeared, and they were in each other's embrace.

With her arms wrapped around his neck, and her

joyful tears dampening his cheek, Scott tightened his hold and told her again. "I love you!"

How many times those words had been on the tip of his tongue, and he hadn't been able to say them. Wasted time. The swelling of his heart threatened to overtake him, suffocate him, if he couldn't say them again—shout them for the entire neighborhood to hear—but Emily's lips found his own and claimed them with a fury and passion he eagerly returned.

Every luscious curve of her body pressed against his, and it took all the strength he could muster not to explore its mysteries right there in the soft glow of the street light. His head reeled with intoxication as he fought his desire to sweep her up and carry her inside.

When finally they broke apart, he rested his forehead on hers and whispered the words again. This time, she said them too, and his heart threatened to burst.

"I thought you'd never say it," Emily said. "You don't know how much I've wanted to hear that from you."

"I was taking it slow." He smoothed her hair from her forehead. "It took forever for you to go out with me. I didn't want to rush you."

"Thank you for not giving up. Your patience and tenacity are among the reasons I love you." She kissed him again, a slow, lingering kiss that made his head spin above the clouds.

Rowdy teenagers packed tightly in a rusty sports car drove by, whistling and catcalling at Scott and Emily as they passed.

Scott wrapped her in the security of his arm and escorted her back to the door. "I'll be so glad when you can move from this apartment. It doesn't seem safe here."

"Oh, it's fine. Occasionally I can hear the kids getting a little crazy as they drag down Main Street, but it's usually quiet." She fingered her keys but made no move to unlock her door. "It'll be awhile before I can move into the house, anyway. Roger found some rotten floorboards in the kitchen and had to rip everything out to replace them."

"Ouch. That'll set him back some. Any idea on the new target date?"

"Several weeks beyond his original estimate. That doesn't mean I have to wait until then to move in, but I'd like him to finish with the kitchen and at least one bathroom before I do. And I'd like to have the place rewired. It's fine now, I guess. But before I go spending the night, I want that worry eliminated."

Scott wrapped his hand around hers, keys and all. "I'm looking forward to waving to you on the balcony." He kissed her goodnight.

Soon, she'd be sleeping right up the road from him. The thought was too exciting to safely ponder for long.

29

The next morning, Emily sat up in bed and arched her back in a luxurious stretch, arms out, mouth wide in a yawn. Considering how little sleep she got last night, she felt amazingly rejuvenated. She clasped her knees to her chest.

He loved her! He'd finally said it.

Joyous warmth spread through her, leaving her energized and anxious for their date this evening. He didn't tell her where they were going, but the wish in her heart was for Zabaglione's. A little pasta, a little wine, a little diamond of maybe a carat or so...

Thinking about it wouldn't make the day go by faster. She jumped from the bed and headed for the shower. She needed to go to Parker's and check on a claim for the windows that were shattered the other night. Guilt for filing against her insurance so soon had almost prevented her from doing it, but with the expense involved with the rotten kitchen floor, she couldn't afford to replace those windows with anything similar to the originals without the insurance. Choking out the deductible would be hard enough.

Next, she needed to make a trip to Chapman's and browse their kitchen center. While she was there, she could look through the outdoor paint samples and determine the color scheme for—

She frowned at a thought niggling her mind.

The gray hooded figure she'd seen had seemed

vaguely familiar, but she couldn't be sure and would have to go to Chapman's to find out.

There was only one way she could go without being recognized.

She showered, dressed, and, by ten o'clock, headed out the door.

****

At a quarter after twelve, Scott turned on Emily's street. She wasn't expecting a lunch date, but after last night, the thought of waiting until this evening to see her again was just too much to bear. Her favorite meatball sub sandwich steamed in the paper bag next to his club sub and a couple bags of potato chips. As he neared her apartment, he caught sight of a little old lady hobbling through the front door.

Millie.

He hadn't seen her around in weeks, and while her presence blew the idea of being alone with Emily, he was happy to see that his favorite cat catcher had been out and about.

He went to the door, tapped lightly, then let himself into the cat sanctuary where he caught sight of Emily's chestnut tresses as she headed up the stairs to her apartment.

"Hey, Em!" He glanced around, but saw no sign of Millie. "Didn't I just see—"

Emily slowly turned toward him. "Uh, hi Scott. I wasn't expecting you."

She stood midway up the stairs, holding what looked to be a wig in her left hand and a hair net in her right. Her eyes were downcast, but he was able to study her face. It was lined, and crinkled, and aged...like Millie's.

"You're Millie?" He shook his head and then laughed. "You're *Millie?* I should've known!"

"No way you could have known." As if wounded he'd even suggest it, she tilted her head with a haughty expression. "I've been very careful. Until today, anyway."

"I've always wondered why I never seem to catch the two of you together. Now I know."

As she came down, he couldn't stop staring at that dark hair framing an ancient face. The contrast was astounding and illustrated a skill professional makeup artists would envy.

He emitted a low whistle. "Great job. As close as I was to Millie in the truck the day the journalists were after her, I knew something was a bit...off, but I never thought of this. What causes the limp?"

Emily rested a hand on his shoulder for support, slipped a small, smooth pebble from her shoe, and held it for him to see before sliding it into her pocket with a grin. "Can't afford to lose it. It took forever for me to find one I could tolerate but would still give the right effect."

Scott laughed and shook his head. "So, why the Millie persona?"

She shrugged. A sheepish grin curled her lips. "Millie can do things I can't, go places unnoticed, overhear things. Catch cats without people thinking anything of it."

He chuckled. "That's the truth. She's known for being a bit eccentric. But what made you think of inventing her to save cats in the first place?"

"It's complicated, and it's not just about cats. I like to help people. While she hunts cats, Millie finds people with problems and 'tells' me."

Emily searched his face as if in hope he'd understand. He didn't, but this was the first tidbit she'd ever shared about her private life. He tried to appear sympathetic as she continued, but she must've noticed his confusion.

She blew a wisp of hair from her cheek with a huff. "It's like this—you remember when I first came to you with that kitten?"

How could he forget? He nodded.

"It was one of three I found on the road to Dogwood when I was moving back from Houston. The only one alive. They'd all been hit by a car as if the idiot driver had aimed at them." Her lips tightened a moment before she resumed her story. "While I was staying at the hotel—while I was looking for a place to live here—I saw two more cats get killed. One time, I saw a kitty barely miss getting hit. He darted to the bushes just outside my room, and I tried to coax him out."

"Were you successful?"

"Well, yes—but when I came out of the bushes with him, some kid said, 'Look, Mom! A cat lady!' and I realized I was quite a sight. I had been in the process of changing clothes and got distracted, I don't remember how, but I was wearing a pair of orange capris and a red suit blouse that clashed horribly."

"That explains her sense of fashion." Scott pictured the scene and couldn't help chuckling. "But why did you go into this cat-catching business full time? And what does it have to do with helping people?"

"I let the boy play with the kitten and got to talking with his mother. She opened up to me and told me personal things I doubt she would've told me as...well, as *me*, and not as an eccentric cat lady. I was able to help her and still protect my anonymity—"

The door flung open behind them, and Paul Goodrich burst in. His scrutiny absorbed the scene in an instant—the wig, the makeup, Millie's polyester pants. He grinned.

"Nice to finally meet you, Millie. Or should I call you 'Emily'? Or maybe—" his smile broadened— "I should say Mrs. Wade Coulter."

30

Under her old-lady makeup, Emily's face turned ashen. She fled up the stairs and slammed the door to her apartment.

Scott's brain, unable to process what he'd just heard, simply went blank. His feet remained rooted in place, and he presented himself as a fine rubbing post for Daisy, who curled around one leg and then the other and purred with a volume easily heard in the silence.

"What just happened?" He turned to address Paul. "What was that all about?"

Paul cleared his throat. "Sorry, man. I hate to be the one to break it to you."

"You'd better fill me in on what's going on. What is it you just broke to me?"

"That's it. She's married to Wade Coulter, a con man the Texas Rangers finally caught and put behind bars a couple of years ago. I don't have all the facts yet, but it looks like our little charity auction coordinator may have been a partner in his scams." He blew out a breath. "Again, I'm sorry. I know you're fond of her, but maybe it's best you steer clear."

"Maybe it's best you get your facts straight before you go smearing her name." Scott snarled. "I may not know what's going on, but I know Emily's not capable of conning anyone."

"You didn't know before today that she was

Millie, did you? Didn't know she was married?" Paul placed a hand on Scott's shoulder. "Doesn't that mean she conned you?"

Scott couldn't say anything, couldn't meet the man's eyes.

After a moment, Paul gave his shoulder a squeeze and turned to go.

Scott stopped him. "Give her a little time to explain. I'm sure she can. Surely she has an explanation."

With his hand on the door, Paul said, "I won't run with the story until I've verified the facts. I don't work that way." He looked over his shoulder at Scott. "For your sake, I hope I'm wrong." He left.

Scott rubbed his forehead. All this was related to Houston somehow, but Emily had given him no clues to help him piece together the puzzle. Nothing that could help him understand.

Still, until he had all the facts, he wasn't about to jump to the same conclusions Paul had. The journalist was confused, had the wrong woman. No way had Emily Taylor ever been married, much less been involved in a felony.

But doubts blanketed certainty. The girl he'd known would never be in trouble with the law. But the woman she'd become? She'd been gone for ten years. Anything could've happened. Did he really know her?

For the first time, he heard her sobs from her apartment and bounded up the stairs. He tried the knob, but it was locked. "Emily, let me in."

"No, Scott. Just go away."

Tears laced her voice, and he ached to reach her. "Please, Emily. Talk to me. Trust me. Haven't I proven you can?"

"Yes, but—" She sobbed. "I can't talk right now. I can't. Please understand."

Rubbing his neck, he exhaled an exasperated breath. He wanted answers, but not like this. Not through a closed door. Still, one question burned in his soul. "Answer me this: Are you now, or have you ever been married?"

Silence pulsed for several long moments. His heart caught in his throat, and the pain of it choked him. "Em, answer me. Have you?"

The longer the silence stretched, the more he wanted to slam his fist through the door. But then, he heard her voice, weak and sad, from the other side. "Yes."

****

Although he was in no mood for company, Scott unlocked the passenger door on his pickup to let Roger join him inside. "Hey."

"Hey, yourself. I've been looking everywhere for you." Roger slid into the seat and slammed the door. "Man, I'm disappointed."

Scott scowled. In his current mood, hearing Roger's boisterous voice grated on his nerves. "About what?"

"Finding you here. I've already been by your clinic and the house. My next stop was your mom's. Too bad I found you here first. I could've scored a fried chicken or a pot roast if I'd paid a visit to Miz B." He thrust his chin toward the paper cup in Scott's hand. "How many of those have you had?"

"Three. And I don't really want this one." Scott sighed and handed over his root beer float. "You want it?"

"Ain't pot roast, but it'll do." Roger pulled the straw out and ran it through his lips to clean it, then flipped it over and reinserted it into the plastic lid. "I'd forgotten how good these things are."

"So why were you looking for me?"

"Got a call from Lauren about an hour ago. She sent me after you."

"Word gets around fast." Scott huffed out a breath. "She talked to Emily?"

"Yep."

"And?"

"And she wants you to get your butt back over to Em's apartment and let her explain."

"Explain what? She's married." Scott stared without interest at the carhop skating down the sidewalk. His heart felt heavy, as if it had solidified into cold lead in the past hour. He rubbed his forehead. "She's married. There's nothing to explain."

"Seems to me, if the woman I'd been dating for the past several weeks was married, I'd want to know why she didn't bother to tell me." Roger sucked on the straw and smacked his lips. "Fact is, she ain't married."

"She told me herself she was."

"*Was* being the operative word. Lauren said that Emily said that *you* said—man, this sounds like some stupid soap opera. Or a kid's drama. Don't you feel like we're back in high school?"

Scott flashed him a black look. "What did Lauren say Emily said?"

Roger raised his hand defensively. "Look, she said that the way you asked if Em was married didn't leave her much of a way out. You said, and I'm quoting here, *Are you now or have you ever been married?*"

"Right. And she said yes."

"She said yes to the 'have you ever been' part." Roger put the sweaty cup in the holder and rubbed his damp hands down his pants legs. "She was married for a few hours to a con named Wade Coulter who got arrested the same day they got married. They never even had a honeymoon. Emily got the marriage annulled soon after. She tried to tell you, but you'd left."

"What did she say about being involved with the cons?" Scott shot back bitterly. "Did she bring that up? Did she explain that?"

Shock registered on Roger's face. "Involved? She wasn't involved. She testified against him. She was as much of a victim as everyone else."

"That's not what Paul Goodrich believes. And if he can verify it, he's going to run an article all but accusing her of scamming Dogwood citizens with this auction she's planning."

Roger shot out a breath. "She didn't do anything wrong. She just fell in love with the wrong guy."

The words crashed through Scott's chest. She'd been in love with someone else. He shouldn't be surprised. Most people in their thirties had fallen in love at least once. But not him. She'd always been the only one for him, and he'd never declared his love to anyone else, never said the words until last night.

Roger gaped at him. "You don't believe what that reporter says, do you? You don't honestly think Em could be involved in a felony?"

Scott shrugged. Too many questions remained unanswered. "We're thinking of Emily Taylor, the high school valedictorian. This Emily has lived a life apart from us for years. What do we really know about her?"

"We know she was raised better. We know she's a Christian—"

"—who has only been to one church service since she returned, and that was when Micah proposed to Mom."

"But she's still a Christian." Roger drew his lips tight. "Look. All I know is, when I'm with her, she seems like the same ol' Emily. Lauren is comfortable with her. Those two fell in together as if they'd never been separated. I don't believe she's changed that much in ten years."

Emily, Millie. Married, single. Con artist, victim. Scott's head reeled. He didn't know what to believe.

Another tap on the passenger side jerked his attention. Roger lowered the window, and a pimply-faced kid on skates scowled at him. "Mister, we can't have empty vehicles taking up our slots. You need to move it."

"What difference does it make if I order from this pickup or that one, as long as I order?"

"You haven't ordered," he insisted.

Roger leaned over and studied the menu board outside Scott's window. "Gimme four jalapeño burgers—Trey will eat two by himself—one order of chili-cheese tater-tots, and two of onion rings. Oh, and add three more root beer floats. Kids'll love 'em."

When he turned back around, the kid was glaring at him. "You've gotta punch the button. From your own vehicle."

Roger rolled his eyes toward Scott.

"That's all right. I need to be going anyway. Thanks for the info," Scott said.

Alone again in his pickup, he sat hunched over his steering wheel. True, he needed to be going. Question was, where? Dani had clinic duty for the evening. He didn't want to see his mom, didn't want to face her questions. He couldn't go to Emily's. He wasn't ready for that.

He prayed she'd told Lauren the truth about having her marriage annulled. The idea he'd been kissing another man's wife was more than his soul could take. He prayed everything she'd said was the truth, and that she was single and not complicit in the cons this Wade Coulter dude committed.

But even if she had told the truth, she hadn't trusted him with her past, with the things on her heart—not even with her double identity. Maybe he would've understood if she had just told him, but what kind of relationship could they build without trust? He wanted a woman he could confide in, one who would confide in him. A wife, a lover, a best friend.

Apparently, Emily wasn't the one.

31

Emily sighed and toed the Friday newspaper, which was spread out on the coffee table. It held nothing about her; neither had Thursday's or Wednesday's.

For three days, Paul Goodrich had failed to reveal her secret to the town's population. Maybe Dogwood's "soft touch" had become old news. Maybe he had finally decided to concentrate on the arsonist instead of harassing her. Wouldn't that be wonderful?

Other than stepping out to retrieve the *Dogwood Daily*, Emily hadn't left the sanctuary of her apartment. She tended the cats in her pajamas every morning, and was still in her pajamas when their nighttime feeding rolled around. Her days were centered on old movies and the "how-to" channels, and her nights brought little sleep. Dark rings had formed under puffy eyes. She needed a shower. Badly.

Scott hadn't called once since he'd discovered her secret and hadn't answered when she'd called him. After that first day, she quit trying.

She'd been so careful to keep her past from everyone. From him. Well, the truth was certainly out now, wasn't it? Only Scott didn't have half the facts Connor and Lauren did. He just knew she'd been married. For all he knew, she was still married.

How had Paul found out? What had sent him searching through the Harris County records? He didn't seem surprised to see her as half-Emily, half-Millie, so he'd already figured that out...probably through Sheriff Bailey. Just because she and Scott had denied her ownership of the house the night it was vandalized didn't mean the sheriff had. Why would he? As far as he knew, her ownership was a matter of public record.

Apparently, Paul searched the records and discovered both her house and the refuge were owned by All Creatures, Inc. It hadn't taken him long to add two and two.

But that still left the question of how he had discovered her marriage. Did it really matter? He knew, and soon everyone else in town would know.

Although why anyone would care was beyond her. She sniffed and scrubbed her face with both hands, and wished for the millionth time Scott would let her explain.

He wouldn't even talk to her.

How could he yank his love away that easily? How tenuous would a relationship with him be if he disappeared every time he got mad at her? If he wouldn't listen to her, or even confront her and fight out their problems with her?

Wasn't she worth fighting with? Fighting for?

Bitterness roiled in her stomach and burned in her throat. For the second time in her life, a man claiming to love her had lied.

Fine. She didn't need him.

She vaulted from the couch and marched to the shower. Time to focus on something besides Scott. Something like her house. She still needed to determine her paint scheme, pick out the hardware for her new kitchen cabinets and drawers, figure out whether she wanted laminate or marble countertops. Plenty of things to keep her mind off Scott. Instead of waiting by the phone, she'd be out and about, heading to the home improvement store in Tyler. Chapman's didn't have what she wanted, and the road trip would do her good. She would crank the radio loud and drown the clamoring thoughts about Scott.

After her shower, she pulled on some jeans and a red T-shirt, then loped down the backstairs to her car.

She drove toward the Victorian and slowed when she saw Roger's truck. She parked at the curb.

Roger strutted to her car. "Hey, princess! You heading out to see Scott?"

"No, just taking a road trip." The fact she would drive right past Scott's house hadn't dawned on her. Or maybe it had on some level, but she hadn't consciously planned it. Oh, well. She was miles away from the alternate route and wasn't about to backtrack now. "How's it going with the house?"

"We're getting the cabinets installed, and the new beveled windows will be delivered this afternoon. We'll put those in tomorrow."

She climbed from the car and walked with him toward the house. "I'll be glad to see those windows in, but don't you think we should leave the plywood up just in case?"

"I suppose we could. Whoever did this is probably still on the loose. I haven't heard about him getting caught, have you?"

"No, but I think I know who it is."

Roger stopped walking. "Who?"

She bit her lip. "He looked like someone I've seen at Chapman's."

Roger rubbed his chin. "Wow." He thought a

moment, his dark brows drawn tightly over his nose. "That would make sense in a way. The acetone could've come from there. Are you going to turn him in?"

"I don't know. He's just a kid. If I'm wrong, I could ruin his life."

"Yeah, I can see why you'd be hesitant." He studied her for a moment. "That's not the only thing bothering you, is it? Hasn't Scott called?"

"No." She snorted. "Was he supposed to?"

"I had hoped. You two need to clear up this mess."

Her lips tightened. "Lauren talked to you?"

"Of course she did. She tells me everything. I tell her everything." He rested a hand on her shoulder. "It's called 'having a relationship.' Something you and Scott need to work at."

"That's not going to happen. He thinks I'm married."

"No, he doesn't. I told him you weren't Tuesday night, soon as I got off the phone with Lauren." He grinned. "That's called 'being a buttinsky.' "

Emily's heart plummeted. "So he knows about the annulment?"

He nodded and gave her shoulders a sympathetic squeeze.

She bit back tears.

Scott knew and still hadn't called.

****

Scott closed the gate to the pasture and strode toward his house in time to see Emily's car speed past. For a moment, his heart stopped. Then he mentally booted it back into gear. With her new house being just up the road, she'd pass his place every time she headed out of town. He might as well get used to it.

His fist clenched around his key ring. Maybe someday, some distant day, he'd find a woman who would trust him, and Emily Taylor would be a long forgotten episode in his past. Well, no. Not forgotten. In her previous absence, he hadn't forgotten her. Perhaps the best he could do was let time distance him from this present pain, the constant gnawing ache in his heart, the persistent questions running through his head.

He growled, ordering his mind to shut up, and unlocked his truck. Before he could climb in, a car honked, and he looked toward the highway.

Parker Milligan's black lab, Chica, rode with her head hung gleefully out the passenger window of a maroon SUV; her ears blew back and her pink tongue dangled out of the corner of her mouth. When Parker slowed and pulled into Scott's drive, she barked enthusiastic greetings to him, the horses, and the sparrows flittering nearby.

Parker's window lowered. "Hey, Scott. Got a minute?"

"Sure." He slammed his truck door and strolled over. "What can I do for you?"

Inside his vehicle, Parker snapped a leash on Chica's collar, then climbed out with her on his heels. "Sorry to bother you at home, but Dani said you'd be here, and I don't have a lot of time before I have to get back to work."

"It's no problem." Scott scratched the lab's ears. "Something wrong with Chica?"

"No, no. I wanted to take a look at Scotch Bonnet. Spencer's been sulking around lately. He hinted you'd have to get rid of the horse soon. I wanted to take a look at her."

"Come on back."

Once there, Parker tied his dog to a fence post and followed Scott through the gate and into the field.

The bay roan lifted her head from the fresh grass and gazed at them warily as they approached. She'd calmed down considerably under Scott's care, but she was still a bit leery of strangers. Scott clicked to her, but she skittered away a few yards before stopping, her eyes and ears focused on the two men invading her pasture.

Parker shook his head. "She seems awful flighty."

"She's not used to you. You should see her with Spencer. One click of his tongue, and she comes galloping."

"Really?" Parker rubbed his neck, eyeing her beneath thoughtful brows. "He'd certainly love to have her."

"They're good together. Good for each other."

"Found a place for her over on Sorrel Ridge."

"Nice place."

He grunted an agreement. "Just need to figure out how to get her there."

"I've got a rig. Want me to take her?"

"You wouldn't mind?"

"Not at all." With the coolness of a businessman, Scott stretched out a hand to shake on the deal, but inside, he squelched the urge to whoop like a kid. At least someone would get what he wanted, and if it couldn't be himself, he was glad it was Spencer. "When do you want me to take her out?"

"His birthday's a week from Sunday. Reckon we can get her stabled the day before?"

Scott winced. The auction. He'd promised to help and wouldn't renege regardless of where things stood with Emily. "That Saturday won't work. I'm booked. How 'bout after church on Sunday?"

"That's fine." Parker gave Scott's hand an extra shake before releasing him. His expression held an excitement Scott hadn't seen in a while. "Boy's going to be excited when he finds out he's a horse owner. I want to see his face when he gets a load of the animal in her new home."

Scott clapped him on the shoulder. "I'd like to see that, too."

****

Emily took the long way home from Tyler so she wouldn't have to pass Scott's house. Catching sight of his lean form this morning as she drove by was more than her heart could bear—and it had ruined her trip.

With everything that had transpired since her house was vandalized, she felt fragile. Racing past Scott's home without the freedom to seek the shelter of his arms, or even offer a wave in greeting, crushed her.

She'd continued on her way, made it to Tyler and the home store, but once there, couldn't concentrate well enough to coordinate the colors she wanted, and she was already doubting the hardware she'd chosen for the new cabinets. She couldn't focus on anything but him and the last time he'd kissed her. She raised her fingers to her mouth now as if still able to feel the warmth of his lips lingering there.

A gas station's neon lights glowed ahead, and she glanced at her gauge. It registered just above a half tank, not worth stopping. The grocery store occupied a corner lot farther ahead. She flipped her blinker and prepared for the turn. Scott probably wouldn't be bringing cat food and kitty litter around again, so she'd better pick some up, and a few other things while she was at it.

Inside, she grabbed a cart and wheeled it to the pet aisle. She bent for a ten-pound bag of cat food and transferred it into her basket just as a raven-haired beauty entered the lane. Amber Goodrich. Emily tried to turn and run before the woman could see her, but—

"Oh, hello—uh...Emily? Is that your name?" Amber's cheeked flushed crimson, no doubt uncertain what to call the woman with three aliases.

Paul had probably told his wife about Emily's multiple personalities. Nothing she could do about it, and she might as well get used to the curiosity of others.

"Yes, I'm Emily. Nice to see you again, Amber."

"Honey, I found the—" Paul stopped in his tracks and flashed a dazzling smile at Emily. "Well, hello. I've been hoping to run into you again."

Emily steeled her spine and raised her chin. "I can't imagine why. You don't need me anymore. You've already discovered who Dogwood's *soft touch* is. Although why you haven't run it in the paper is beyond me."

"I was waiting until my interview at the prison next week. Being the soft touch may not be the only newsworthy item about you."

"The prison?" With brows drawn, Emily squinted at him. "What are you talking about?"

"You know, where your *dear* husband is incarcerated."

Emily's blood roiled through her veins. "He's not

my husband, and if you were half the investigative reporter you think you are, you'd know that! Next time you go spouting your mouth, make sure you've got your facts straight."

"I'll be sure to ask Coulter to verify the facts while I'm there," he growled. "Anything else you want to share with me?"

Emily was on the verge of whacking him with the cat food bag when Amber put a hand on his arm. "You two are creating quite a scene. Paul, let's just finish our shopping."

He drew a breath and stepped back. "You're right, honey. I'm sorry." He reached for their grocery cart, and with all the civility of a British butler, gave Emily a slight nod. "Good to see you again. Have a nice evening."

Seething, Emily watched as they disappeared around the corner. She wanted to ram her cart into the dog biscuit display, but she took a deep breath instead. If she hadn't already created a scene, knocking down a cardboard case in a fit of anger certainly would. Her mind was void of any grocery list she'd stored in it, so she snatched the cat food out of the basket and dashed for the counter, leaving the cart in the aisle.

****

"You should've seen him, Lauren," Emily balanced the phone on her shoulder as she refilled the cats' food bowls. "He was so smug, telling me he was going to verify my marital status with Wade."

"I hope Wade tells him the truth."

"I don't understand why Paul doesn't just search the Harris County records." She carried the water bowl to the faucet in the back. "The annulment is a matter of public record. If he found out I had married Wade, he could certainly find out I unmarried him without having to go all the way to the prison."

"Wait. You think the only reason he wants to talk to Wade is to find out whether you two are still married?"

"What else could he want?"

"Oh, no. Didn't Roger tell you? Paul isn't trying to confirm your marriage. He's trying to establish you as a co-conspirator in Wade's cons."

Emily's hands trembled, and she dropped the bowl, sloshing water all over herself and the utility counter. "But I wasn't involved. I didn't even know—"

"I know that. But Paul doesn't. He told Scott he wanted to verify your involvement before he printed anything."

"He told Scott his suspicion?" She leaned her back against the wall and slid down. "Scott thinks I'm a con artist?"

"I don't believe he knows what to think. Roger says he's confused and is still trying to sort things out." Her voice grew stern. "But you haven't given him much to work with. Why didn't you ever confide in him?"

"I was so ashamed." Emily sobbed. "I didn't think he'd want me if he knew."

"Sweetie, he loves you. He's always loved you. And you didn't do anything wrong."

Panic charged through Emily's nerves. "Wade won't leave Paul with that impression. The board denied his parole. He's probably boiling with hate toward me right now. He'll probably confirm every nasty thought Paul has about me."

"You've got to talk to Scott. Tell him everything. Tell him the truth."

"He won't believe me. Besides, I haven't heard from him all week. He won't answer my calls. He's not interested in my side of the story."

"You've got to try." Urgency filled Lauren's voice. "I'm getting off the phone now. Call him. Then call me."

"But—"

"Do it!"

Emily wiped her face and sighed. "All right. I'll try again."

They disconnected, and she took a couple of deep breaths before trying Scott at his house. No answer—of course. But just in case he really wasn't home, she tried his cell, too, and got his voice mail. For a moment, she felt torn. He'd already proven he didn't want to talk to her. She should leave the man alone and get on with her life. But she couldn't allow him to have the impression she'd participated in Wade's crimes. She thought about telling him everything in a voice mail message, but changed her mind. Instead, she left yet another request for him to call that would probably go unanswered.

She gathered herself, dried the counter and floor, and then refilled the cats' water bowl.

What was it with Paul Goodrich? What had she ever done to him to make him want to destroy her life, just as she was getting it back together? Couldn't he leave her alone? No telling what Wade would stuff his ears with, and that greedy journalist was likely to publish any lie told him. If he printed his suspicions, everyone in town would believe the worst of her.

She'd have to step down from the fundraiser.

Would probably have to leave Dogwood to find someplace she could live in peace.

But there was nowhere else to go.

Ninny.

The word came out of the blue, and accused her worse than anything Goodrich said about her. She was being a ninny—it was true. She had decided to hide from her accuser instead of fighting him. So, Goodrich was going to the prison?

Fine. She would, too. At least she could discover Wade's attitude toward her, find out what he had to say. Confront him.

How liberating! She was sick of hiding. Sick of worrying he would find her. Instead of cowering like the ninny she'd been for the past year, she'd see for herself how much anger he harbored against her and then take whatever precautions were necessary to protect herself from him.

She ran up the stairs and consulted her calendar. The auction was a week away, and she still had follow-ups to make. When Lauren was in town, she'd been the frontrunner, talking with the auctioneer, the caterer, and the manager for the community hall, and allowing Emily to remain in the background as planned.

Now, Emily would have to do everything. Not that it mattered. Since she was going to confront Wade anyway, she had no need to remain in the shadows about the auction.

The prison wasn't too far away. She could probably make the run in half a day and still be able to finalize plans for next Saturday. She called Connor at home and asked him to arrange for her to meet with Wade.

"Are you nuts?" Connor shouted. "I thought you

were afraid of him!"

"I am, but I'm tired of it." As far as she knew, Connor wasn't aware of what had transpired over the past several days, and she chose not to tell him. "With the auction coming up and Lauren gone, I don't have a choice but to step up to the job. I don't want to have to worry about cameras and media. It'll be best for me to confront him. Who knows? Maybe you've been right all along, and I've just been paranoid. Unless I see him, I'll never know whether he's angry with me, and I'll spend the entire week nervous."

Connor drew a breath and let it out in a huff. "All right, I'll see what I can do. But it's not like I can just call down there and make an appointment. You'll have to go during general visitation."

"When is that?"

"I don't know, but I'll find out Monday." His voice took a fatherly tone. "It may not be until after the auction. Will you be all right with that?"

"I'll have to be, won't I?"

But what about Paul? Would he have to go during visitation, too, or would he have special privileges as a journalist? If he got to the prison before she did, how could she counter what Wade told him?

How could she prove her innocence to Scott?

32

Not five minutes in his mother's home for Sunday dinner, and Scott already felt a comfort only moms could provide, the kind that came with familiar scents and cushioned hugs and the inevitable complaint of, "You're too thin. Do you eat enough? Come on in here and let me fix your plate." She heaped double portions of everything and handed it to him.

"Don't give me all that."

"You're skinny. Eat."

"Mom, I'm fine. I do eat."

"Oh yeah? What? When?" She tried to pinch an inch from his waist and got a pinch of empty shirt instead. "Uh-huh. You've lost weight. Come on. Sit down."

They blessed the table and then Rita leaned close. "So what's going on with you? I haven't seen you all week. My grass is three feet high! I'm almost scared to go out there. Who knows what all's hiding in them weeds. We're close enough to Louisiana, you know. Could be 'gators out there."

Scott chuckled. "I get the hint. I'll mow right after lunch."

"Not in your good Sunday clothes, you won't."

"I've got some jeans in the truck. I'll change first. Happy?"

"Happy." She filled her fork with peas and poked it in her mouth. The comfortable silence between them stretched as they concentrated on their plates.

Scott was an instant away from believing he could enjoy lunch without his mother's trademark nosiness, when she asked, "So, how's Emily these days? Does she like her new house? How are the auction plans? You never tell me anything."

"I don't know much about Emily anymore." Scott lowered his fork. He'd been dodging her calls all week, the most recent of which was last night. They needed to talk, she'd said. Needed to clear the air. Maybe when he could breathe again after having the wind knocked out of him, they could. Right now, he didn't want to. "We're kinda not seeing each other for a while."

"What?" Rita rubbed her hands on the dishtowel in her lap. "Something happen between you two?"

"She has some secrets, Mom. Some things she really should've told me."

"Oh, posh! Every woman has secrets. Our hearts are a hotbed of things we'd just as soon no one knew."

"Like she's been married before?"

Rita raised a brow. "Well, now, sounds like that's one she should've let you know. I'll agree to that. How'd you find out?"

Scott didn't want to describe the awful scene in the cat refuge, and since he'd never mentioned Millie to his mom, he'd have a rough time trying to catch her up on all he'd learned that day. "Let's just say, I didn't find out from her. At least, not immediately."

"She confirmed what you'd heard?"

Scott nodded. He pushed away his plate, his appetite gone.

Rita rested a hand on top of his. "Did she explain?"

"I didn't give her a chance."

"Well, you should. A sweet girl like Emily doesn't take marriage vows lightly, and for her to be single again, something awful must've happened. Something truly awful."

Scott hadn't thought of that, but it was true. The Emily he'd known would never leave the man she had vowed to love, honor, and cherish. She took those vows seriously and wouldn't marry carelessly. Roger said she got an annulment soon after Coulter's arrest. Had she known when she married him what kind of man he was?

"Of course, if you're not interested in Emily anymore, Pat and Carol are still single. Either one would be ecstatic to have a date with you."

Scott huffed in exasperation. "Mom."

"I thought not." She pushed his plate back to him. "Eat. This tastes a whole lot better than that crow you'll be munching before long."

He retrieved his plate but couldn't convince himself to eat. Instead, he pushed his peas around with his fork like he did when he was eight. Questions about Emily's years away still niggled at him. She'd changed—he'd said it before. Sometimes, he didn't even recognize her. Did her changes extend to her moral character?

Mom had said no. Roger had said no. Why couldn't Scott be as certain?

****

Roger's pickup sat in the driveway of the old Farley place—Emily's place. Her car was nowhere in sight, and Scott felt a surprise twinge of disappointment as he pulled in behind the truck. The front door to the house hung open, so Scott went inside and called out. "Roger?"

"Back here," came a muted reply. Roger sprawled on the bathroom floor with his head and shoulders in the cabinet under the sink. He stuck an arm out. "Get me that wrench, will you?"

Scott found it and slapped it into Roger's palm. "Working on the Lord's day?"

He grunted and then asked for the oil can. "Kids are out, wife's away, not a decent football game on until later this afternoon. What else am I supposed to do?"

"Well, you put it that way, working on a sink sounds perfect."

"Glad you think so." Roger scooted over a bit. "Come down here and hold the light for me."

Scott wriggled his upper torso under the sink and shined the light at the pipe Roger was wrestling. "Nasty mess. You going to be able to get it off?"

"Yep. Even if I have to use a blowtorch." Roger grunted again. Rust flaked and fell to his sweaty face, and he wiped it off with his forearm. Then, with both hands and a mighty twist of the wrench, he forced the pipe threads to turn a quarter inch. "What you doing out here?"

"Coming home from Mom's."

"Yeah? She feed you good?"

"Always. She worked it off me, too. Weekly lawn maintenance." Scott watched the pipe scratch loose a slip at a time, amazed that Roger had managed to get it moving. "Got a question for you."

"Shoot."

"When did Emily figure out Wade was a con

artist?"

Roger arched a rust-flaked brow. "You mean, did Em knowingly marry the man and participate in his crimes? Is that what you're asking? I think you know the answer to that."

"Yeah, Mom thinks I should know, too. It's just that—"

"—that she didn't confide in you and you were shot off balance." After the final twist of the wrench, Roger yanked the pipe free from the sink. "Scoot out."

Scott got to his feet.

Roger squirmed from under the sink and wiped the rust from his hands and arms on a rag. "I can't deny she should've told you, but you've known for five days now. You should be hearing her side of the story from her, not trying to piece together tidbits of truth from third-hand sources."

Scott rubbed the back of his neck. "I don't know how to approach her. What to say."

"Just show up at her door. She'll know what to say." He turned to the sink and grabbed a screwdriver. "But help me with this first."

"What would you have done if I hadn't shown up?"

"Oh, I would've gotten it done. It just would've taken longer." Roger pried up the aluminum ring around the sink and then ran the screwdriver around the sink itself. They got their fingers under the lip and forced it away from the stained countertop. "I got it now."

Scott relinquished his hold and followed Roger as he went outside to the refuse pile. In the city, plumes of smoke danced in the air over the downtown area. Scott shook his head. "The arsonist is at it again."

Roger tossed the sink on the pile and looked toward town. "Aw, man. I wish they'd catch that guy. Em thinks she knows who it is. I wish she'd go ahead and turn him in."

"Did she tell you who she suspects?"

"Someone from Chapman's. She's hesitant to tell the police because he's just a kid, and if she's wrong, she could wreck his life." Roger watched the smoke and shook his head. "I say, turn the guy in and let the authorities sort it out—"

Scott barely caught the last of Roger's words. He yanked the keys from his pocket and sprinted to his truck.

33

As a kid, Emily had never lacked company. Her childhood home had been like Lauren's, one of the popular hang-outs among her friends. Now, with Lauren gone and Scott out of the picture, she sat alone at the local fast food restaurant, idly twirling a french fry as she stared out the window.

An old car pulled up, battered and faded, just like the woman who drove it. She and four frail-looking kids climbed out. They must've ranged in age from six to twelve; the older ones held hands with the younger, and they trailed their mother like ducks on a pond.

Emily eyed them carefully from under her lashes.

The little family wore clean clothes, but all were faded and patched, and the youngest girl's little summer dress with daisies at the hem hung too loosely around her fragile body. The mother ordered four of the smallest hamburgers on the menu and one super-sized soda. The oldest boy took the cup and filled it with orange soda at the self-serve fountain and then grabbed five straws. They chose a table close by.

Emily looked at her own cold sandwich. Even if she hadn't taken a couple of bites of it, she couldn't offer it to the mother. Such action would be perceived as charity, and Emily didn't doubt the woman would be too proud to accept. If she were Millie right now, she'd figure out a way to give food to the family without offending the mother, but Millie no longer existed.

Too ashamed to throw her food away in front of the kids, Emily wrapped up her sandwich and fries and then went to the counter for a sack. After she bagged her lunch, she slipped a couple of twenties from her purse. With the bag in one hand and the soda in the other and her purse strapped over her shoulder, she fumbled her way to the entrance, dropping the money near the small family's table.

"Hey, lady!" The oldest boy called to her.

Emily quickened her steps.

"Hey! You dropped your money!" He picked up the twenties and headed toward her.

She rushed to her car and locked herself in. As she drove away, she saw him standing at the door waving her money at her.

Forty bucks wasn't much. If Millie had been there, she could've arranged for a lot more. Emily could've done the same, but somehow, being dressed as Millie—a harmless eccentric—gave her an inroad that Emily couldn't achieve as herself. Millie could say and do anything; Emily couldn't. She missed Millie.

She rounded the corner toward home. A violent roil of smoke billowed over the historical district, and Emily's heart cramped.

Not again. She couldn't let this go on. She pulled into her parking place behind The Litter Box, and called 9-1-1 on her cell. With her phone to her ear, she climbed from the car and strode around to the front of the building.

There, not fifty feet from her, was the same young man in a gray hoodie she'd seen leaving other fires. Leaving her own house. He casually strode opposite her direction, but she recognized his walk, the way he kept his hands in the pockets and his head down.

She had no choice but to turn him in.

Once she made her report, she watched the smoke from the fire, which was about three blocks away.

Behind her, tires squealed to a stop, and she glanced over her shoulder.

Scott emerged from his truck, making her heart leap to her throat. But it soon plummeted when she saw the look on his face. Whatever emotion was reflected there seemed stronger than she felt ready to face. She wrapped her arms around her midsection, a protective shield from whatever darts he planned to shoot.

As he closed the distance between them, she realized the emotion radiating from him was worry. For a moment, she held a glimmer of hope he'd been worried about her. She turned to fully face him. "Hello, Scott."

He stopped a few feet away, nodded at her, and rocked on his heels.

He seemed so distraught, her arms ached to enfold him. But he'd yet to look her in the eye, and his distance kept her anchored where she stood. She switched to business mode—cool, aloof, professional. "Is there something I can help you with?"

"I need to know..." He cleared his throat and tried again, this time looking at her. "Roger said you know who's been setting all these fires. Can you tell me who it is?"

She studied him for a moment. Why did he want to know? If she was wrong, she'd be smearing a young man's reputation. But she'd kept so much from Scott, and because she had, they now stood opposite each other like total strangers. She bit back a sigh. Whatever his reason, he seemed to need her answer. "I think it's a kid named Spencer. Spencer Milligan."

He grimaced. "Are you sure it's him?"

"Reasonably sure. I thought I recognized him at my house the other night, but I wasn't certain." She rubbed her hands up and down her arms and stared at a crack in the sidewalk. "I wanted to be positive, so I dressed as Millie—that day you found me in costume—and walked to Chapman's where I'd seen him before. He was there. It was him."

"But Roger said you weren't sure."

"I was sure he was the guy I'd seen at my house, but not that he was the one I'd seen walking away from the fires. Now I am. I just saw him again."

"You did?" He looked up and down the street, but Spencer had already turned a corner. Scott shot out a breath from between his cheeks. "Did you do anything about it? Have you told the authorities?"

"Yes, just a few moments ago."

He strode back to the truck without a backward glance. His pained look before he'd turned tore at her, and a cloud of guilt engulfed her. Though she didn't know how, she'd hurt him. Again.

****

"Scott and Parker are friends, and he feels close to Spencer," Lauren explained. "He coached him all the way through Little League and kept up with his junior varsity baseball."

Poor Lauren. Every time Emily called, she had to listen to a new tale of woe. But Emily didn't know where else to turn. "Maybe I shouldn't have turned Spencer in."

"No. You had to do what was right. And if you're sure—"

"I am sure. I hate it, but I'm positive the boy I've been seeing at all these fires is Spencer."

"Then you have nothing to worry about. Scott will come around."

Emily sighed. "I know you're busy. I'd better let you go tend to your sister. Thanks for being a sounding board."

"Not a sounding board," she said. "A friend."

"The best." Emily disconnected and rested her phone against her chin.

So far, Scott hadn't shown any sign of "coming around," and after shoving his friend's son into the hands of the authorities, she didn't expect things to get better.

Being the one to turn Spencer in twisted her stomach. He'd seemed like a good kid when she'd met him at the store, and she certainly liked his father. Parker had been quick to settle her claim about the windows.

The ones his son broke.

Seeing Parker in the future would give "awkward" a new meaning, especially if she was called to court as an eyewitness against his son. She clenched her lips. Once again, she'd managed to get herself into a mess. She'd hurt both Scott and Parker. She couldn't apologize to Scott because he wasn't speaking to her, and she couldn't apologize to Parker, because no apology could cover the pain he must be feeling.

She placed the phone on the coffee table, rose from the sofa, then wandered to the kitchen window where she could see billowing smoke tinted with the gold and red of the fire beneath. What would cause a boy to start fires? What sickness devoured him? Did Parker know, or would this take him by surprise?

Anguish smothered her. So much pain all around her—not the least of which was scorched into the hearts of the homeowners whose house this latest fire consumed. She'd have to add them to the list of fund recipients from the charity auction. A fundraiser might help them, but who would help Parker? Spencer? She had to do something.

She twisted away from the window, picked up the cordless, and placed another call to Connor at home.

He listened to her plan. "You're going to get penalized for early withdrawal, you know."

"I know."

"Are you sure you want to do this?"

"Absolutely."

34

The vending machine at the Dogwood Police Station spit out a second soda. Scott handed it to Parker and then lowered himself to a cushioned vinyl bench next to his friend and popped the top of his own can.

The grueling afternoon had ended with Spencer being arrested on several counts of arson. Even now, he was being detained in the juvenile center.

The boy's mother had left earlier, weeping against her live-in's shoulder whenever she wasn't shooting daggers at Parker. It was obvious whom she blamed for Spencer's situation.

Parker hunched forward, forearms on thighs, and rolled the soda can between his hands. "I don't know what happened to the boy I raised. He was a good kid."

"He still is. Somewhere beneath that tough-guy façade, he's still a good kid. He's just got a lot of anger."

"That he does. It's been building for six years—ever since the divorce." Parker blew out a breath. "Parents splitting up is hard on a kid, I know, but they adjust. Don't they? Don't they usually adjust? I mean, think about it. All those kids from broken homes—they don't start fires and get into trouble. Spencer's had six years to get used to this. What happened?"

"Maybe there's more to it. Have you talked him?"

He snorted. "I quit trying. All we do when we're together now is fight. And if he's not fighting, he's moping. I figured it was typical teenage rebellion, figured he'd grow out of it." He twisted his head and met Scott's eyes. "Did he ever tell you anything? Do you have any clue why—when all this started?"

Scott raked a hand through his hair. "No, man. I'm as lost as you are."

"Well, it's apparent who his anger is directed at. He thought all those houses he burned were insured by my company. Thought he was getting back at me."

An image of Emily's house flashed through Scott's mind, and he shook his head. "What happens now?"

"He'll be arraigned, I guess. Tried. I hope they try him as a juvenile, but he's old enough to be tried as an adult. They said—" Parker's voice cracked. He paused, took a couple of deep breaths that wavered on the exhale, then tried again. "They said he could be charged with first-degree felony arson because so many houses were destroyed. Ninety-nine years max. *Ninety-nine years!*" Parker broke down and sobbed.

Scott could do nothing but awkwardly pat the man's back.

After a bit, Parker scrubbed his face. "I guess I'd better be heading home. Nothing more I can do here."

He rose, and Scott rose with him. "Anything I can do for you?"

"You've done it," Parker said. "Just being here helped."

As they walked toward the parking lot, Scott said, "Look, I'm crazy about Spencer. He's a good kid. I don't know what happened, but the good in him is still there, somewhere inside."

"Thanks." Parker's smile was limp.

"Let me know what's going on."

"Yeah. I'll make sure you're in the loop."

Scott whispered as he drove home, "Lord, everything's so messed up, and I don't know what to do." He just wanted to wind time back to where he and Emily were happy. He wanted to discover in his memory some hint to Spencer's behavior. He wanted all the burned homes to rise from the ashes. But nothing he wanted was likely to happen, and he felt helpless. Prayer was his only recourse, so he prayed. For Parker and Spencer. For all the people who'd lost their homes. For Emily. He prayed for wisdom and direction.

He prayed until he pulled into his drive and shut off the engine.

****

A charred-wood smell curdled the humid morning air and irritated Emily's nose as she stepped out of the cat refuge. The scent soured her stomach, and she hurried to her car to get away. The sun shone dully behind a film of last night's smoke, and the overall effect dampened her mood—not that she'd been walking-on-clouds giddy. Today was Monday, though, and she couldn't give in to the temptation to curl up and hide as she had last week.

That the auction was only a few days away kicked her into panic mode. Last night, she'd made a list of everything she needed to do and had contacted Lauren about the coupons to designate the services donated for the auction.

First on her list was the Down Home Diner; then she needed to track down everyone else who'd offered a service for the auction. Lauren had e-mailed her coupon designs, and Emily had printed samples to show to each of the donors for their approval. Of all who'd offered services, Clara was the only one Emily didn't dread seeing. Micah was next on the list, then Scott's mom, then Scott himself.

"Dread" didn't begin to cover the way she felt about seeing him. Maybe she could get Rita to show his coupons to him and get back in touch with her later. Yes. That would work.

Before she dared to pull into a slot at the diner, she drove past and studied all the cars. At the top of the list of people she didn't want to see—right next to Scott— was Paul Goodrich. But not finding his car among those parked near the diner unnerved her just as much. Had he already been there and she'd missed him? Or was he on his way to see Wade?

Nothing she could do about it if he was.

She shook the journalist from her mind and pulled into a parking spot directly in front of the diner. Inside, a quiet buzz emanated from the few tables where moms shared social brunches and retirees swapped tales. Midmorning appeared the perfect time to come.

Annie mopped around the tables in the back, and Clara checked receipts at the register. She glanced up, and a broad grin crinkled her cheeks as she scooted from around the counter.

"Well, look here. Give an old lady a hug." She opened her arms wide, and Emily stepped into them. "Let's find you a good table. What'll you have this morning?"

"Nothing, thanks." She fumbled through her purse for the diner's coupon. "Lauren and I just wanted to see if this works for you."

On the coupon, Lauren had drawn the diner's blue-canopied façade with the name displayed across the large storefront window and "six dinner specials" printed along the bottom of the pane.

"Oh, these look fine. Just fine."

"I want to see." Annie had apparently put her mop away and stood by them now, wiping her hands on her apron.

Emily warmed at the sight of her. The little bump under her apron promised a new Crawley this winter. She rubbed the younger woman's shoulder in greeting. "How's A&K's Barbecue coming along? Will you be able to open soon?"

"By the end of next month," she said with obvious pride. "We're so excited about it. Our first ad runs tonight during the six o'clock news—wait, how did you know about it?"

Emily bit her tongue and scrambled for a good answer, but Clara glanced up from the coupon and winked. "She's a friend of Millie's, remember? Took the net to her that time she'd left it here."

"Oh, yeah." Annie drew out the words as if something had dawned on her, and she returned Clara's wink. Before Emily could ask to be let in on the joke, Annie's expression changed. "I miss Millie. We never see her anymore. Where has she been? Is she ill?"

"No, she's fine. She's...away." Emily eased the coupon from Clara's grasp. "Since this has your seal of approval, I need to make it larger and have it laminated." She stuck it back in her purse, and gave a little wave as she reached for the door. "Lauren will be so happy she pleased you. Thanks again for contributing!"

Outside, Emily turned to look in the window. What had those winks been all about? She had the acute feeling they knew who Millie was—not the first time she'd wondered that about those two. But she couldn't be sure, and as long as Goodrich hadn't announced Millie's identity, Emily needed to be far more careful not to do it herself.

Micah was next on her list of people she least dreaded seeing, but she couldn't make her rounds according to that list, not as high as gas prices were. Between the diner and Micah were Scott's mother's home, his animal practice, and his house. By the time she got to Micah, she'd be a wreck. Actually, she might never even get there. Judging by the way her stomach churned at the thought of seeing Scott, she might turn tail and run long before she reached the parsonage in the country.

But the morning was still early. Scott would be working, so a quick visit to Rita's should be safe. She turned left at the drive-in restaurant and drove to the familiar red-brick house. She sniffed the air the moment she stepped out of the car and knew Rita had been baking. Perhaps she'd score a position as guinea pig.

Rita greeted her at the door with flour on her cheek and a dishrag in her hand. "Emily! It's so good to see you. Come in. Come in."

Emily did and received her second fortifying hug of the day.

"Come on back to the kitchen. That timer's about to go off." Rita led the way to her cluttered kitchen, where Emily saw the first layer of what looked to be a wedding cake, covered in a soft ivory fondant, and a series of pale pink camellias, beautifully formed out of pastillage and set carefully off to the side to dry. "What can I get for you? You hungry?"

"No, thank you. I'm good—"

"Oh, posh! You look like you haven't eaten all year. Let me make you a sandwich."

"That's way too much trouble, Rita. I just came by to show you the coupon Lauren designed for your cake giveaway for the auction."

That stopped the older woman's fussing for a minute, and she came to rest by Emily's side as she dug the coupon out of her purse.

Rita wiped her hands again before taking the coupon from Emily. For this one, Lauren had drawn a traditional three-tiered cake, with white lilies, beading, and swag accents. "Looks like the one I did for her and Roger back when they got married."

"Actually, I think it is."

"Well, you tell her I'm honored she remembered." Rita handed the coupon back. "How long they been married now? Ten years? Longer?"

"At least sixteen. Trey's expecting to get his driver's license next spring."

"My goodness, they do grow up fast, don't they?" She fluttered around the kitchen again, pulling a cake from the oven and resting it on a metal rack. "Are you sure you don't want something to eat? I'm starved for something that doesn't have sugar in it. Won't you have lunch with me?"

Emily glanced at the wall clock. Eleven. Scott didn't usually take his lunch breaks until twelve, not that he would come here to eat. Or maybe he would. She didn't know what he did with his time anymore.

Rita pulled a bowl from the fridge. "Chicken salad sandwich? Or would you rather have roast beef?"

Her expectant look denied Emily the ability to say no. "Chicken salad is fine."

They worked together to prepare lunch and then sat at the table. Rita offered thanks to the Lord, and with "amen" barely out of her mouth, said, "Now, what's all this about you being married?"

Emily sputtered. "I'm not married. Who told you I was?"

"Scott. Well, he didn't say you were still married, just that you had been once."

"What else did he tell you?"

"Not much else. Just that you had secrets you wouldn't share with him. That'n there was a whopper. You should've 'fessed up."

Emily sighed. "So I've been told."

Rita stepped away from the table and returned with a bag of chips. She offered some to Emily, who shook her head. She didn't even want her sandwich anymore.

Rita grabbed a handful and put them on her own plate. "I told him women have secrets. And we do best to keep them to ourselves. But once you let a doozy like that get loose, a man's gotta wonder what else you're hiding. He's going to wonder if he can trust you. You'll need to tell him."

"I'd love to, if he'd ever give me a chance." Emily's lips tightened. "He won't talk to me. And I really messed it up between us when I turned Spencer Milligan in for starting the fires."

"That was you?"

"Yes, ma'am. I'm afraid so."

"Scott know?"

Emily nodded.

"You know for a fact the boy did it?"

"Yes."

Rita leaned back in her chair and studied her. "Scott loves that boy."

Emily's throat tightened, squeezing off her ability to speak. She bowed her head.

"He loves you, too."

Without looking up, Emily slowly shook her head.

Rita put her hand on Emily's arm. "Honey, I know my son. He's hurting. He's confused. But once he gives his heart, it's gone for good, and he gave his heart to you years ago."

Emily's tears spilled over, and she couldn't stop the flow.

Rita patted her arm. "He's got to process everything, but he'll come around. Give him a little time."

"I have no choice." She sniffed and reached for her purse. "I have his coupons here, too. Would you mind giving them to him? If he likes them, you can call me. I don't need them back, I just need to know whether to prep them for the auction or have Lauren redesign them."

"By the time I see him, the auction will be over. He only comes by on Sundays. Maybe you should take them out yourself." She glanced at the clock. "It's almost noon now. If you catch him, you can have lunch with him, too. Sure hope you're hungry."

She wasn't. By the time she left, she felt drained. She couldn't share Rita's belief that Scott loved her. His coupons still occupied a slot in her purse, right next to Micah's. When she pulled up to the intersection, she couldn't decide between left for the ride to the clinic or right toward home.

Her cell phone jangled, and she jumped. As shaky

as she was, she didn't need to be talking and driving, too. She turned right, then right again, into a parking lot, and answered her phone.

"Well, you're scheduled," Connor announced. "Visitation is Thursday, 3:00 to 5:00 PM."

Emily's nerves locked with dread. No matter that she'd wanted this, that it was her idea. The thought of seeing Wade again scared her.

"Emily? Are you sure you want to do this?"

"No, of course I don't want to do it." She drew a breath and spoke what she knew in her heart to be true. "I have no choice. I have to know what's going on in his head, or I'll never be free from this fear."

"Do you want me to go with you? I could clear my schedule and drive you out."

"Thanks, Connor. I appreciate the offer, but I think this is something I have to do by myself." She hit the *end* button and leaned back against the headrest. If she was going to conquer her fear, meeting with Wade was definitely something she'd have to do herself. So was meeting with Scott. She had to be able to shove her feelings aside and tend to business.

She took a moment to buy a soda for her dry mouth and then headed out for the clinic.

35

No Monday in recent history compared to this one. Scott's head throbbed with tension, and every high-pitched yap the Yorkie on his exam table emitted pinged through his cranium. He inserted a thermometer into the dog and then squinted at the clock. Nearly noon. Judging from the line of critters he'd seen in his waiting room, he'd have to snag a power bar from his desk drawer—and a strong pain killer.

He palpated the Yorkie's stiff belly and questioned the owner about the dog's diet, only partially hearing the answer. He already knew. Pudding, the Yorkshire terror, had a bacon addiction and when indulged, she swelled to the size of a pot-bellied pig. A quick glance at Pudding's chart told the truth of how frequently she was indulged.

"Mrs. James, you can't keep giving in to your dog. At her age, she shouldn't be eating fatty foods."

The silver-haired widow twisted her hands. "I know. You've told me. But she begs so, and I can't help but to give in."

"Try, Mrs. James. She's miserable, the same as she is every time you let her have her way." He gave her his sternest look but had to temper it with a gentle smile. At the slightest sign of discord, the woman would cloud up and sob into her Irish lace hanky until he was totally at a loss how to soothe her. He'd learned to tread lightly. "Do you have any bloat medicine left?"

"Yes, some."

"I'll write you a new prescription. You know what to do, don't you?"

"Yes. I know what to do."

"And no more bacon, right?"

"I'll try."

Scott lifted a brow. "Mrs. James?"

She sniffed. "No more bacon. I promise."

She gathered her purse and the prescription he handed her, and lifted Pudding delicately into her arms. "Mustn't beg, Pudding. Mustn't beg!" She toddled down the hall.

Scott finished charting his notes and rubbed his temples. His headache could no longer wait. When he stepped toward his office, Dani hollered for him.

"Dr. Barlow, Emily's he—"

"Shh, don't bother him. I'll just leave these here." Emily's hushed tones diverted him from his mission, and he changed course for the receptionist desk. The sound of her voice washed him with a relief from...homesickness. Being separated from her had made him homesick. He hadn't realized.

"Nonsense. He'll want to see you." Dani lifted her voice again. "Doctor—"

"He can call me later," Emily said. "Just be sure he gets those."

Scott reached the front desk in time to see Emily scuttle out the door. The shaft of light bouncing off the concrete pavement outside made him wince and halt his pace, but when the pounding in his head eased, he strode to the door to follow her.

She sat in her car with the engine running as she strapped her seatbelt on.

"Emily!"

She pulled out of her parking space and drove away.

He eased the door shut and clamped his jaw against the pain. Whether his head or his heart hurt worse, he couldn't tell, but surely a pain reliever would help one of them.

In the waiting room, a young woman shushed a Peke-a-Poo with watery eyes, and another woman stroked a panting Chihuahua. His morning appointments had waited patiently far beyond their time slots. With a smile and polite nod to the Chihuahua lady, he stepped to Dani's desk.

"What did Emily want?"

"Just to show you these."

Happy dogs and cats adorned "degenderization" and flea dip coupons for the auction. Three coupons each. Scott snorted. "Degenderization." Lauren had coined a new word.

"Give me a minute before you send the next appointment back."

"Sure. You going to call her?"

"Non'ya business, Dani."

"You know I'll snoop."

"Then snoop me up a sandwich from somewhere. Those power bars don't sound good today."

At his desk, Scott balanced the phone on his shoulder and rummaged for the pain medication. Three rings on Emily's cell phone, and she still didn't answer. Four. Five. Voice mail. "Emily, the coupons are great. They'll work just fine for the auction. Hey, I, um...I'd like to...uh..."

Before he could figure out what he'd like to do, her phone beeped. Disgusted with himself, he disconnected. What *would* he like to do? Apologize? He probably should.

But she should, too. And she should explain. Something she should've done long ago.

Still, he hadn't really given her a chance lately. Maybe he could catch her later in the day, and they could sit and talk and hash things out until everything became clear in his mind. Maybe he could hold her again, feel her next to him, kiss her memories of Houston into oblivion.

Maybe he could get rid of his headache before then. He downed the pills and massaged his temples again.

****

Emily didn't want to go. After the emotional morning, she didn't want to take the short drive from Scott's clinic to Micah's parsonage. He might not be there anyway. He could be at the hospital or the nursing home or a homebound invalid's house. He was a working man, after all. His job didn't end on Sundays.

She scowled and sat up straighter in her seat. If Micah wasn't at the parsonage, he might be at the church, and if he wasn't in either place, she could leave the coupons with his secretary.

Emily needed to quit making excuses and find him. She had work to do and couldn't afford to give in to self-pity.

His car wasn't at the parsonage, so she drove farther until she reached the church. She stared up at the twin spires and felt a tinge of melancholy. The few times she'd dared return to the church with Scott had touched her with a sense of coming home. In a way, it was like coming home, back to the church she'd been raised in.

Micah hadn't been the pastor when her parents passed away, but their services had been held in the sanctuary, and they'd been laid to rest in the tiny cemetery at the back of the church property.

She'd been denying herself a return to her church home because she'd been ashamed. But she hadn't done anything wrong. She wasn't the one who'd lied. She wasn't the one who'd taken money from generous, unsuspecting people. And because they'd had so little time between the simple ceremony and the charity ball, they'd never consummated her fraudulent marriage. She'd never been with Wade that way.

Now if she could only convince Scott of that.

She lifted her purse from the passenger seat and headed into the back of the church and toward the pastor's office.

Micah was hunched over his desk, pen in hand, surrounded by opened volumes of thick books. His glasses sat on the end of his nose; he looked over them at Emily and then slapped his pen down and shoved from his chair. "Emily. This is a nice surprise."

The hug he gave her felt right—comforting, parental, just like the hug she'd received from Rita. A lump clogged her throat when she realized she might never receive hugs from these two people again if she and Scott didn't patch things up.

"What brings you out this way?"

From her purse, she pulled a coupon sporting a grinning fish jumping out of the waves and handed it to him. "Lauren made this for you for the auction, but I'm tempted to keep one for myself once we get them made. I haven't been fishing in years."

"Pretty soon, we'll be family, you and I, soon as you marry Scott and I marry his mama. You could come fishing any time you want. You can, anyway." The broad smile on his lips didn't undermine his compassion. The hint for her to respond, to open up to him, was far too obvious. He apparently knew what had happened between her and Scott—Rita had undoubtedly told him, if Scott hadn't.

But she wasn't ready to discuss it, so she kept her own smile in place. "Then we just saved a coupon for the actual bidders." She offered a light laugh, and he chuckled in return. "Do you like it?"

"I think it's great. Is this what the winning bidder will get?"

"Something similar, yes. Just bigger and laminated. If you like it, I'll get it ready." She turned to go, and he walked her out. "You'll be at the auction?"

"Rita and I wouldn't miss it. What about you? Will you be here for midweek service Wednesday night?"

From the door at the back of the church, Emily could see the small cemetery. She hadn't been back there since her parents died—they weren't there anyway, just their shells. But memories of them crowded this chapel, and she seemed more aware of them while Scott wasn't here to distract her.

She sighed. "I'd like to. I'd really like to come."

"So what's holding you back?"

He gave her that look again, the knowing look, the *talk to me* look. She might not be ready to respond the way he'd like, but she did feel ready to return to church. "Nothing is holding me back. I'll see you Wednesday."

****

Emily pulled into her parking place behind the refuge. Even though it was only three-thirty, she wouldn't go out again today. She'd change into her grubbies, pop some popcorn, and settle down in front of the old movies channel. A comedy was coming on at four, and she needed a good laugh.

The answering machine light on her home phone blinked, and she jabbed the button.

"Uh, hello? My daughter's birthday is coming up and I'd like to get her a pet. Do you have any kittens left? You can call me at..." Emily grabbed a pen and wrote the information on a scratch pad beside the phone. Since she'd retired Millie, she didn't have any more kittens, and she'd become so attached to Daisy and Bulldog, she couldn't part with them. Scott usually had notices of free kitties tacked on his cork board at the clinic. The lady could call Dani.

After the beep, Lauren's bright voice perked her ears. "Where've you been? I've been trying to call your cell all day. I've got a surprise for you. Call me?"

The computerized voice said, "End of messages."

Emily grabbed the cordless and poked in Lauren's number. Then, while she waited, she checked her cell phone. The battery was dead. While she plugged it in to recharge, Lauren answered.

"Hey, ladybug," Emily said. "What's the surprise?"

"I'm coming home."

"In time for the auction?"

"Yes, ma'am."

Emily squealed. A weight had been lifted off her shoulders, and the freedom allowed her a little dance in the kitchen. "When are you coming?"

"Friday morning."

"What about Tracy? Surely her legs haven't healed that fast."

"No, but the doctor recast them with those walking dealies on the bottoms, so between those and the crutches, she can get around a little easier. Besides, with the kids in school, there isn't that much for me to do anymore. David rearranged his schedule so he can pick them up and do the errands." This time it was Lauren's turn to squeal. "I'm so excited! I'm anxious to get home. I feel like I've been exiled for an eternity."

"I can't wait to see you. You've got to call me as soon after your homecoming with Roger as possible."

"Of course. Let's plan on lunch at the diner." Emily agreed. Then Lauren's voice took on a business tone. "Now, catch me up. Where are we on the auction? What needs to be done?"

Emily recited her list, which they discussed, and then recalled the one detail she'd been dreading most. "We still need the autographed golf card and book from Paul and Amber Goodrich."

"Oh, it's a good thing I'm coming home. You leave that for me. I don't want you anywhere near him."

"I can't say I was looking forward to it, but those two items could bring in a good bid."

"Has he talked to Wade yet?"

"I was hoping you would know."

"Me? How would I know?"

"Well, if Wade talked to Paul, Paul would probably talk to Scott, and undoubtedly Scott would tell Roger, and Roger told me he tells you everything. So-o-o..."

Lauren laughed. "What a grapevine. Yes, as far as

I know, Rog does tell me everything, and this particular subject hasn't come up. Do you think Paul backed out?"

"Backed out? No way. Not that hound dog."

"Maybe he hasn't done it yet—or even better, maybe he *has* done it, and Wade didn't give him the dirt he wanted, so he let it drop."

"Wouldn't that be wonderful?" Emily sighed. "But I can't picture it happening. Wade was unscrupulous to begin with, and he was furious with me during the trial. I can't imagine him passing up an opportunity like this."

"Did you ever talk to Scott? Explain your side to him?"

"I quit trying. He won't answer his phone." Emily wandered into the den and dropped onto the couch. "But I've made a decision. I'm going to confront Wade."

"Are you out of your mind?"

"No, I'm not. Think about it. Everything that's wrong in my life right now centers on my fear of that man. And I don't even know if I have a reason to be afraid. He's a con-man, not a murderer."

"Yes, but he's still the man who can feed Paul Goodrich a line of bull. What if Paul believes him? What if Scott does?"

"I'll just have to figure out a way to counter whatever he says."

"Can you do that?"

In her mind's eye, Emily pictured an old file where she'd packed what was left of her entire relationship with Wade—which boiled down to newspaper articles of the fiasco, a marriage certificate, and an annulment decree. But it was enough. "Yes. I think I can."

36

By the time Scott tended his last patient, the clock had ticked an hour past closing. In between appointments, he'd tried Emily's cell phone, and when it became obvious he couldn't reach her that way, he'd tried her home phone—which buzzed a busy signal in his ear every time he called. Here they were in the twenty-first century, and Emily didn't have call waiting?

He discovered she didn't have call forwarding either, when he'd finally got her phone to ring, and she never picked up.

Or was she screening him?

Turnabout was fair play. He'd avoided her calls for days; maybe it was payback time. Still, he needed to see her and had every intention of going to her apartment. He'd barge in, if he must. The time had long passed to settle things between them.

He checked his in-patients one more time, wadded his lab coat for the laundry, and headed out. This time the late afternoon sun didn't hurt his eyes. His throbbing headache had settled to a dull pain he could tolerate. As he locked the clinic's door, his cell buzzed against his hip.

"Scott?" Parker Milligan's voice sounded strained. "I need to ask a favor of you."

Within twenty minutes, Scott was sitting beside Parker on a weathered wooden bench outside the juvenile detention center. Parker looked as though he'd dropped ten pounds since Spencer's arrest. His eyes were shadowed, and his lips maintained a grim, rigid line, as if the moment he relaxed, they'd quiver. He didn't seem to know what to say.

Scott started. "Did you find a lawyer for him?"

"Yeah, good one, too, I think."

"Look, I know it's none of my business, but if you need help...you know. If I can pitch in and help pay..."

"Thanks, but I don't think I'll need it." Parker rubbed the back of his neck. "You remember the anonymous source who helped that kid with cancer?"

Scott nodded.

"I guess whoever it is has decided to help me. I got a letter. Recommended some big-name lawyer and held a check for his retainer or to use on an attorney of my choice. After that, the lawyer is supposed to charge whoever this person is. I'll never see a bill."

Scott nodded. He'd received such a check too, for an "equine clinic." It held no clue showing who it was from on the envelope, the check, or the letter. Totally anonymous. But only two people knew his dream, and his mother didn't have that kind of money. "Well, that's one thing off your mind."

"Yeah." Parker stared at the juvenile detention center's entrance. "They said I could visit him today."

"Have you been in yet?"

Parker shook his head. "I went yesterday, but he wouldn't see me."

Scott waited, watched Parker breathe as if he had to remind himself to inhale. His gaze landed somewhere over Scott's left shoulder, but Scott doubted he saw anything. Finally, he ran his tongue over his front teeth and focused on Scott.

"Would you go in? Would you talk to him? He's always confided in you before. Maybe he will now."

Scott hesitated, not sure he wanted the responsibility, but finally he nodded. "I don't know that he'll talk to me, either, but I'll try. Anything you want him to know?"

"Yeah. Tell him..." Parker's breath caught, and he pinched the bridge of his nose before continuing. "Tell him I love him."

****

The room was gray. Gray walls, gray floor, gray metal table separating gray metal chairs. Even the light battling through the dirty fixture seemed gray. No windows.

The door scraped open and Spencer shuffled in, wearing a prison-orange jumpsuit and slide-on sandals.

"Fifteen minutes," the burly guard grumbled and then closed the door as he left.

Spencer stood next to the chair opposite Scott and studied the floor while Scott studied him. A kid. He was just a kid. Scott had known him since T-ball and pizza parties. If the ache in Scott's heart remotely resembled the ache in Parker's, Scott hurt for him. How does a man survive seeing his son in a prison uniform?

"You want to sit down?"

Spencer plopped down and slouched in the seat, slinging an arm over the chair back. But he still wouldn't meet Scott's gaze.

"They feeding you good?"

A shrug.

"You sleeping all right?"

Another shrug.

"Your dad misses you."

That earned a glare.

Scott shifted in his seat, trying to appear as casual as possible in these surroundings. "He does, you know. And he loves you. He doesn't understand this."

Spencer picked at something on the table, giving it his full attention, but his mouth twitched downward.

"Spence, look at me." Scott waited. "Please."

The boy glowered at him. "Why are you here?"

"Because I don't understand, either. Why, Spencer?"

Nothing, just a dull, dispassionate expression.

"Your dad said you targeted houses you thought he insured. You were getting back at him for something? For taking your driving privileges away?"

Spencer snorted and looked away.

"It has to be something more than that...the divorce? Your parents split up years ago. Surely it's not that." Scott gave him a moment to say something, but he didn't. "How can you carry around that much anger and hate? What did your father do to make you hate him so much?"

Red-faced, Spencer slammed his fist on the table. "Me hate him? Ask him why he hates me."

"He doesn't—"

"Oh, don't give me that. He hates me. He let me believe it was my fault he left Mom in the first place. Do you remember when he left? Do you?"

Scott kept his tone level. "Maybe you should remind me."

"Six years ago. I was ten and pitching against the Olta Pirates. Remember that game?" Spencer didn't wait for a response, but Scott nodded anyway. "Last inning, we were up by two, but there were two on the bases. Gil Stevens was at the plate. He'd hit everything I'd thrown at him all night, so I decided to go to the split-finger fast ball."He paused and looked at Scott as if he should understand.

"I remember the game," Scott said. "We lost by one. But what does that have to do with your dad?"

"We lost by one because Gil hit a homer off my fast ball—the one Dad told me I wasn't ready to use. He said I needed more practice, needed to work on it before I used it in a game. He was so disappointed in me he didn't talk to me all the way home. Next day, he took a suitcase and moved out." His gaze penetrated Scott. "You tell me. What kind of father leaves his family because his son didn't win a little league game?"

Scott leaned back in his chair, flabbergasted by the way the kid's brain worked. "That's what you think? He left because of a stupid game?"

"What else was there? I lost, he left. What was I supposed to believe?"

Scott shook his head. "Your parents never told you why they split?"

"No. All Mom would say was 'ask your dad,' and Dad wouldn't say anything at all. He'd just look at me and then get in some sort of mood. I finally learned not to ask. I just assumed it was my fault, and he never said or did anything that made me believe otherwise."

Scott shook his head. How much should he tell the boy? After a moment, he said, "Spence, how soon after your dad left did Marcus move in?"

Spencer's brow twisted. "I don't know. I don't remember."

"You were only ten years old when your parents split up. Adults don't always tell their kids when they're having troubles. Your dad told me things weren't right between him and your mom, told me what he suspected—what he'd been able to prove. It had nothing to do with you. Do you understand what I'm trying to say?"

"You're saying Mom cheated." He sneered. "I kinda have that figured out now. No thanks to him."

"So you understand now that it wasn't your fault." Spencer nodded in response, leaving Scott totally confused. "Then why? Why start fires now?"

"Because he thinks he can rule me." Spencer exploded from his seat, and his chair slammed against the floor with a metallic ring. "He thinks getting me on weekends and a few weeks in the summer gives him the right to order me around. Take my car keys. Tell me what time to be home. He lost his right to do that when he left."

"He's your dad," Scott said evenly as he watched the boy's angry prowl back and forth across the table from him. "He loves you, and part of that love means he has to raise you right. Even though you two don't live in the same house, he's still your dad, and disciplining you is still his responsibility. Maybe he made a mistake not explaining things to you earlier. Maybe you both made mistakes. It happens. You're human."

Spencer snorted.

Scott wasn't getting through. He leaned back and shot out a hot breath. "He came to see me last week. You know that? You know what he wanted?"

Spencer shrugged, ran a hand through his hair, paced.

"He wanted to see Scotch Bonnet."

Spencer stopped moving. His profile maintained a sullen, suspicious expression as he stared at the floor, but at least he was listening.

"There's a terrific place to stable horses called Sorrel Ridge, and he rented a stall for her. He was going to give her to you for your birthday."

Spencer's lips quivered. He sniffed.

Scott moved toward him and stopped, an arm's-length away. "He loves you, Spence. Even now, he loves you."

The ragged breath Spencer drew exhaled on a whimper. His face screwed up and twitched between his refusal to cry and his inability to deny the tears already dampening his cheeks. With a sob, he sought Scott's arms and cried until he could catch a smooth breath again.

Scott held him until the last tear fell.

The boy's swollen, red face turned up to his. "Do you think he could ever forgive me?"

"He already has."

37

After a two-day search, Emily finally caught sight of the folder at the very bottom of her lower bureau drawer. Why it hadn't been in her filing cabinet along with the rest of her important papers remained a mystery. She eased her hand under the winter sweaters, pulled it out, and plopped on the bed.

Inside the slightly worn file sat the remnants of her two-year romance with Wade Coulter. She'd given her diamond-crusted wedding band to her attorney to return to him, but a picture of it on her hand rested inside the file, along with other photos of their private ceremony. She pulled out the shot of her and Wade—the happy newlyweds. Holding a small bouquet of red roses and pink lilies, she wore a white satin tea-length dress and the radiant smile of the foolishly naive.

In his dark suit, Wade looked like one of those famous bachelors in tabloids who had just been ripped from circulation. Wavy, walnut-brown hair dipped roguishly over his forehead and curled over his collar. Cunning eyes stared directly into the camera. His smile reflected victory more than happiness. What had he been thinking? And why hadn't she realized the kind of man he was?

She flipped through the remainder of the photos and shuddered. No one needed to see these. Ever. She bounced off the bed and fed the pictures to the shredder in her office. She considered shredding the marriage license too, but thought better of it. It marked part of her history, and a lesson learned the hard way.

Paul popped into her mind, and she scowled. Everything she held in her folder, with the exception of the wedding pictures, he could've found himself. What kind of a reporter was he? What did he have against her that he was willing to take a convict's word over hers? Still, he hadn't published anything yet.

Maybe she had time to talk to Scott before he did. All this could've been avoided if she'd just told Scott what he wanted to know when he'd asked. If she had just spit it out and confessed, he wouldn't have had to include keeping secrets from him in his list of things to forgive her for. She had to figure out some way to get him to listen.

Like catching him at church Wednesday night.

****

From her seat on the last row, Emily could scope out the entire congregation unnoticed while the announcements were being read.

Scott and Rita sat close to the front, with Roger and his daughter, Michelle, directly behind them. On the left of the sanctuary, Trey Norris, his girlfriend, Carla, and a dozen more teenagers filled the first two rows, the traditional seats for the youth group since Emily was a teen. She, Scott, Roger, Lauren, and a host of others had occupied those pews over the years.

A smile tilted her lips at the memory of Scott sitting next to her when they were kids. All it took to make his neck flush was a look from her. If she touched him, he'd reward her with a full-face blush and a goofy grin. He'd been so cute, even then.

Emily caught sight of Paul and Amber Goodrich a few rows behind the youth group and drew a shaky breath. If he turned a little farther to the right, he'd see her. What expression would cross his face if he did?

She didn't want to know.

Knowing where he sat ruined her pleasure in the evening service. As they stood for the praise music, she carefully shifted to hide behind the taller man in front of her. When they resumed their seats, she slid to her left to eliminate the possibility of being accidentally spotted. She was out of his line of sight, but he wasn't out of hers, and during the entire service, she kept refocusing on him.

Questions crawled like a ticker-tape through her mind. Had he interviewed Wade? What did he say? Did Paul believe him? Was he going to tell Scott the lies Wade fabricated...or had Wade told the truth? Dare she hope?

Paul seemed to be keeping an eye on Scott, just as Emily was keeping an eye on him. She noticed every time he glanced Scott's way, and the questions running through her mind intensified.

When the service ended and the notes from the final song had faded, Paul headed toward Scott.

Emily headed for the door, her car, and the file resting on the front seat.

****

After the service, as Scott chatted with Roger, Paul Goodrich materialized at his side. "Got a minute?"

Inside, Scott cringed and prepared himself for more bad news, but he shoved a smile into place and shook hands with the journalist. "Sure. What's on your mind?"

Paul seemed hesitant to speak in front of Roger, so Roger excused himself. Paul nodded at him, looked around, and then spoke in a low whisper. "You know what I told you about Emily Taylor being married?"

"Of course."

"I jumped the gun. Right after her house was vandalized, I found an old article in the *Houston Chronicle* about her and Wade Coulter, calling him her husband, but I didn't check it out. Truth is, their marriage was—"

"—annulled?"

"Yeah, she tell you?"

"No." Scott crossed his arms and widened his stance. The man's accusation had busted a solid year's worth of Scott's attempts to get Emily back into his life. What was Paul going to say now? *Oops, sorry?* That wouldn't cut it. "I haven't spoken to her since I talked to you at the cat refuge."

Paul winced. "Wow, I'm sorry. Look, I interviewed Coulter yesterday—"

"You went to the prison?"

"Just to confirm a few things."

"The man's a con artist." Scott's voice climbed with his anger. He checked the curious glances in his direction and lowered his tone to a whisper. "What makes you think he told you the truth?"

"I believe he did." Paul kept his voice low. "He told me—"

He gaped at something over Scott's shoulder.

Emily barreled toward them with a file in her hand.

"Here." With an expression balanced between anger and pain, she shoved the manila folder at Scott.

"Take it."

"What's this?"

"Your answers. Everything you need to know. This is what happened in Houston. Read it and decide for yourself what the truth is." She glared at Paul and then returned her attention to Scott. "Decide whether you're going to believe him or me."

Before either man could say a word, she spun on her heel and raced out the nearest door. After a stunned moment, Scott rushed after her, but by the time he spotted her in the parking lot, she was driving away. Seemed he always caught her taillights these days.

Roger appeared at his side and rested a hand on his shoulder. "You'd best leave her alone for a bit. Let her calm down."

Scott clenched his jaw. "Did you know she was coming tonight?"

"Nope. Haven't talked to her lately. But you should—just not right now."

"How long you reckon I should wait?"

"Well, I'd wait until she was the one doin' the calling. If I know women, she'll probably call you soon to get your reaction to whatever's in that folder." Roger shoved his hands in his pockets. "What's it about, anyway?"

"Houston, I guess."

"I'll be so glad when you two straightened this out. It's gettin' exhaustin'."

"Yeah." Scott gave the retreating convertible a final glance and then returned to the sanctuary. Paul and Amber were leaving, but Scott caught his arm. "You want to finish our conversation?"

****

Emily's hands shook, whether from anger or shame, she didn't know, but they shook enough she didn't dare hold her glass of tea. Ever since she'd returned home, she'd passed the time alternating between fuming and kicking herself. She'd called Lauren the minute she walked in the door.

"I don't even know if it was me they were discussing. I just marched up like I knew what I was doing and butted into their conversation." She stopped her pacing and withered onto a chair. "My first official day back in church, and I make a spectacle of myself."

"Well, don't worry about it. Whether or not they were talking about you, Scott needed that information you provided. Maybe you finally got through to him."

"I got through to him, all right. I illustrated what a high-tempered idiot I can be."

"Stop that. You're miserable. Scott's miserable. What you did tonight may be just what he needed to bring an end to this mess."

Emily felt certain the end to the mess loomed near—and how it was resolved rested entirely in Scott's hands. She'd done all she could.

38

Emily took a break at a gas station, refilled her tank, and bought a bottled water for her parched throat before resuming her trip to the prison. She'd kept herself busy all morning with the caterer, the auctioneer, the decorations for the auction, but now she had nothing to do but drive and think. And the thoughts crossing her mind provided no comfort.

She'd finally checked her voicemail and heard the message from Scott telling her he liked the coupons, but whatever else he'd had to say was chopped off. He'd called her several times, but not since last night—which meant he'd taken Paul's word over her own. Whatever that word was.

Not that it mattered. If Scott wanted to take the word of a man he'd known for a few months over the woman he'd known all his life, so be it. Best she discovered where his loyalties lay now rather than after they married.

Married. Her giddiness over the prospect of a proposal from him seemed eons ago.

The rational side of her brain reminded her she didn't know what Paul and Scott were talking about last night, and she was pole vaulting to conclusions.

Still, whether or not they were discussing her, she needed to see Wade for herself. She couldn't wait to shove away the cloud of fear that had hung over her for far too long.

A road sign told her she had twelve miles to go, and her body grew tense. She hadn't seen Wade in over two years. What would he be like after all this time in prison? What must he think of her?

She whispered a prayer for strength.

****

Emily shifted on the hard bench and clenched her hands in her lap. Taut nerves held her back erect and her legs locked at the ankle.

To her right, several men, dressed in red pullovers and khaki pants, worked between the rows of a large fall garden, where pumpkins and butternut squashes peeked from healthy green leaves.

To her left, a pair of small girls squealed and ran giggling into the open arms of a man who smothered them with kisses. A woman approached, speaking excitedly in Spanish, and he put his girls down to crush her in a passionate embrace. The little family found a spot among picnic tables crowded with families that had made the special trip for their monthly visit.

Behind Emily, razor wire topped a cyclone fence that stopped at a guard house where she'd signed in and left her bag. All she had in her pockets were her driver's license and a chit to retrieve her purse. In front of her loomed a brown-brick two-story building and a high guard tower. The windows in the tower were angled in such a way that those inside could have a clear view of everything happening in the prison yard and around the buildings below.

The sight of it made Emily shiver. She wasn't quite sure where to direct her gaze. She tried not to stare at the tattooed men and women occupying the nearby tables. For some reason, she'd associated "white collar crime" and "minimum security prison" with a more refined type of prisoner. As she looked around from the corner of her eye, she wished she hadn't turned down Connor's offer to drive her.

"Not a champagne crowd, is it?" Wade flashed a smile she'd once found appealing, but her thudding heart responded to her anxiety more than his straight, white teeth. Although he seemed fit and tan, his eyes held a hardened look in addition to the cunning she'd always misinterpreted as an alert interest in life. The combination made him almost intimidating, and she struggled to maintain her composure.

She looked at him but couldn't return his smile. "It's not quite what I expected. The people look a bit rougher than I'd thought."

"You thought everyone would be charming con men, didn't you?" He sat down across from her and tilted his head to his left. "Carter over there is in for rape. Next to him is Milt, a child abuser. Sanchez, in the corner, sent his wife to the hospital with broken ribs. Juarez, assault with a deadly weapon. Menendez, involuntary manslaughter. Those guys run a gang that keeps the rest of us leery."

Emily bit her lip. This wasn't at all what she'd imagined. "How do you cope?"

"For starters, I stay away from those guys I just named. But I got friends." He nodded toward the garden. "D'Shawn is in for two counts of burglary, and Patterson's here for fraud. There's another guy back in the cell that ran a con game in San Antonio for eight years until he finally got caught. We play cards." He snorted. "A *lot* of cards. It helps pass the time."

She didn't know what to say so said nothing.

He studied her, taking in her hair, her face, her shoulders. She squirmed under his scrutiny.

"I was sorry you wanted an annulment," he said. "I really loved you. I thought we'd be together forever." His words didn't match the look he gave her. The slightest sign of a smirk, the gentlest tinge of humor, dared her to fall for his line. The artist's con.

"You can't help yourself, can you?" She shook her head. "I'm immune, Wade. Pretty words have no effect on me anymore. Perhaps I should thank you for that."

He snorted again, rested his forearms on the table, and leaned toward her. "Why are you here? You obviously don't want to give our marriage—short as it was—another try, and you couldn't possibly be concerned for my welfare. So, what do you want?"

She looked toward the parking lot beyond the fence. She should've anticipated his question. She knew what she wanted, what she needed to know, she just didn't know how to express it. *Are you still mad at me? Do you want to kill me? Do I need to fear you?* She shook her head against all the questions and took a different path. "You ruined me in Houston."

"Is that what you're here for? An apology?"

"That would be nice, but no, that's not why I'm here." She took a breath. "The parole board didn't grant your request."

"Nope."

"Why?"

He sucked in a breath and looked away. "There's a woman from Abilene who came out for the hearing. Seems I ruined her husband, too. He killed himself."

Emily grimaced at the pain that shot through her heart.

Wade continued. "They found out later that he'd made some bad investment decisions all the way around, not just with me. But I'm the one she blames."

"Are you sorry? Sorry for your part in it?"

His lips tightened. "Yeah. And I'm sorry for what happened to you, too." He looked at her again. She studied his face and saw the pain there. He meant it. At least she thought he did. Wanted to believe...

Boisterous laughter from the corner caught her attention. The men in the gang were pointing at several of the wives in the picnic area and making comments Emily couldn't understand, but she was certain she didn't want to. Lewd gestures, cat calls, vulgar expressions. The men behaved like a dog pack. Chests puffed out, eyes hard and cold. They gained their strength through their numbers and apparently used that strength to intimidate everyone who crossed their path.

Wade had said he was leery of them.

She believed that to be an understatement. If his parole bids kept getting rejected, he was looking at another five years in this prison. Five years of living with fear. Unimaginable.

"You never did tell me why you're here."

She focused on him. "To tell you I forgive you."

****

In the Down Home Diner on Friday, Lauren gaped at Emily. "Do you really think he was sorry?"

Emily toyed with the lettuce protruding from the second half of her club sandwich. "It doesn't really matter. I meant it when I forgave him."

"What did he say about Paul? Has he talked to

him?"

"I don't know. I forgot to ask."

"But that was the point of going."

"Well, not entirely. I needed to see how he felt about me now, whether he still hated me."

Lauren drew her brows together. "So if you can't be sure he was sorry, you don't know whether he still hates you, right?"

"I don't believe he does. I doubt he's changed his ways, but I didn't really get the impression he harbored any anger toward me. Besides..." She tilted her head. She hadn't thought of this until now, but it was true, "I feel at peace about it."

"And Scott? Do you feel at peace about him, too?"

Emily's stomach soured, and she shoved the remains of her sandwich away. "I'm working on it."

"Have you heard from him?"

"No. And at this point, I'm not sure I want to. Think about it—he knows I got the marriage annulled, and if he's read that file, he knows I testified against Wade and was exonerated of all charges. And he *still* hasn't called." She frowned. "If he's still angry that I didn't tell him everything earlier, there's nothing I can do about that."

"You're right. There's nothing you can do. I personally would like to take a bullwhip after him, but there's nothing I can do, either. You two need to figure this out yourselves."

"It's figured, and I'm going to accept it. Apparently he feels that what I've done is unforgivable, and I'm not going to continue trying to gain his forgiveness when he has no intention of giving it."

"You don't know that he won't forgive you."

"How could I know? The only message I've received from him was that the coupons were all right." She balled her napkin and chucked it on the table. "I'm not going to waste another moment worrying about him. It's time to move on."

Lauren gave her a skeptical look but shrugged. "Maybe you want to 'move on' with me to Paul and Amber's house to get their donations."

"Oh, no. I'm not in that forgiving of a mood." Emily grinned. "They're all yours."

39

Thirty minutes before the auction guests would begin to arrive, white-shirted waiters bustled around in the community center's professional kitchen, arranging appetizers and canapes on silver serving trays. Crudités with spinach dip, bacon-wrapped scallops in a peach-brandy glaze, crimini mushrooms with crab stuffing; the savory scents filled the kitchen and proved a temptation beyond Emily's resistance level. She popped a scallop in her mouth and moaned with pleasure. "Karen, you've outdone yourself."

"I'm glad you like it." Karen Fitzhugh, the caterer, prepared some glass flutes to serve her mimosas in. A mid-price champagne chilled in the refrigerator alongside a few gallons of mint tea so guests could have their pick.

"You don't know how much I appreciate this. Donating your time and skills to this cause goes beyond generous."

"Well, one of those houses belonged to my aunt. I think this is the least I can do." She winked at Emily from under a shock of sandy blonde hair. "Besides, good food leads to happy contributors, and happy contributors tend to bid higher at auctions."

"Then we're in good shape. With your food as our secret weapon, a toothpick could go for fifty dollars." Emily passed the chocolate tuxedo strawberries awaiting space on a tray and snitched one on her way to the swinging doors, which opened into the auditorium. A flurry of activity filled the large room.

Lauren had recruited the help of the church youth group. They swarmed the auditorium, using peach bows to secure white linens to long tables, arranging auction items on display stands, and bringing in more items from the trucks outside. Lauren roamed from table to table with the auctioneer, their heads bent close together to be able to hear over the din.

Emily whispered a thankful prayer as she looked over the crowded tables. The auction was destined to be a success. She considered joining Lauren for a closer look but glimpsed Scott and Paul toting in a custom-made cedar chest and thought better of it. She retreated, and the door closed behind her on the sound of Lauren's voice ordering the men where to put the chest. Lauren was handling everything just fine.

Emily preferred to stay out of sight in the kitchen and away from Scott and Paul and any reminder of Wednesday's fiasco.

The fact the two men worked together so congenially caused an uneasy feeling to rise in Emily's chest. Since Scott still hadn't called, she didn't want to think of their chumminess.

With her mood soured, she went to the sink and washed her hands.

Karen was spreading a sun-dried tomato and ricotta mixture over slices of baguette, which she had already grilled and coated with pesto.

Emily grabbed a towel and stood by her side.

"Can I help with the bruschetta?"

Karen placed a completed slice on the tray and reached for another. "Don't you think you should get ready for the big show?"

"I'm not part of the big show." Emily grabbed a spatula and began spreading. "I'm more of a behind-the-scenes girl."

Before long, the noise from the auditorium grew exponentially as guests arrived, hopefully with big bank accounts or fat wads of cash.

Emily stole a glance at the laden tables. The cake Rita had been decorating the day Emily had visited held center stage on the front table. A masterpiece, as were all her cakes. Emily didn't know whether Rita planned to auction it or serve it, but she hoped for the latter.

Lauren caught sight of her and scowled as she headed toward the swinging doors. Dressed in an amethyst shift and five-inch heels guaranteed to kill her feet before day's end, she slammed into the kitchen and confronted Emily. "Why aren't you dressed? Everyone is arriving. It's hopping out there."

The blood rushed from Emily's face. "I'm staying in here."

A server excused himself so he could get out.

Lauren grabbed Emily's elbow and drew her aside. "I thought you'd be out there helping me."

"And I thought you understood I wanted to remain anonymous."

"That was before this whole episode with Paul Goodrich, before your visit with Wade," Lauren whispered harshly. "It's moot now."

"I know. It's just..." Just that she didn't want to see Scott, or Paul—or anyone else who'd witnessed her outburst Wednesday night. "I'm not ready to hobnob in big crowds yet. I'm a bit out of practice."

"Oh, and you think I'm experienced? You roped me into this."

Emily winced. "I know. You're doing a great job, too. Please don't drag me out there."

"Fine." Lauren puffed a breath through her cheeks. "Are you going to stay in here all day?"

"As long as Karen needs me."

"Then what?"

Emily shrugged and stepped away to straighten the strawberries on the tray. "I may hover in the background for a while and see how things are going. We'll see."

Lauren studied her for a minute, with questions and skepticism drawing her lips taut. "You're not hiding from Scott, are you?"

"Yep. Scott and Paul. Both of them. I don't want to be cornered by either of them." Her honest answer seemed to elicit sympathy from Lauren, or maybe it was her pleading tone, her trembling voice, her shaking hands.

"Well, I hope you hang around. It'll really get good when all the bidding starts." She smiled and became more animated, talking as much with her hands as her excited voice. "Did you see all those women examining Rita's cake? I can't wait to see what her coupons go for. And they're planning to start the bid for the bass boat at seven thousand dollars. Can you imagine? The golf cart will go for almost as much, I'm sure. We'll be able to provide a decent-sized check to each of the families who lost their homes. Isn't it exciting?" Lauren slipped back into the auditorium.

Her enthusiasm lightened Emily's mood. But it dampened quickly when she saw Scott and Roger deep in conversation with Paul. She turned and found Karen, who was washing red grapes at the sink. Emily smiled. "How's it going?"

"Everything's under control."

"Good." She slipped out the back door.

****

Scott smiled at Lauren as she approached and slid into Roger's open arm.

Paul gave her a smile, too. "Looks like you've got a success on your hands."

"Let's not start counting chickens," she said. "The bidding won't start for a while, and we won't know how we did until long after the final 'sold.'"

"Well, you and Emily managed to gather quite a collection of goodies." He glanced around the auditorium. "Where is your partner? I haven't seen her all day."

"I haven't, either," Scott said. "I was wondering whether she would come."

"Oh, she's here somewhere. I'm sure she's just been busy." Her voice sounded casual, but she gave Scott a pointed stare.

After a moment, he understood. No way was she going to announce Emily's whereabouts in front of the journalist.

She returned her attention to Paul. "I overheard a group of young golfers carry on about that score card you donated. Even so young, they knew who Arnold Palmer is."

"The man's a legend." Paul lifted his tea glass in acknowledgment of someone across the room—Amber, who waved an invitation for him to join her. "Excuse me. Catch y'all later." He maneuvered through the crowd.

Scott stood closer to Lauren. "Now, where is

Emily?"

"She's in the kitchen, where she plans to stay until certain people"—she jerked her head toward the retreating Goodrich—"are gone. Probably for the duration."

"She's not hiding from me?"

"Oh, yeah. You, too. She's under the impression you don't want to talk to her."

"That's not true. I do want to talk to her."

"Then why haven't you called?"

"Someone told me not to." Scott jabbed Roger.

"You have got to be kidding me. Since when did you start taking love advice from Roger?"

Scott hung his head. "Well, it kinda made sense."

Lauren glared at him.

Roger clapped Scott on the shoulder. "Buddy, you're on your own. You guys don't need me for this conversation." He watched a server toting a full platter of scallops. "I'll catch you later."

"I kept missing Emily on the phone," Scott explained once they were alone. "Then, after that episode Wednesday night, Roger said I should let her calm down. Let her be the one to call me."

Lauren smirked. "Well, he got it half right. You did need to let her calm down a bit. But that was Wednesday night. This is Saturday. You should've called."

"I'm not sure whether it matters. She hasn't been answering my calls. Was she screening me?"

"I don't know, but maybe you should stop relying on the telephone. She's here now. Get off your duff and go to her."

A lump formed in his throat. Familiar shyness washed over him and sent any semblance of confidence swirling down the drain. "Do you think she'll talk to me?"

"Won't know if you don't try." She grinned as she threw his own frequently used words back at him.

40

With everyone she knew safely tucked away at the auction, Emily set to work on the crown molding in her parlor. Working off her anxieties on top of the ladder seemed superior to glooming around her apartment and crying into her cats' fur.

A fan blew the chemical odor of tung oil out the only two windows that weren't boarded up from the vandalism. Another fan was angled up to blow on her as she worked. Even in September, the temperature hovered close to ninety, and the temptation to set up the window unit air conditioner she'd bought in Tyler lost to the need to work in a ventilated area.

She'd parked her car in the back near the garage just in case anyone came looking for her—"anyone" being Scott. Since the Queen Anne sat on Scott's route to just about anywhere he'd want to go, Emily had reached a decision: She'd flip it. She'd refurbish it and put it up for sale and continue to live in the apartment until she found another house less likely to be on his path.

By the time she finally turned the corner in the room and took on the home stretch, sweat from climbing up and down the ladder glued her clothes to her.

She could cover the oil drops along the drywall with the wallpaper she'd designed and then sand the paper glue off the paneling before applying the tung oil to it. Once the walls were done, she'd refinish the floors, put up the new drapes, and rent a truck to haul the furniture back from Jefferson. A few pictures and doo-dads, and she'd be done. One room down, a half-dozen more to go.

A couple of years could pass before she would be finished with the house—especially since she would have to wait for funds. Right now, even her charity account was zooming toward a zero balance. If she wasn't more careful, she'd be joining the cats for surf-and-turf in a can.

Her phone sang, and she stepped off the ladder to read the caller ID. Scott. With a sigh, she dropped the cell back in her purse. Whatever he called for, she was no longer interested. Seeing him buddying up to Goodrich had told her all she needed to know about whose side he chose after reading her file. If he read it.

She prayed God would give her the strength to let him go. Then she prayed he'd allow a comfortable friendship between her and Scott someday. She wasn't willing to give up her friendship with Lauren, and having an easy relationship with him would prevent any awkwardness whenever they were together.

In her head, she had it all figured out. But her heart implored God with far different prayers.

****

Scott snapped his phone shut and shook his head at Lauren. She turned to Karen, who was pouring another round of mimosas. "Are you sure she didn't tell you where she was going?"

Karen filled the last glass and wiped the lip of the pitcher with a towel. "No. She didn't give me a clue.

One minute she's watching out the swinging doors, and the next she's heading out the back. I thought you had upset her."

"Not that I know of." Scott walked to the service doors and looked out the small square of glass. In the auditorium, crowds browsed the display tables, registered for the auction, or fanned themselves with their bidding placards. He squinted at the third set of entry doors where he had been standing when Lauren joined them from the kitchen—where he had stood with Paul Goodrich, Emily's imagined arch-enemy. Once a couple sipping from champagne flutes strolled past, he had a clear view of the corner.

Just as Emily undoubtedly had earlier.

He winced. "I think I know what happened."

At Lauren's quizzical look, he explained.

She propped her fists on her hips. "All right, this has gone on long enough. You two need to start communicating. I can't have my two best friends at odds like this. Fix it. And bring her back here." She shoved open the door and marched out of the kitchen.

Lauren's unusual shot of temper left Scott slack-jawed, but he quickly recovered. His mind slammed into gear and developed a plan. A glance at his watch let him know he had a couple of hours before the bidding began. Would it be enough time?

41

"God, why did you waste all those extra arms on octupusses?" *Octopi*? *Octopies*?

Emily didn't know for sure what the correct plural was, but that didn't change the sentiment. Regardless of how many times she'd hung wallpaper in the past, she always wished for more hands. She smoothed out the corner panel, tucked it up to the crown molding with a trowel, and sliced off the excess. She stepped down from the ladder to admire her handiwork. She had only one wall left—the one holding the most windows, which was the very reason she'd saved it for last. Papering between window frames was tedious work.

She moved the ladder and then climbed to measure the space between the first window frame and the crown molding. As she stretched with her tape measure, someone pounded on the front door. She groaned and debated answering. It was probably nothing. A salesman or something. No one knew she was there. She continued with her measurement, but the knocking became more persistent.

Finally, she climbed down just far enough to peek out. A gray haired man raised his fist to knock again. For an old man, he sure could hammer the wood. Whatever he wanted, he probably wouldn't be there long. She'd shoo him away as politely as possible and get back to work.

But he didn't shoo easily. The man barged in and gave her a long, appraising look from under a furry brow. "You ain't Millie."

"No, I—"

"I was told I could find her here. Where is she?"

He looked for all the world like Mark Twain, sans cigar. Wild, white-gray hair; thick mustache; a wiry unibrow stretched under a crinkled forehead. His stooped shoulders jerked with every step as if trying to yank his legs up with them so he could walk.

"Mister, Millie isn't—"

"Millie!" He hitched his way up the stairs, one step at a time. "Millie! Where are ya, girl?"

Emily flipped her hands in dismay. What was she to do with the old man? She followed him up the stairs. "Really, mister, Millie isn't here. She doesn't live here."

He whirled on her. "What? Where is she?" He hobbled back to peer at her. Thick brows quirked, his mustache twitched. "What have you done with Millie?"

"Nothing. She doesn't live here. She never has."

"Bah." He looked around, making a smacking sound as he did. He poked his head into each vacant room. "Millie? You in here, darlin'? Don't go hidin' from ol' Jake now, honey. Millie?"

Emily stood on the landing and watched him, feeling she'd slid headfirst down the rabbit hole. Even as Millie, she'd never seen the man. Was he a client at the food bank? She couldn't remember, but even if he was, he wouldn't know Millie.

Finally, he returned. "She's not here." He eyed her again, head to toe, and a broad grin lifted his scruffy cheeks. "Hey, you're a looker. What do you say, cutie? Wanna go catch the early bird special?" The old coot actually clicked his tongue at her!

"Now, look. I don't know who you are, but—"

"Jake. Jake Falco, at your service." He struggled into an arthritic bow and then used the banister to straighten up.

Emily caught a whiff of his cologne, and squinted at him suspiciously. "Scott?"

He chuckled. "Not very convincing, was I?"

"Are you kidding? You had me totally fooled. How did you know I was here?"

"I didn't. I was on my way to your apartment when I caught a glimpse of your car out back through my rearview."

"I was under the impression you didn't want to see me again." She swirled away from him and headed down the stairs. "It took a while, but I got your message loud and clear."

He scrambled down the stairs behind her. "I just needed time to sort things out."

"Well, you certainly took your time, didn't you? Not a call, not a chance to explain, nothing." She hit the bottom stair and continued toward the door, intent on showing him out. He needed to leave before she lost every thread of self-control she held in her tentative grasp. "Your silence told me you didn't want to see me again. And since you never broke that silence, I had no other way to interpret it."

"I'm sorry. That's not what it meant." He grabbed her shoulder and turned her to face him. "I've missed you. I've been wanting to talk to you."

"Why didn't you ever take my calls? I could've explained. Or why didn't you call after I gave you all my information? Didn't that explain everything well enough?" She scowled. "What you're saying now doesn't match your actions of the past couple of weeks."

"Yeah, I know." He lowered his head for a moment and then looked at her. "Everything I learned about you that day took me by surprise. You'd been married before. Didn't you think that would upset me a bit?"

"Yes," she whispered. "That's why I never told you. I didn't think you could ever forgive me."

"So you chose to lie to me instead?"

"I didn't lie, I just—"

"You just dodged every opportunity I gave you to tell the truth. To trust me." He rubbed his forehead, removing some of the makeup in the process. "That's what hurt the most, Em. Did you think I wouldn't understand?"

"How could I expect you to understand when I didn't?" A lump in her throat choked her, making her voice sound small, tormented. "I don't understand how I could've been so blind, how I could've missed seeing what that man was." She stalked away from him, flinging a hand out in frustration. "And now with Paul Goodrich on the scene...I don't know what that man has against me, or what kind of lies he's been telling you—"

"He's told me nothing different from what was in those articles you gave me."

She twisted back to face him. Had she heard him right?

"Didn't you notice Paul never published anything about it in the paper?"

"Well, yes, but I thought he was still digging, still trying to find some dirt on me."

Scott shook his head. "Paul's moved on. He said

there was nothing else to discover."

Emily's jaw slackened. "Why didn't you call me? Why didn't you let me know? You had to have known I'd be worried over what that man said about me. He thought I was a con artist like Wade was. And it floors me that you would believe him even for a moment. I may have done some things wrong, but never like that. Never anything like that."

Under the makeup, the wild mop of hair, and the bushy brows, Scott looked miserable. "I didn't believe him. Not really. I was just...mad. Hurt. Not thinking right."

Emily clamped her lips tight. She could understand how he'd felt, and the idea she'd hurt him so terribly washed her in a new wave of guilt.

A wry smile spread across Scott's lips as he reached into his pocket. He withdrew a cashier's check from his wallet. "What was this about? Was 'Millie' trying to fix things between us?"

He tried to hand her the check, but she clasped her hands behind her back. She shook her head. "I didn't mean it like that. It was..." She didn't know what it was. Maybe a small part of her wanted to buy his pardon, but that hadn't been on her mind when she asked Connor to send the money. "It was just an impulse."

"Like the impulse to pay for Spencer's attorney fees?"

The heat in her cheeks intensified. "How did you know about that?"

"Parker told me about the mysterious check he received. It wasn't hard to figure it out from there." His expression softened. "You—Millie—*y'all*—have been helping everyone in town, haven't you?"

She turned away from him. "How is Spencer? What's going to happen to him?"

"It's still too soon to tell, but from what I understand, if Spence pleads guilty, they'll try him as a juvenile, and he won't have to serve as much time as he would have. Afterward, they'll send him through a rehab center." He rested his hands on her shoulders and her heart took a joyful leap at the familiar touch. "It was nice of you to help Parker and Spencer. Spence is a good kid. He just got turned around somehow. Don't feel guilty for turning him in. No one blames you. Parker wouldn't blame you either, if he knew. He's relieved his son was stopped, relieved he will get help."

Emily nearly collapsed with her own relief. She sat on the stairs and whisked an errant tear with a shaky hand. "So it worked out?"

Scott joined her and settled his arm around her shoulders. "It worked out just fine."

"Lauren said you'd worked with Spencer through the horses. Kind of a therapy for him."

"Well, that's not quite right. I'm not qualified to be a therapist. But he sure took to Scotch Bonnet. I think they would've healed each other given time."

The cashier's check was still in his hand, and she closed both of hers around his. "Use this. Open a rehab clinic for horses. Maybe the county can add to the funds, and you can extend it for juvenile rehab, too. Maybe the county can hire a therapist who's qualified."

"It would be worth looking into, wouldn't it? Maybe Sheriff Bailey can steer me in the right direction to get it set up." As he tumbled her idea through his mind, his thoughts played across his features almost legibly. Finally, he mumbled, "It could work. I bet it could work."

"So you'll keep the money?"

"In a trust account, until I find out whether the idea will fly. And even if it does, I'll only use it if you'll be my partner."

"Me? I don't know anything about it."

"I don't either."

"You know how to work with horses. I don't even know that much."

"I can teach you. Besides, either you come with the deal, or there is no deal."

She smiled, wanting very much to be his partner. She shoved out her hand. "Deal."

The smile on his face became sensual as he leaned toward her. "I have a better way of sealing it."

Oh, how she had missed the taste of his kiss, the security of his strong arms around her. What a magical feeling, being loved by Scott Barlow. His kisses lifted her heart far beyond the clouds and then resettled it topsy-turvy in her chest. It thumped crazily with joy, making her lightheaded and breathless. And she wanted more.

But he broke off the kiss and cuddled her instead. "I've missed you."

"I've missed you, too." A lump in her throat pitched her voice higher, and tears threatened to stream down her cheeks, but she didn't care. She nuzzled closer.

"No more secrets?" he asked.

"No more secrets."

Another kiss, another trip around the solar system. "Still love me?"

"Always." She met his eyes, which were peeking

from under shaggy brows. "Even when you're that age."

One more kiss. "Lauren gave me strict orders to bring you back to the auction."

She looked down at her sweat-stained work clothes. "Well, I can't go like this."

Scott waggled his brows. "And I'm not going like this."

42

The auctioneer's gavel slammed on the table. "Sold to paddle number sixty-three. Come claim your prize, little lady."

As a young woman in a pumpkin-orange blouse excused her way up front, Scott and Emily skirted the crowd and found a vacant spot at the wall near the kitchen. Emily glanced around, excited to see the boisterous bidders, and then she tapped Scott's arm. "I'm going to the kitchen and check on Karen."

"Don't be gone too long. I've spent enough time without you as it is."

She smiled and gave him a peck before slipping through the kitchen door. After sending savory appetizers out during the brunch-to-lunch hours, Karen now prepared a few sweet trays for the early afternoon.

"Looks like everyone's happy out there." Emily eyed the puffed pastry pouches on Karen's tray. "What's the filling?"

"Mascarpone with a hint of amaretto." Karen sent the tray out and then crossed her arms. "And you're wrong. *Almost* everyone's happy. Lauren's been checking in every thirty minutes asking for you. I wish you'd told me where you were going."

"I guess I should have. Sorry." Emily found the bowl of mascarpone filling and started to dip her finger into it. Karen rapped a spoon on her fingers, retrieved a small bowl from the counter and scooped a bit into it.

Emily tasted the lightly sweetened, soft tart cheese with a tinge of almond flavor. Heaven. Karen knew what she was doing in the kitchen. "Is Lauren mad?"

"Not mad, I don't think. Worried. That's all you get. I need every bit of that for the next round."

"Sorry." Emily stuck her finger into her mouth and savored what little bit of filling she'd scored.

"You should be out there apologizing to her right now." Karen shooed her away. As Emily neared the door, Karen called, "Oh, and congratulations."

"What for?"

"You and Dr. Barlow made up, didn't you." It wasn't a question.

"How did you know?"

"He and Lauren were in here earlier looking for you. I could tell by the conversation that something was up." She gave Emily a saucy grin. "Comparing the mood you're in now with the one you were in earlier, I'd say you two have reconciled."

Emily shot her a wink and a smile and then pushed through the door.

When the first person she spotted on the other side was Paul Goodrich, she stopped short, almost getting smacked by the door as it swung closed. He saw her, pointed her out to Amber, and the two of them made their way toward her through a crowd of enthusiastic bidders.

She edged back. She could still slip into the kitchen and dash out the back. Scott might be friends with Paul, but Emily didn't have a reason to trust him. He'd spent too much time stalking her for her to feel comfortable now.

The door bumped her, and a uniformed waiter with a tray on his shoulder excused himself so he could get by.

She stepped aside, trapped against the wall.

"There you are." Lauren appeared at her side, and she jumped. "Where did you go? Is Scott with you?"

Emily continued to watch Paul. "He's around here somewhere."

"What's wrong with you?"

She lifted a discreet finger and pointed toward the advancing couple.

"Oh, dear." Lauren moved closer to her. "Just keep your cool. He's not here to report about you. He's here for the auction. Even brought his wife, right?"

"Reporters tend to get their stories wherever they can."

"Right." Scott joined them and took Emily's hand. "But you don't have anything to worry about anymore. He's moved on, remember?"

Scott's touch, more than his words, fortified her, and she planted on a smile as Paul and Amber greeted them. At least she hoped it was a smile. Her face felt frozen into something more resembling a grimace.

Paul shook hands with Scott and offered a smile that included both Emily and Lauren. "Looks like you two ladies pulled off the event of the year. Everyone is having a great time and spending enough to bring in a serious chunk o' change for the arson victims."

"I've already spent more than I intended," Amber said. "But it's for a good cause, right?"

"It is," Lauren said. "What did you buy?"

"Someone donated some costume jewelry to be sold in one lot."

Emily tried to listen to Amber's bidding victory

but couldn't help stealing glimpses of Paul.

He caught her looking and stepped closer with a mischievous gleam in his eye. "How's Millie? I haven't seen her around lately."

Scott tightened his hold on her hand—or was she the one with the vice grip? Either way, it helped. Emily raised her chin a notch. "She's gone. We're not likely to see her again."

"Wow, I'm sorry to hear that. I wish I could've met her. She seemed to be quite an adventurous little lady." He gave her a pointed look, which seemed to convey that her secret was safe now. "If you do see her, tell her we miss her around here. Too many cats are wandering around downtown now that she's gone. We need her back at work."

Amber stopped her conversation with Lauren and turned to Emily. "I've been wanting to adopt a cat from The Litter Box, but every time I go by these days, the place seems closed. I do hope Millie hasn't gone out of business for good."

"She's gone?" Lauren looked disappointed. "I never got to meet her."

"You will." Scott slipped his arm around Emily. "She'll be back."

Paul nodded at her, gave her an honest smile. A quiet assurance that Millie's identity was safe, and probably the closest thing to an apology Emily would ever get from him. She offered a tentative smile in return. The man had kept her secrets and joined her church. Peace between them would make life much easier.

Roger joined them with his hands full of cream-filled pastries. "Have you guys tried these? They're great."

"You're going up another belt size in a single day if you don't quit." Lauren rubbed a dab of cheese from the corner of his lip. She grinned at the others. "He hasn't passed a single tray he could resist."

The auctioneer called the next item for bid. "Cakes by Rita. Everyone here knows the quality of Rita Barlow's cakes—and if you don't, where were you when she served up the one she donated for today's activities?" After the crowd's laughter settled, the auctioneer opened the bid. "Let's start at five hundred, a cheap bid for a great cake."

"Five hundred."

"Five-fifty."

The bidding climbed higher and higher with each paddle shoved into the air. The auctioneer's call echoed around the room, and Emily's blood pressure spiked as the bid soared over a thousand.

A paddle shot up with the shout "Fifteen hundred," and the crowd hushed. Everyone turned to see the bidder, but another grabbed their attention with a shouted bid of two thousand.

Rita and Micah made their way to Scott's side as the bids continued to climb at five hundred dollar increments.

"Well, I never. Never in my born days!" Flushed with excitement, Rita fanned herself with her placard. "Can you believe how much these people are willing to pay for a little ol' cake?"

"Not just any cake, Rita." Micah beamed. "Now you know what the rest of us have known for a long time. You're the best baker in all of East Texas."

"Now, go on with you." She swatted his shoulder with her fan, but her grin broadened.

The gavel finally landed on fifty-five hundred, and

Scott let out a *whoop*. He hugged his mother and then held her at arm's length. "Are you crying?"

She sniffed and swiped her tears. "I feel like I've actually made a worthy contribution. Like my work counts for something."

"It always has, Mom."

Emily watched the two of them, with Micah still beaming like a beacon next to Rita, and felt a wave of wistfulness. She missed her parents and loved Scott's mom and her future husband as if they were her own.

If he'd ever get around to proposing, maybe she could call them her parents, too.

43

Emily ran her hand along the smooth surface of her new countertop. The gentle pearl gray soapstone perfectly complimented what she'd done with her Queen Anne kitchen. Instead of aiming for the dark, rich tones often found in Victorian homes, she'd opted for sunnier, warm colors.

The cabinets and drawers sported a soft peach tone and acrylic pulls made to look like crystal. The salmon-colored walls contrasted with the cabinets, and another touch of peach on the baseboards, crown molding, and door and window frames served as the perfect accent.

Add the brushed stainless-steel appliances, the pecan-stained wood floor, and the sink's tile backsplash adorned with a painting of a dogwood limb, and the effect was perfect. With the glow of November sunlight filtering through the windows, the place felt homey, like an English country kitchen.

The bulk of her current installment on the sale of Deck the Walls went to pay Roger and his crew, and she'd be living with a tight wallet for a while until her next installment, but the house was finally functional enough for her to move in. The bathrooms, while not remodeled, at least worked, and a good scrubbing had done them a world of good. The electrician had changed out the wiring in October, so she no longer feared burning the house down, and Roger had shored up the balcony outside her bedroom. With some plants, a table, and a couple of chairs up there, she'd be ready to wave at Scott as he headed into town from his clinic.

The parlor was all but finished. Just last week, she'd dressed the windows with the new drapes she had designed, and the only thing missing was the furniture she still made monthly payments on. As much as she would love to just pay it off and bring it home, she had to resist or she wouldn't have much money left to live on for the next six months. But once she moved her comfy furniture from her apartment into her house, she'd be all set. At least she'd have something to sleep on in the bedroom and a cozy couch and TV in the den.

She took a few more minutes to look around, to daydream over her plans for the dining room, and then locked the house and headed for home. She had a wedding to get to. The November day held clear skies and moderate temperatures, perfect for the pot-luck reception on the church's picnic grounds. The late-afternoon wedding and the promise of a beautiful sunset during the reception filled Emily with a sigh of romance. When it was her turn, she wanted to get married on a day just like this one.

****

The skirt rustled on Emily's tea-length sapphire-blue dress as she hurried through the foyer to the closed sanctuary doors. Opening one just a crack, she peeked in at the murmuring wedding guests and at Micah and Scott on the dais, both looking suave in their dark suits. The pews were adorned with sky blue ribbons and white-flocked pine cones with sprigs of needles. Simple, but elegant. Perfect for a winter wedding.

Emily had thought Scott would give his mother away, but for reasons of her own, Rita chose to walk down the aisle without him. Micah had asked him to be his best man, since his son Ezra would be performing the ceremony. He stood on the dais with them, a taller, thinner version of his father. With the exception of Emily, the whole wedding was a family affair, and she had felt like she didn't belong.

Rita had "poshed" her protests, though. "You'll be family soon enough."

Emily rushed back to the dressing room and reported her findings to the bride. "You've got a full house out there. It won't be long."

"So many people?" Rita fidgeted with the delicate lace on her ice-blue cocktail dress. "You'd think they'd find something better to do on a Saturday afternoon."

Emily gave her a hug, careful not to muss her hair. "You are so loved. Of course everyone wants to be here for you. For both of you."

The music changed in the sanctuary, and one of Rita's friends waved to her. "It's time."

In a flurry of nerves, Rita sought out her bouquet of white roses and then came to a stop before the mirror. "I feel jittery as a young bride."

"There's reason for that," Emily said. "You are a young bride."

"Oh, posh!" She patted her hair and nodded at her reflection. "Might as well do this, what with Micah waitin' and all."

Emily grinned. "Yes, ma'am. Might as well do this."

She escorted Rita to the entry into the sanctuary, took a moment to compose herself, and then nodded at the two young men who stood there now to attend the doors. They drew back the doors, and Emily stood framed in the opening. The look on Scott's face when he saw her made her feel as though she was the bride, and she felt herself blushing like one. To the slow, easy beat of an instrumental song she didn't recognize and barely heard, Emily walked down the aisle, momentarily the center of attention—but hers was focused on Scott.

She took her place on the first step of the dais, gave a subtle wink to Micah, and turned to watch Rita's grand entry. As she stepped into view, Micah whistled softly.

"She's a beautiful woman," he whispered.

"You're one lucky man, Pop." Ezra whispered back. He leaned toward his father's ear. "She's a keeper."

Rita didn't glide down the aisle like a dreamy-eyed bride. Her step held purpose, in keeping with her personality. But her focus remained on Micah, and her smile radiated sunshine throughout the room. When at last she reached the dais, Micah helped her up the two steps. Once she settled beside him, he folded her hand on his arm and gently covered it with his own. He gave a nod to his son. "Better get started before she changes her mind."

****

Rising to her knees on the familiar blanket Lauren had spread on the grass for the reception picnic, Emily caught sight of Scott coming from the back of the church. As he strode toward her, he gave her a cross-eyed look, and she knew exactly what he meant. So many wedding pictures. The fact that either of them could even see surprised her. Still, having been asked to pose with the family left her with a warm sense of belonging.

With the hand holding his ham sandwich, Roger waved Scott over. "C'mon. Loosen the tie on that monkey suit and relax. The good ladies of the congregation concocted quite a feast for your mama and the preacher man."

With a wink at Lauren, Scott asked Roger, "Did your wife cook?"

Lauren swatted at him. "Yes, I did. I made chicken lasagna, and you'd better eat some."

"Yeah, you'd better get you a taste," Roger said. "It's not too bad. But to make sure you don't go hungry"—he pointed toward the far end of the service tables—"Karen's stuff is over there."

This time, Lauren swatted at Roger—and connected.

Scott offered a hand to Emily. "Care to join me?"

Still laughing at their antics, Emily let Scott pull her up and then smoothed her dress. A cocktail formal wasn't exactly the best dress for dinner on a picnic blanket, so she was glad they'd be taking their plates to the table set up for the wedding party. As they walked to the buffet line, she asked, "Did Rita ever tell you where they were going on their honeymoon?"

"No, they're keeping that secret behind tight lips. But knowing Micah, he probably talked her into a fishing trip somewhere."

Emily laughed. "Somehow I just can't see it."

"Don't sell Mom short. Who do you think taught

me to fish?"

Just beyond the banquet tables, some of the church's musicians had assembled with their instruments, prepared to play for the evening dance.

Scott nodded toward the makeshift dance floor. "How about a waltz later?"

"How about several waltzes?" Even though she'd enjoyed the pleasure of his arms almost daily since they'd made up, the thought of having them around her as they danced in the cool evening air made her nerves tingle with anticipation.

As they made their way through the line, the happy couple appeared at the back door. Those nearest started a wave of applause that ripped throughout the picnic grounds and escorted them to their table. Rita blushed, Micah waved, and they both beamed with the happiness expected from newlyweds.

And Scott teared up.

"You're not going to cry again, are you?" Emily smiled.

"Me? I didn't cry. Not crying now—just a delayed reaction to the flashes during the photo session."

"Uh-huh." In spite of her doubting tone, she grew tenderhearted toward this man who loved his mother as much as he did. He'd make a great father, a wonderful family man.

After dinner, a round of toasts were made with blue Dixie cups filled with sweet iced tea. The couple cut the cake—the one Rita baked because, as she'd said, she wasn't going to "pay no five thousand dollars for someone else to do what I can do for fifty." Lights flashed as candid photos were shot with disposable cameras. Jokes and stories about Rita and Micah caused roars of laughter. All this wedding romance made Emily want to rush Scott into proposing. She gave her head a little shake. He'd do it in his own time.

The band started to play, and Micah extended a hand to his bride. They swept out to the dance floor and waltzed with slightly arthritic hitches to their steps but beautifully just the same.

Scott escorted Emily to the floor, and the two danced until Scott tapped Micah's shoulder, and they changed partners. Emily stepped into Micah's beefy embrace and received a warm smile as he danced with the music.

"You'll be next, you know," he said. "I hope you'll let me perform the ceremony."

"Now, stop that. He hasn't even proposed, and I was just telling myself not to rush." She winked. "But when he does, I wouldn't have anyone else perform the ceremony but you."

Between dancing with Scott and laughing with Lauren and Roger and all her other new friends from church, Emily was stunned to find the evening had drifted away on gossamer wings.

The boys from the youth group brought Micah's vehicle around for the couple to make their exit. They'd scrawled "Preacher's got a Bride" along the sides and "Just Married" across the back, and tied two groups of a half dozen balloons each onto the rear bumper. The sober black vehicle had morphed into a carnival truck. A line of celebrants holding tiny bags of birdseed formed between the couple and their getaway vehicle.

Micah laughed as he held out his arm for Rita. "Well, my love, ready to run the gauntlet?"

She turned to Scott and held him for a few moments and then giggled and joined Micah in the closest thing to a mad dash a couple their age could achieve.

"I feel like I'm seeing my kids off." Scott stood behind Emily and circled his arms around her waist. "It's so good to see her happy."

She leaned against him. "It is good. They make a terrific couple."

"Um-hmm. So do we."

Rita turned from the passenger door to toss her bouquet into the crowd. As it flew into the air and the young ladies scrambled to catch it, she climbed into the truck, then waved out the window as they drove away.

After a few moments of silence, Scott sighed. "Let's see if we can get another dance or two in before we have to start cleaning up the place."

He cued the band for a slow dance and eased her into a one-step across the dance floor.

After everyone had grabbed their pot-luck dishes and left, Roger and Lauren joined Scott and Emily, and the four of them filled trash bags until the church picnic area was spotless.

Roger dropped an arm across Scott's shoulders. "Lauren told me it'd be rude to ask, but I've never been one to stand on ceremony. When are y'all getting married?"

"Roger." Lauren's mouth gaped in mortification.

"Well, doncha think it's time?"

Emily's pulse quickened as a flush crawled up Scott's neck. She hated that Roger had pressured him, but she couldn't wait to hear his response.

"I don't believe you." Lauren glared at Roger. "He'll propose when he's good and ready and probably at Zabaglione's or someplace nice. Not standing in the church parking lot with the two of us staring at them." She turned to Scott. "Isn't that right?"

"Well, the truth of the matter is—"

"I just wanted to know what's taking him so long," Roger said. "Seems to me, they oughta be engaged by now."

Emily glanced from one to the other. Scott had started to say something, but he never finished, and with Lauren and Roger going at it, he probably wouldn't. He caught her eye and shrugged. She smiled. What else could she do? She couldn't yank the rest of his sentence from him. But as Lauren fussed at Roger for not having the sense God gave a turnip, Scott eased to Emily's side and slipped his hand in his pocket. He withdrew a tiny box and held it in the palm of his hand as he searched her face.

"I've been carrying this thing around with me for months. I wanted to wait until after Mom got married before I asked you, and, well, she's married now." He opened the box, and a one-carat marquis sparkled from its platinum perch above the twelve round-cut diamonds flanking it. "What do you say? Will you marry me?"

Tears caused her vision to shimmer, and her breath caught, choking her throat. The ring dazzled her. She didn't care that they weren't at a quiet table for two in Zabaglione's, didn't notice the church parking lot with its twinkling white lights from Rita's reception, and she was barely aware of her friends watching them. The focus of her entire being centered on Scott.

"Well, you gonna say yes?" Roger demanded.

Emily nodded. Scott let out a victory shout, and she laughed as he swung her around.

"Yes," she cried when her voice returned. "Yes!"

He slipped the ring on her finger, and Lauren grabbed her hand to see it. Even in the soft glow of the strings of twinkling lights, the diamonds put on a fiery show.

Emily returned to Scott and rested her hands on his chest. The love radiating from him matched the intensity she felt in her heart, and again her words were trapped in her throat.

So she let her kiss do the talking.

44

Spring

The amber-eyed calico keeps easing herself into the corner, and I don't think she can arch her back any higher. She's planning her escape, I just know it. I have my net, but I don't want to have to use it. Cats go nuts when caught in the web.

"Go slow. She's spooky."

"I know, I know." Jake casts me an irritated glance, and the cat darts between us and heads behind the courthouse.

"You took your eyes off her."

"Well, so did you, old woman. When are you going to learn how to catch a cat?"

I stick my tongue out at him, and he laughs.

I have to admit, having him hunt with me makes the job far easier. He brings a cat carrier with him. I've had far fewer scratches now that I don't have to carry frightened felines anymore. Jake takes 'em straight to the clinic. We can't do this too much longer, though. In another few weeks, the baby I'm carrying will stretch my belly so far, this old woman get-up will look ridiculous. When that time comes, "Millie" will have to go into hiding again.

Jake hobbles over to me, smacking his lips like old men do, and gives me a devilish look. "You're lookin' hot today, Mrs. Falco. How's 'bout you an' me have us a little date?"

His bushy brows waggle, and I can't stifle my giggle. In my orange tee shirt and purple polyester pants, I doubt I look "hot," but beauty is in the eyes of the beholder, right? Besides, I'll go on a date with him any time. He doesn't have to ask me twice. "Where we going?"

He reaches in his front pockets and turns them inside out to reveal how empty they are. "Can't afford much. How about A&K Barbecue or Down Home Diner?"

"How about both?" He's fibbin' about being broke. I saw him slip a fifty in his wallet just this morning. "We'll do A&K for lunch and the diner for dessert. I've got a hankerin' for one of Clara's brownies with ice cream on top."

Jake steps closer to me, but it's Scott's eyes I see, beaming love at me like I'm the center of his universe. "Anything you want, little mama."